THE CORPSE IN THE GARDEN OF PERFECT BRIGHTNESS

THE CORPSE IN THE GARDEN OF PERFECT BRIGHTNESS

MALCOLM PRYCE

BLOOMSBURY PUBLISHING
LONDON • OXFORD • NEW YORK • NEW DELHI • SYDNEY

BLOOMSBURY PUBLISHING
Bloomsbury Publishing Plc
50 Bedford Square, London, WC1B 3DP, UK

BLOOMSBURY, BLOOMSBURY PUBLISHING and the Diana logo are
trademarks of Bloomsbury Publishing Plc

First published in Great Britain 2020

A catalogue record for this book is available from the British Library

ISBN: HB: 978-1-4088-9529-0; eBook: 978-1-4088-9531-3

2 4 6 8 10 9 7 5 3 1

Typeset by Integra Software Services Pvt. Ltd.
Printed and bound in Great Britain by CPI Group (UK) Ltd, Croydon CR0 4YY

To find out more about our authors and books visit www.bloomsbury.com
and sign up for our newsletters

To Squeaky for her eighteenth birthday

Author's Note

The first volume of these memoirs described the events during the winter of 1947 when, after a lifetime's loyal service to the Great Western Railway, my employment as a railway detective was terminated. The four great railway companies were dissolved and on the stroke of midnight, December 31st, a mooncalf called British Rail was born.

My final case, prior to this dissolution, resolved the greatest mystery in all the annals of railway lore, namely the disappearance from a train in 1915 of a party of twenty-three nuns travelling from Swindon to Bristol Temple Meads. A case that the press dubbed 'The "Hail Mary" Celeste'. This second volume details my subsequent fate in the early months of 1948.

Chapter 1

IT WAS A MORNING in early April, shortly after dawn, when Cheadle Heath brought me the letter from the Countess.

I was making my way back to the engine sheds after working the night shift on the permanent way gang. I trudged home, cold and worn out and holding a simple lamp fashioned from a piece of rope alight in a can of tallow. The same design, they said, that illuminated the builders of the Great Pyramid of Cheops. The outline of Weeping Cross South signal box resolved from the gentle fog: a faint grey shape, soft as a watercolour wash, standing sentinel over the tracks. The air was thick with the scent of tar. A tiny light gleamed like a morning star in the opaque windows of the signal box, betraying the presence of a man who also would have spent this night hard at work, although with the considerable advantage over me of a blessed kettle and a teapot.

The common man thinks firing a train is the hardest job on the railways, but all railwaymen will tell you there is no harder labour than the permanent way gang in winter. The men who do it are made of hammered iron. Out at night, in all weathers, clearing the tracks of snow and ice, putting down detonators on them to warn of fog, and sometimes walking into the path of the very train they are trying to warn. One of these men of hammered iron was Ifan, a Welsh miner's son who had partnered me during the night. Back in January there had been nights when we waded through drifts up to our waists and struggled in the teeth of blizzards strong enough to blow a man clean off his feet.

Just before we reached the water tank I parted from Ifan and took the path that led under the arch of the viaduct and alongside a brick wall black with soot and taller than a man. From afar came the sad wail of an engine and the thuds and last clunk of goods wagons being shunted. Those soft sounds seemed only to accentuate the silence of the morning. Then the stillness was disturbed by the appearance of a man's head at the top of the wall. He peered over and, not noticing me, began to clamber down, lowering himself gingerly, feet pedalling wildly at an invisible bicycle, searching for purchase before he lost his grip and fell to the ground. Lumps of coal spilled onto the path.

He lay there for a second or so, looking slightly dazed. I walked across and stood over him.

'Stealing coal, are you?' I said. 'You scoundrel.'

He looked up at me and narrowed his eyes as he focused his gaze. 'Jack!' he said. 'Jack Wenlock. Is it you?'

I peered at him. 'Cheadle? Cheadle Heath?'

My gaze darted to the spilled coal and back to him. 'Oh, Cheadle!'

2

He looked sheepish. 'If you had told me six months ago that I would be doing this … times are hard, Jack.'

'We used to chase men who stole coal. We used to box their ears.'

'Yes we did. Now look at me. Blotting my copybook again, eh?' He said it with a sad laugh as if it were indeed comic, but it also epitomised so much of the ill fortune that had attended his life. Cheadle and I had both been members of the Railway Goslings, that fabled cadre of detectives that haunted the carriages of the Great Western Railway until 1947. He lost his position in 1936 for a sin that was never exactly specified at the time. They told us he had blotted his copybook. Later we learned he was punished because of a tryst in Ilfracombe with a shopgirl called Florence.

The letter terminating my employment as a railway detective had landed on my desk three months ago. For a lifetime's devoted service, two weeks' notice.

'Jack, I do not normally do this.'

'I am relieved to hear it, Cheadle.'

He sought to rise, and I helped him up.

'All the same,' he said, 'I don't suppose the men who dug that coal would begrudge a few lumps to a poor man to warm his hearth in winter.' He narrowed his eyes as if recalling an event long ago. 'Do you remember the works outings? The special excursions to Cornwall from the Railway Works?'

'Of course!'

'Did it never strike you that life was like that? An excursion to Cornwall that lasts barely a week?'

'I can't say it did.'

His voice became hushed with awe, as if he were revealing a profound truth.

'It's as if we are walking along a road at night, in an unfamiliar part of town, and we hear music and laughter, so we follow it to a glittering house. The door is open and we walk in and up some stairs, through a curtained doorway, and blink in surprise to find ourselves in a theatre, with a play performing on the stage. The play is our life. Don't you see?'

'Yes, I see what you mean. I had never thought of it like that.'

'I have been thinking of that time with Florence.' He grew suddenly animated and his eyes sparkled. 'Oh how gaily I blotted my copybook!' He gripped my arm. 'You must blot your copybook, Jack, blot it, I say! Blot it for all you are worth!'

'But how, Cheadle? Stealing coal? I could never do such a thing.'

He moved closer to peer into my eyes. 'There was a time when I would have said exactly the same thing. But consider who you would be stealing it from. The railway company who sacked you after half a lifetime's loyal service. Those who taught you never to blot your copybook.'

I considered his words. Had he really changed so much? Was he right to think like this?

4

'Cheadle,' I said, 'all those years we served together, so loyally, we did not care who owned the railway, it didn't matter. We loved her like our family and viewed those who stole from her as an intruder found in our own home.'

'Yes!' The word fizzed like a firework in the cold morning air. 'Yes, and now they have nationalised her and thrown you out of your own home. Soon they'll sell the home, or close down half the rooms in it.'

'Do you think so?'

'The little lines will be the first to go,' he said with solemn certainty.

I thought of those lovely old branch lines. Spreading out across the map like capillaries, some with just a single carriage pulled behind a tank engine going no faster than a horse, they were the glory of the land. 'How can you know?'

'It is the way of this world, those who cannot pay their way, whether man or machine or beast, will be for the chop. What happens to the pit pony when he can no longer work, Jack? He is sent to the glue factory.'

I looked at him, confused. 'All the same, theft is theft … isn't it?'

He shook his head sadly. 'The times are changing, Jack. The coal belongs to the people now, and so do the railways.'

'Surely this nationalisation cannot last long. A new government will be returned and restore the railways to their rightful owners.'

5

'You mean to rich men in top hats, meeting in rooms far away from the railway lines? People who know nothing about trains, only how to make a profit from the labours of men like you?'

'That may be true of other industries, but the men who presided over the Great Western Railway loved her as much as any of us.'

'Perhaps. But those days are gone, can't you see?'

'Tell me, Cheadle, how is it that the common man who never owned anything before the war now has enough money to buy a railway?'

He peered into my face with an air of concentration, and a hint of sadness in his gaze. 'Jack,' he said tenderly. 'Those men bought the railways with the blood of their fallen comrades.'

I wondered how it was that such a thought had never crossed my mind. Was it true?

'In truth, Jack,' Cheadle said, 'I didn't come here tonight to steal coal. I really came to see you, to give you something. This.' He took a letter from his overcoat pocket. 'I've been asked to deliver this to you. It is from a lady in Cornwall, a very wealthy lady who I am given to understand has very important information to convey to you. She couldn't find you, and I've struggled too; you have gone to ground and seem to be using the name "Cunningham".'

'There are some chaps looking for me, Cheadle, men who mean me ill.'

'I will not pry, Jack, but I must tell you that yesterday, as I looked for you, I was approached by a man dressed as a post office special messenger. He was far too old for a position that's usually given to boys. His face was terribly burned on one side, and his eyes were colder than those of a dead fish. He asked me if I knew you, and not liking the look of him at all, I told him you had left this town long ago.'

'But how did you find me, Cheadle?'

'We are creatures of habit. If someone asked you to find me, where would you look?'

'I would say, Cheadle Heath takes a pint in the Railwayman's Arms every evening at half-past six.'

'And I would say, Jack Wenlock can no more survive away from the railways than a frog can live away from a pond. I asked the men, Jack, and it didn't take long to find some who had seen you. If you are in danger, you need to hide yourself better than this. Go and see Mr Jarley at the Weeping Cross Railway Lost Property Office and ask him for a better disguise.'

'That is excellent advice, Cheadle, thank you.' I tried to sound unconcerned, but, in truth, his words had kindled a sense of foreboding in my heart.

He pressed the letter into my hand, picked up the lumps of coal and tucked them inside his coat. Then, without another word, he ambled off. I watched him leave and then moved over to the penumbra of a railside light to examine the letter. The envelope was stiff, the colour of curd. Inside there was a train ticket to Wisskirriel and a note written in fountain pen on thick, creamy paper embossed with a crest. It was stationery of a sort I had never held before, and I sensed it cost more for a box than I earned in a month.

Dear Jack,

I hope you will forgive the curt nature of this note, I lack the skill to announce this matter in a manner that befits it. I wish I could prepare you for what I say next because I know it will greatly astonish you. If I understand correctly, you know nothing at all about your mother. Well, I have recently been in receipt of information regarding her fate that may greatly interest you. In the hope that you will wish to learn more, I am enclosing a return railway ticket along with a promise of accommodation at the local inn.

Yours
Lady Susan Seymour

In the goods yard a tank engine passed. There was a whoosh of escaping steam and a thousand sparks glittered in the sky above me for a few seconds, as if a magician had emptied his top hat above my head. My hand trembled. This was the most astonishing event of my life.

I had never met my mother, but the account of my nativity had been told to me so often at the orphanage that I saw her quite clearly in my dreams.

It was late in the evening of January 23rd 1914 when she stepped off an omnibus outside the Saint Christopher's Home for the Children of Railwaymen. Snow was falling in thick drifts upon the town of

Weeping Cross. She was big with child and nervous. She drew the bell pull; there was a tinkle from within, and after a suitable wait she was admitted. She was taken the same night to the railway engine sheds nearby, where in a special maternity annexe a bed had been arranged so that she might have there her confinement. Nurses in starched tunics embossed with the letters GWR helped her down into her cot, calling for warm water and towels. They chafed her hands and dabbed the moisture from her brow. There came shouts and the noise of shunting. A whistle wailed, more shouts, and out of the midnight gloom a steam engine appeared with the regal mystery of a whale rising to the surface of the ocean. It was a 4–6-0 Saint-class locomotive, engine number 2904 Lady Godiva. She had a domeless parallel boiler, raised Belpaire firebox and boiler pressure of 200 psi. She came slowly to a halt before the parted thighs of the young girl. The strange ritual that was about to be enacted had been staged in accordance with the ethological discoveries of a German scientist called Oskar Heinroth, who had shown that the gosling of the greylag goose imprints as its mother the very first thing it sees after hatching from the egg. The driver pulled on the whistle. There was a shriek, a column of smoke and steam shot up into the night. The mother groaned and I, the Railway Gosling, was born. The first thing I saw in this world was a Saint-class locomotive, engine number 2904 Lady Godiva.

Chapter 2

DAWN GLIMMERED THROUGH THE fog. The north-east wind picked up. It was icy and held the cold scent of rain to come. I walked through the town to my digs on Dandelion Hill. On the slopes preceding it there was a recreation ground, and since taking this job it had become my custom to sit awhile on the bench at the top and look down on the town, and wait for an hour to pass before going home and waking Jenny.

I didn't wish to wake her too early, even though sleep seldom came easily to her. I imagined her lying in the dark, worrying about what would become of us, listening to the snores, or sounds of perpetual bickering, from the Grimshaw family who lived on the other side of the drab curtain that partitioned the room we were obliged to share. When I arrived home she would force the features of her face into a smile and cook me the powdered egg that was my breakfast. And I would say, 'Aren't you having some too?' and she would say that she wasn't hungry.

I sat on a bench and thought about what had just transpired. I reread the letter and then put it back in my pocket as carefully as if it were a little bird. What could it mean? I could not begin to imagine what news the writer of the letter might have about my mother. I struggled to resist a dangerous hope that began to rise in me: if she was as grand as she made out, might she not be in a position to help us? She might take pity on us. Because our plight was dire. We were three weeks in arrears with the rent and, as far as I could see, there was no honest way of making it up.

At the Orphanage we had been discouraged from inquiring about our mothers. All I knew about mine was the strange manner of her confinement, and that as part of this arrangement she was subsequently sent to the Colonies, where a domestic position was to be found for her.

The Railway Gosling programme was soon abandoned, but had originally been intended to create a new cadre of hero for the boys of the realm, one they could look up to, and in so doing acquire a measure of British 'pluck'. It was felt that this particular quality had been sadly lacking during the recent wars in Africa. Of particular concern had been the Battle of Isandlwana, in which a force of British and Colonial troops armed with the latest Martini-Henry breech-loading rifles had been bested by an army of Zulus armed with spears.

During that famous battle a solar eclipse occurred. Many believed this was God firing a warning shot across the bows of the Great Ship Britannia, telling us to pull our socks up.

On the southern horizon came the first puffs of smoke from the 7.47 Hereford train. Smoke rose, too, from the chimney of Chumley's biscuit works. Barges moved slowly along the canal, its waters black and in places flashing silver in the morning light. I had loved God's Wonderful Railway, but she had not loved me back. It was a hard time for a man to lose his livelihood, especially a man who had confounded all the odds and expectations and found for himself a wonderful wife. I had never thought to marry, of course. My life had been one of unstinting devotion and sacrifice in the name of the GWR, and most of that time, when not apprehending ruffians making a nuisance of themselves on the trains, had been spent in the company of chaps, all of whom – with the exception of Cheadle Heath – knew about as much about the mysteries of the flesh as I did, which is to say precisely nothing. For all that, I would say my new wife Jenny and I make a good team. As for those practical matters of the flesh that exist between man and woman within a marriage, I will say only that Cheadle sent me a handbook complete with instructive diagrams that has proved most helpful.

Our room was at the top of four flights of stairs, from which the carpet on the top three had been removed and replaced with nailed-down jute. It imparted a dry, dusty odour to the air, whereas the rest of the house was

dank, and smelled of boiled cabbage, lavatory disinfectant and chilblain ointment. I climbed with weariness
not so much from my night's loss of sleep but from the
question in my heart about what future lay ahead. I
hoped against hope that I did not encounter my land-
lord. Folk passed me on the stairs on their way to work,
rubbing sleep from their eyes and grunting greetings.
On every landing doors ajar led to rooms in which the
wireless was on, tuned to the Home Service. In our
room Jenny was sitting on the bed, watching the door.
She smiled when she saw me and jumped up, embracing me, then pulled back and looked up into my face.
'Pleased to meet you, meat to please you,' she said. I
could tell she had been crying.

'Meat?'

'At an early stage in its development. A prototype
chicken.'

'What I would really like is powdered egg. I don't
suppose we have any?'

'You're in luck.'

'I'm in luck every day,' I said playfully.

Despite the dark lines around her eyes, she smiled
and the smile reached her eyes. 'How was your night?
Was it very hard?'

'I'm afraid it was all rather dull. Not too cold. I was
partnered with Ifan again. I caught a chap stealing
coal.'

'Oh really? And knowing you,' she said with a hint of
mischief, 'I expect you wanted to box his ears.'

'Actually, no,' I said. 'I … I thought … I didn't think I ought to begrudge a chap one lump of coal for his fire.'

She drew back slightly in surprise. 'Really?' She looked pleased.

'Yes, why not?' I said feeling slightly guilty. 'It could have been Ifan's brother who mined that coal.'

'Oh, Jack!' said Jenny, her eyes glittering with what appeared to be pride. 'I'm proud of you!'

She went to the stove wedged between the bed and the window, and buttered a slice of bread to go with my egg. 'I thought today I would go and ask at Quails the nicotine throat pastille makers, the mothball warehouse, the creosote wholesaler and the Coal Tar toothpaste people.'

'You asked at all those not two days ago, Jenny.'

'There's not much to do after I clean the saucepan.'

'Why don't we go for a walk instead?'

'Don't you want to sleep?'

'No.'

I had met Jenny four months before, when she proved to be the last client to walk into my office. In so doing she provided me with the opportunity to resolve, as my swan-song case, the mystery of the 'Hail Mary' Celeste. As a child you no doubt shivered to read about it: a party of twenty-three nuns travelling from Swindon to Bristol Temple Meads who vanished into thin air.

Jenny and I were married on the stroke of midnight on New Year's Eve 1947, just as the Great Western

Railway vanished from existence and British Rail was born. Our wedding ceremony took place on the footplate of number 4070 Godstow Castle. In those days the driver of a mainline express was still empowered by an Act of Parliament to perform the marriage ceremony, a privilege also granted to the captains of ships and hydrogen-filled dirigibles, although since the tragedy of the *Hindenburg* this last office was seldom performed. At the precise moment that we said 'I do' every train in the land tooted its whistle to salute or lament the birth of British Rail. That collective choir of tooting whistles had been dearer to my ears than church bells.

We put on our coats and walked to the end of the street, and through the gate out onto Dandelion Hill. The children's swings and roundabout were still, the boating lake had been drained during the war. The town lay below us and a sense of it stirring, like a hive waking, could be felt. We held hands and walked into a breeze never stiff enough to threaten my hat. Smoke from the factories and the gasworks filled the sky, but here and there the blue broke through like a jumper patched at the elbow. To the south another train appeared, puffing plumes of white smoke into the sky.

'What's that one, Jack?' said Jenny as the train crawled across the horizon with a languor that contrasted with the energy of the smoke.

'I'm sorry, I don't know.'

16

I could feel her disappointment. 'There was a time when you knew them all.'

'Yes, but there are new ones now. A new timetable.' I felt like a farmer who could no longer remember the names of his cows.

I recalled the December afternoon when she walked into my office. The room filled with the beautiful reek of sulphur and steam, gushing in glorious chuffs through the broken window, as the 17.17 to Hereford passed outside. I told her without needing to look that the engine was number 4070 Godstow Castle, a 4-6-0 Castle class, the sort with a sloping throatplate in the firebox, which meant that even after the modifications to the blastpipe and chimney, the steam superheating still fell short, betraying its presence with the characteristic double cough in the chuffs. She looked at me and said, 'Golly', barely able to believe that a man could discern so much from a few chuffs, so I laughed and pretended I was joking, but of course I wasn't. To a man brought up in a railway servants' orphanage a chuff is an encyclopedia, containing the life story of the engine, a sound as dear and identifiably specific as the cry of a baby to its mother, or the bleat of a lamb lost on a hillside.

The sound of Jenny's voice brought me back to the present.

'Will you teach me to drive a train?' she asked.

I laughed.

'I'm serious.'

'I know. But why would you want to learn such a thing?'

'Why shouldn't I?'

'I'm not saying you shouldn't, I'm just curious to know why you want to.'

She hesitated, as if naming the precise motive was not easy. 'Because of what you said.'

'What did I say?'

'You know very well.'

Indeed I did, or at least had a good idea, but it was more fun to feign ignorance. I moved behind her and enfolded her with my arms, resting my chin on the top of her head. 'In the time I've known you, Jenny, I've said many things about the railways, some would say I talk about little else.'

'You said that there were times when the engine is running fast and firing beautifully and all is going well and that … that the feeling is … rather wonderful.'

'That's true.'

'In fact, you said more than that.'

'Did I?' A half-smile tugged at the corner of my mouth.

The factory hooter from Chumley's sounded, faint and far away. A man near the boating lake was walking his dog. It was the only other sign of life this morning.

'You know very well you did.'

'You'll have to remind me.'

'Don't pretend you don't know.' There was a hint of exasperation in her voice. She knew she was being teased, but realised, too, there was no retreat.

The man threw the stick. The dog chased after it, stopping for a second at the rim of the empty boating lake before continuing after the stick.

'If it's what I think you mean,' I said, 'I've never heard it cited as a reason to learn to drive a train.'

'You said it was like the pleasure a man takes privately with his wife.'

When I had stopped laughing, I told Jenny I had an extra shift that afternoon. In truth, I intended catching the train to Exeter St David's and from there taking the connection for Wisskirriel. But first I would ask Ifan to cover for me.

I did not tell Jenny about the letter because I knew it would arouse the same unjustified hope in her that it had in me. If it should prove to be a cruel hoax, or simple mistaken identity, it would be very hard to return and tell her. All the same, I could not entirely extinguish the hope in my own heart. I knew well that if Jenny failed to find a job soon, I would not be able to pay the rent arrears we owed; we should be turfed out onto the street.

Chapter 3

THE LAST MEETING OF the Board of God's
Wonderful Railway took place on 19 December 1947. Various business was transacted.
The house at 10 Florence Road, Ealing was bought
from the organisation 'Homes for Motherless Children' for use as a GWR hostel. Six Hillman Imp motor
cars were bought to serve as company cars, at a cost of
£2,968 13s 6d. Monies were allocated for the refur-
bishment of the Kingswear–Dartmouth ferry, the
Mew. The awards for the best station gardens were
announced: £6 each to Cholsey & Moulsford; Swindon Town; Creech St Michael; Halt; Symonds Yat;
Pontllanfraith; Peterston; Pembrey & Burry Port. It
was like a man about to be executed renewing his order
with the milkman.

That final year, 1947, had been a hard year, starting
with snow, ice and blizzards. Coal was still in short
supply and the government prohibited excursion trains,
including those intended to convey supporters to the
F.A. Cup semi-finals in April. Throughout the land men
and women of the railway laboured in dreadful condi-
tions, to serve the public and keep the railways open.
Signalmen battled to work across drifts higher than
hedges, wading through snow waist-deep or sometimes

crawling on all fours. Often the snowploughs got stuck and the driver and his fireman would dig her out with spades. And sometimes that too didn't work and the men sat in the guard's van where there was food and tea and coal for the stove, and waited for relief.

One member of the permanent way team died in a storm that winter. Lost and confused in a snowstorm at night, he was hit by a train. He left a wife and seven children and the Great Western Board awarded her £707 10s.

What made those men labour so heroically in that winter? The Great Western Railway was our home. At Swindon the company built the houses for the workers and provided a hospital, school, church and swimming baths. In March 1947 the Great Western Railway Music Festival was opened, for the last time, in Reading Town Hall by the Mayor, Lady Phoebe Cusden. For six days it went on, morning, noon and night: orchestras, soloists, recitations and the highly popular production of *The Rebel Maid* by the GWR operatic society. In July the Minister of Transport lifted transport restrictions to permit the Annual Swindon Works Outing to take place. Between 5 and 8 July, twenty-four special trains took 20,000 workers to the seaside.

There was also accommodation at the Swindon Works for the busiest man of all, the funeral director. Because death was never far away. People had heart attacks, or contrived to open the carriage door at 80 mph and fall out. Some choked to death or choked each other. Some leaned out of the window too far and lost their heads. Desperate people threw themselves into the path of a train and destroyed their own lives and gave the men on the footplate nightmares for the rest of their lives. Some chaps on the footplate were scalded to death when things went wrong, and some were crushed like a beetle in a collapsing tin can. One boy infamously preferred sleeping in the firebox to cleaning it at 3 o'clock of a cold winter morning. He went up in smoke. A hundred years ago, for a while, there was a train that only the dead could take, from Waterloo to Brookwood cemetery in Surrey. I regret to recall I occasionally found dead babies in the lavatories. We were all touched by death, but we did not dwell on it. The only death we were not prepared for was the death of our beloved Great Western itself.

Lady Seymour had sent me a first-class ticket. I sat alone in the richly upholstered compartment and contemplated the pickle I had got myself into as a consequence of solving the case of the 'Hail Mary' Celeste. The disappearance of the nuns turned out to be the result of a foul plot in which His Majesty King George V was implicated. As a consequence, I found disfavour in the eyes of a shadowy organisation called Room 42, who were determined that I should not disclose the role of the King.

I knew little about them apart from the fact that they seemed to operate in a clandestine way within the government. The name derived from a time-honoured practice in which chaps who let the side down were expected to retire to a hotel with a revolver and bottle of whisky, book room 42, and blow their brains out in it. I had good reason to believe that they had a similar fate in mind for me – thus it was that I had been living under the name of Cunningham. But if Cheadle could find me, it was clear that so could they.

A chap called Bates met me at Wisskirriel Station and took my small overnight case. He told me lodging had been secured for me at the local inn and he would take me there later, then showed me to a Rover parked in the station yard and ushered me in.

It was a ten-minute drive from the town, through a narrow lane that twisted and turned around a hill, gradually rising until we broke clear of the hedges that obstructed our view. All at once we could see the ocean, grey-green against a leaden sky, and set against it, on the promontory, stood a grand house that was situated in parklands dotted with trees where deer grazed. The house itself was made from grey stone, obscured with ivy and adorned with crenellations and fake towers, the sort they have on railway stations and that one doubts would be much use in a real siege.

We parked on a gravel forecourt and a maid came out of the main door and curtsied before me, then led me inside and into a drawing room where she requested me to wait. The room was gloomy, filled with mahogany fur-niture, heavy curtains, and oil paintings in which little could be discerned except perhaps the red tunic of a chap on a horse and a patch of silver that represented a body of water. At the far end, French windows opened on to a conservatory, which in turn looked out onto the lawn.

The sideboard was covered with bric-a-brac, includ-ing a carriage clock, a brass shell case acting as a vase for some dried flowers, and a framed photo of a young man in battledress of the Great War. There was also a bronze statue from India showing a god with four arms. The maid brought me a tray bearing a teapot and a single cup and poured. She explained that after I had refreshed myself she would take me upstairs to see Her Ladyship, which she duly did, leading me to the first floor and to a bedchamber commanding a view of the Downs and sea beyond. Lady Seymour lay in a four-poster bed, propped against a mountain of pillows and smoking a cigarette.

'Mr Wenlock!' she said. 'It was so good of you to come.' She scrutinised me, as if examining a purchase. Her hair had once been blonde but was now greying in loose skeins that fell over her shoulders. Her skin was lined and dusted with powder, and her nose sharply sculpted and rather handsome. She looked to be in her seventies. But what struck me most about her was her eyes. The fine lines around them suggested that she had once been gay, and given to a mirth that seldom visited her now.

'Would you care for a cigarette?'

I declined.

'We've met before, actually,' she said without cere-mony. 'But I don't expect you to remember.'

'I'm sure I might, if ...'

She smiled and shook her head. 'The first time was when you were a little boy. I gave a talk at the Weeping Cross Railway Servants' Orphanage and showed some lantern slides of Moon Beam, the Potawatomi Indian princess.'

'I remember that!'

'The second time was in 1935. I sent my niece a birthday package via the Great Western postal service. It contained a postal order for half a crown. But when she opened it on her birthday, the postal order was miss-ing. We reported the matter, not expecting anything to come of it. But the following week you came to see her and apologised. You said you had managed to recover the postal order from the bounder who had taken it, and you made good a restitution. She was so thrilled. You gave her a Gosling's Friend badge, too. That was very kind of you.'

I smiled and brushed it aside with a gesture.

'She always talked about it, kept that badge until she ... she died in childhood you see, pneumonia.' I was about to make an appropriate remark, but she shook her head. 'The point is,' she continued, 'it was jolly big of you, that's all. To take the trouble. I know you couldn't really have found the chap who stole it.'

26

'I don't see why not.'

'Because I never sent the postal order. A month later while cleaning out my dressing room, my maid found it under the bureau. I must have dropped the damned thing.'

I laughed.

She drew thoughtfully on her cigarette, leaning back slightly as she regarded me. 'And now you've got married.'

'Yes.'

'On the footplate of a train.'

I said nothing.

'You really are most curious.'

'I suppose I am. Your letter mentioned … my …'

'Your mother.'

'Yes.'

'I was involved in the early stages of the Gosling programme. I interviewed the prospective mothers. I had a lady's maid at the time – Millie. Your mother. She was sixteen years old, and a real jewel; I was very fond of her. So was my son Curtis, who was fourteen; he doted on her and she on him.' She paused, and her eyes narrowed slightly as if she was troubled by the memory. She exhaled her cigarette smoke slowly, and said, 'Something terrible happened. Some money went missing. Curtis told me he had seen Millie take it.' She paused again, the muscles of her face tightening as she recalled the events of long ago. 'So, with a heavy heart, I had to dismiss her. It was some years later when Curtis found the courage to own up to me that he had taken the money. The guilt has tormented him ever since. After she was dismissed, she immediately left the neighbourhood. No one knew where she had gone. It turned out she was with child. You, in fact.'

Her cigarette was only halfway smoked, but she stubbed it out elegantly and lit another. Dusk was beginning to settle in and the blue smoke curling around her face, caught by the light from the window, shrouded her in a twisting veil of gauze the colour of a dove's plumage.

'Here—' She handed me a photograph. It showed a girl wearing the customary uniform of an Edwardian domestic servant: a dark dress with crisp white apron and cap. She posed stiffly, next to an occasional table in a nondescript hall. She looked painfully young. Her face was soft, childish, with wisps of fair hair tucked into her bonnet.

'That is your mother,' said Lady Seymour.

I stared across an abyss of years at the face of my mother. My heart filled with a feeling that has no name. I stood there thunderstruck and struggled to know even what it was that I was feeling. My mother? A woman I had often dreamed about, but who had passed like a ghost through those dreams, evanescent, a figure for whom I had never imagined a face, and not even been aware that it was lacking. And now I saw it plainly. It struck me that my mother, even at that young age, was very beautiful, and had about her gaze that stared so trustingly at the camera a sweetness and innocent candour.

Lady Seymour carried on as if she had just handed me a receipt for flour.

'It was Curtis who, years later while working in the Colonial Service in London, discovered what had become of her. You see, she had access to my work papers, or rather there had been no reason to prevent her seeing them, so she was well acquainted with the Gosling scheme. Indeed, she had admitted some of the applicants who came here. It seems that she forged one of the invitations, intended for another girl, and sent it to herself. Thus five months later she turned up in Weeping Cross and presented herself for her confinement. Part of the arrangement was that the girls would be given a new life in the Colonies, to deter them from trying to make contact with their forsaken children. For someone in her position it made sense: she could assure a good home for her son and avoid destitution herself. It transpired that she had passage on the SS *Rajah Brooke*, bound for Fremantle. The ship foundered in a typhoon off the coast of Java, with the loss of all on board. So naturally we thought that was an end of the matter.' She paused again, and slightly narrowed her eyes again. The silence extended awkwardly, Her Ladyship lost in thought.

'Did she ... did you ever find out who—' I said.

'The father?' My question snapped her out of her reverie. 'The stable lad. He disappeared soon after, too. Lied about his age and joined up. One of the first to go. He fell in Flanders in November. Curtis was devastated. Despite the difference in status, they had grown up together, like brothers. We don't know if the lad even knew about Millie's condition. It was my husband, Chester, who discovered they had been … carrying on.'

'Your letter said … permitted me to hope … that there was news of her?'

'As I said, we were given to understand no one survived the sinking of the *Rajah Brooke*, but recently Curtis discovered something that suggested this wasn't the case.

'In 1940 he was posted to Singapore in the Colonial Service, and later took up a position with a private firm responsible for turning Malayan tin into those frightful badges, the ones you send off to Robertson's Jam for.'

'Golliwogs, they're called golliwogs.'

'Quite. Then sometime last year, around September I think, he wrote to me about a small article he'd seen in the *Straits Times* describing an unusual item that had washed up on a beach in the East Malayan province of Sarawak. It was a bottle containing some pages from a screenplay. It told the story of an infamous rogue called Captain Squideye, who had bought a white woman at a slave auction in Macassar. The woman, it transpired, was a young English girl called Millie who had survived the shipwreck of the SS *Rajah Brooke*. There could have been two Millies aboard, of course, but Curtis became convinced that this girl was your mother.'

For a moment I stared at her, thunderstruck, and then aware that I should say something said simply, 'I have really no idea how to respond to this revelation.'

She nodded. 'Of course. Of course. I don't blame you.' She stared once more into space, the place where the past is located. 'Curtis immediately booked a berth on the mail packet to Kuching. On the ship he met an American called Sam Flamenco, and they became friends. Mr Flamenco was a Hollywood film producer, or at least had been in his early years – I got the impression that he was very much in the twilight of his career. It turned out that he too had heard about this screenplay and was keen to make a film out of it.

'You might expect two men bent on the same prize to fall out, but that didn't happen. Instead they became friends. In Kuching the screenplay had found a home in the town museum. The curator told them that it was only a fragment, but other fragments had been washed up in bottles on various beaches on the eastern shores of Borneo. The bottles had originally been in the possession of a collector of antiquities in Shanghai, who fled China during the war in his own boat. The ship was torpedoed by a Japanese submarine in 1944, somewhere off the coast of Borneo, but in 1945 a big storm dislodged the wreck from a reef, and over the next two years all sorts of flotsam and jetsam from the ship was washed ashore on

31

the shores of Borneo and nearby islands. Among them the bottles containing the screenplay.

'Mr Flamenco commissioned Curtis to track down the rest of the screenplay, and in return for this service he promised to give him a part in the film he intended to shoot. To this, Curtis agreed. He hired a fisherman with excellent local knowledge as a guide, and took along a stenographer. The plan was to make two copies of each piece of the screenplay they found. One for Curtis and the other to be sent to me.

'In December, he returned to Singapore to wind up his affairs, and in the New Year he set off on his quest. In January he sent me three fragments, and wrote to me that he had reason to believe that Millie might still be alive. I will give you the fragments shortly.

'In February his letters began to arrive with decidedly shaky handwriting, and evidence from their contents that he was not well. Around the middle of February I received a curt letter saying simply, "I now know that which no man should know."

'That was the last letter. After that there was silence. I knew it had been his habit to take his lunch at the Raffles Hotel, so I telephoned the concierge, with whom I have had some dealings in the past. Curtis, he said, had become "unreliable", which I took to mean he had suffered some sort of nervous breakdown. The concierge gave his expert opinion that it was an example of a particular malady called late-flowering Bohemianism.'

She saw the puzzled look on my face and laughed. Throughout our conversation, her face had taken on a sombre cast, but the laughter, soft though it was, revealed this to be a mask. The manner was slightly girlish, and made her eyes crinkle at the corner and glitter. It confirmed my initial impression that she had been quite an effervescent, perhaps irreverent, lady once, but the trials of life had pressed down on her over the years.

'Late-flowering Bohemianism,' she said. 'That's when a chap reaches an age in life where his adventures are over and he settles down to the more quiet demands of the bowls committee or edits the parish newsletter, or at least he should. But then some imp in his soul, unsuspected for many years, rears its head and flatters his vanity into the belief that he is twenty-five again instead of sixty-five. And that, out there in this dark and deceiving world, there is one last adventure that calls to him, one last damsel tied to a tree and in need of deliverance from a dragon. Doubtless you have encountered such types on your trains?'

'If I understand you correctly, yes, I have encountered many such types, generally making a nuisance of themselves.'

'I found out it had something to do with a spat on the Greens committee about emplacing guns on the fairway in anticipation of the Japanese advance, just before the Fall of Singapore.' Her eyes narrowed as if she was trying to picture the disagreement.

'Chaps who were there tell me the Fall of Singapore was quite a blow. The Japs were absolute beasts.'

She nodded and said softly, 'Yes, there were massacres. Although I suspect the blow to British pride was deemed the greater tragedy. The concierge told me that Curtis had been visiting the hotel barber rather more often than was good for a man whose soul was in good health. And there had been whispers, he said, that after his visits to the barber he appeared to be wearing rouge.'

She paused and I tut-tutted.

'I should add this was not his first nervous breakdown. He had one when he was young, shortly after the Great War. There was a boat trip, you see, for the staff. It was supposed to be a day out, a treat. Curtis had just turned twenty-one. They planned taking the boat to Puffin Rock and having a picnic there. Curtis was going too. He was looking forward to it, everybody was. There was a giant tin of Tate & Lyle syrup which some anonymous well-wisher had donated for them. But on the day before the outing he got a phone call ostensibly from the Foreign Office in London urgently requesting his presence the next day regarding an interview. So he missed the boat trip. It turned out that there was no interview and no record of anyone having called him. Then there was a terrible accident out at sea. The engine exploded and the boat sank. No one survived. It was a terrible thing to happen. It hit Curtis hard and he took to his bed for three months as a consequence.'

I struggled to absorb the information. 'Is he still in Singapore?' I asked.

'Apparently, yes, but living in some sort of squalid situation that I was told it would not do for a respectable lady to inquire too deeply into.'

'I see.'

'I want you to go and find Curtis. It seems to me that in so doing you will uncover the fate of your mother. Curtis wrote he had reason to believe she still lived, and that he had a good idea where she might be. I hope this does not appear like a mercenary proposal to you. It is true that I am most anxious about the disappearance of my son, but the fate of your mother has haunted me over the years. It was a terrible injustice that was done to her. My health is not good and my doctor has been candid enough to advise me that I will be lucky to see the year out. If I could make some sort of restitution to Millie it would be ...' She searched for the right word and seemingly unable to find it said simply, 'Well, you can imagine. So, Mr Wenlock, what do you say?'

I stood transfixed. 'Lady Seymour, I ... I have not the slightest idea what to say. Is it even possible that—'

'If you are worried about money, you will of course be well provided for. I propose to give you five thousand pounds. If you are sensible you should go far on that, certainly if you manage to stay out of the clutches of ...' She paused. 'You are aware that Room Forty-Two are looking for you?'

35

'Yes.'

'It seems the information you uncovered in your last case about the former King has upset some powerful people.'

'I discovered that King George V was a scoundrel.'

'Some people wouldn't consider that much of a discovery.'

I was taken aback to hear her say that. The discovery that our King was not a good egg had shocked me deeply at the time, and still did. 'Your Ladyship, I found the revelation quite astonishing.'

'I'm sorry, Mr Wenlock, that was uncalled for. The truth is, you are in a jam. As far as I can see, you only have one way of dealing with Room Forty-Two: you must seek an interview with Princess Elizabeth. She is cut from a different cloth. The King's health is deteriorating, more and more official duties are being devolved to Her Highness. It cannot be long now ... that will be your chance.'

'And why should she worry about a chap such as me?'

She drew long and slowly on her cigarette, and peered at me through the smoke. 'Would it surprise you to learn that she is an admirer of the Railway Goslings?'

'It would surprise me greatly.'

'In many respects she was no different from other children, she read all the Railway Gosling annuals, she longed to meet you and be given a Gosling's Friend badge. But you never turned up on the Royal Train.'

'I was never invited.'

She nodded.

I went on, 'You know of course that I have as much chance of being granted an interview with her as with Father Christmas?'

'Your chances are much better than that, because I intend to write to her and plead your case. You will need to get yourself out of harm's way for the time being though, I don't expect the King to croak immediately. All of which makes the offer I am about to suggest all the more timely. It should see you through until Princess Elizabeth ascends the throne. I have booked you passage on the SS *Pandora*, sailing from Southampton to Singapore. Bates, who collected you from the station, will take care of the details.'

The telephone on the bedside table rang and Lady Seymour answered. 'Yes, put him through.' I waited, aware that Lady Seymour's countenance darkened as she listened to the caller. She whispered, 'Yes, thank you, I will,' and replaced the receiver.

She looked up and informed me that earlier in the afternoon Jenny had been called to the hospital to identify my corpse. Apparently I had fallen into the path of a train.

Lady Seymour explained in a voice hoarse with shock. 'I cannot reveal to you how I know about these matters, but I have a source – reliable and highly placed within Room Forty-Two. I'm told that a man dressed as a post office special messenger turned up at the engine sheds asking for you. The men working there pointed him in the right direction, and later a man said to be you was found on the track, having been hit by a train.'

In the hall I rang the grocer's shop at the end of my street and beseeched him to pass an urgent message to Jenny informing her that I was alive and that she must begin packing at once, and pack only the barest essentials. I took the next train back to Exeter and waited there for the milk train that deposited me back at Weeping Cross at dawn. My heart was in the grip of a pain so acute I found myself clutching it for much of the journey as if it contained a dagger. At Weeping Cross railway station I hailed a taxi, an extravagance unthinkable in the life I had led up until this moment. At Dandelion Hill I instructed the driver to wait and bounded up the stairway of our tenement. The door was half open and Jenny sat on the bed, stiffly erect, with her back to me.

'Jenny,' I said. I waited. She turned her head slowly, like a mechanical doll. 'Jenny,' I repeated, 'It's me.'

'Jack?'

I walked over, sat beside her as she burst into tears. I took her in my arms, muffling her cries.

'Jack, they said—'

'There, there,' and I tightened my arms.

'Jack,' she said again.

I held her face in my hands and stared into her eyes, swollen from crying. 'We have no time,' I said. 'We must leave now.'

Like two ghosts we descended the stairs, carrying a single suitcase towards an adventure that I had no way of imagining. We stepped into the taxi and drove off down Dandelion Hill. As we descended we drove past a man who had just alighted from an omnibus. A man wearing the livery of a post office special messenger.

EXT. SOUTHAMPTON DOCK. NIGHT

The white hull of the steamship *Rajah Brooke* gleams in the bright dock lights. Ticker tape festoons her sides and trails down from her decks to the dock. Passengers throng the deck, pressing against the rail, waving and calling excitedly to their families on the quayside. A brass band plays.

On the quayside, among the derricks, a policeman and two soldiers are searching with hurricane lamps. The policeman holds a 'Wanted' notice bearing the photograph of a girl and the headline WANTED MILLIE TOOKEY. GERMAN SPY.

EXT. SECTION OF THE DOCKS. NIGHT

MILLIE TOOKEY stands amid wooden crates and coiled ropes outside a warehouse. She is wearing her old school mackintosh and has a small, cheap cardboard suitcase. Tied to the suitcase handle is a battered old teddy bear with stuffing leaking from one ear and one eye missing.

She is a safe distance from the search party. They stand between her and the gangway to the ship. If they moved further along, she could slip past unnoticed. A SOLDIER holding a lamp appears from the shadows. He looks at MILLIE and their gazes lock. He is young, no more than seventeen, a year older than MILLIE.

MILLIE TOOKEY

Please do not betray me, Sir. I promise you on all that's holy that I am not a spy. Just a poor girl whose life has gone terribly wrong.

The SOLDIER lets his gaze linger on her for a brief moment as if to consider. He makes up his mind. He moves his lamp away from her and turns as if he had not seen her. He shouts to his companions.

SOLDIER

Nothing here, Sarge!

EXT. DECK OF THE SS *RAJAH BROOKE*.
NIGHT

The ship sounds its horn three times.
A great cry goes up from the crowds
on deck as the ship slowly moves from
the quay into the Solent. Up on the
funnel deck – normally reserved for
walking the dogs of first-class passengers – MILLIE TOOKEY stands alone,
watching Southampton recede into the
night. Tears stream down her face.

TRANSCRIBER'S NOTE:

THE NEXT FOUR PAGES HAVE BEEN
RENDERED ILLEGIBLE
BY SEA WATER DAMAGE.

EXT. DECK OF THE SS *RAJAH BROOKE*.
NIGHT

The typhoon continues to lash the
ship. The bows have sunk beneath the
water and the stern has risen correspondingly a few yards clear. Her

propellers spin in empty air. The ship lists, causing the lifeboats – pitifully few – to foul their lanyards. Crowds throng the deck and cry out in terror. A ship's officer, looking scared, fires his pistol into the air in an attempt to bring the mob to order. MILLIE TOOKEY appears on deck wearing a Mae West and holding her suitcase. An officer spots her.

OFFICER
Where are your mother and father?

MILLIE TOOKEY
In the cemetery, Sir.

The OFFICER takes her suitcase and throws it onto a pile of others. He urges her towards the crowds vainly trying to clamber aboard the lifeboats.

There is a terrible metallic creak and the bows slip further under. Sea water washes a host of passengers off into sea. A great cry of lamentation goes up. MILLIE TOOKEY runs to retrieve her suitcase.

FADE OUT

Chapter 4

'Farewell, England!' Jenny pressed against the handrail of the SS *Pandora* and waved to the dock. 'Farewell!'

A thin drizzle filled the sky, dampening our faces but never quite resolving into droplets. It obscured the town of Southampton, disguising the buildings and turning the lights into fizzing torches. Our hearts fizzed too in a whirl of exhilaration and fear.

We had been in Southampton a week now, while Lady Seymour made travelling arrangements and acquired on our behalf the necessary travel documents.

I had spent the week trying to grasp this sudden receipt of news concerning a mother lost for ever. I felt the same bafflement a South Sea Islander might feel who, never having seen an aeroplane, one day sees a piece of one fall out of the sky.

At first I had been reluctant to believe. In life one seldom dares credit such wonderful things, because of the habit Fate so often has of pulling the rug out from under our hopes. And yet I could not believe that this was some cruel hoax designed to deceive me. It was simply too elaborate. What astonished me most was the reflection that of all the possible explanations for this startling turn of events, the plain narrative given to me by the Countess was probably the most likely.

At the same time, I was troubled by my presentiment that I was leading Jenny into danger. So far I had made a pretty poor husband for her: married on the footplate of a steam engine and the whole of our married life – three and a half months now – had been spent in penury and in hiding from forces who were intent on crushing me. Yet when I shared these fears with Jenny she laughed them off and said that she was rather enjoying the adventure of it. Moreover, she added that my account missed one vital item. Namely that we were happy.

This was true. Until I met Jenny, I had lived the life of a man who spends his days at a cinema where only black and white films are screened, then moves to the picture house down the road and sees for the first time films in Technicolor.

Mr Jarley at the Weeping Cross railway Lost Property office presides over an emporium that, it is said, contains every article that it is possible for a human being to lose. It had been a simple matter to furnish us with luggage and outfits suitable for a trip to the tropics. Jenny had acquired a suitcase that had once belonged to the superintendent of the sales division of a firm manufacturing ladies' trouser suits. It contained a number of sales samples and also a book about the Suffragettes entitled *Trust in God, She Will Provide*.

I had been provided more modestly with a set of pale linen suits and a well-thumbed copy of Chamberlain's

Guide for Travellers to the East. It included information on how to deal with beggars, how to hire a boy, and advice from a doctor stating that once past Port Said one should eat kidneys for breakfast to counteract the heat. In addition, Mr Jarley gave us a small bottle of a tincture called chloral hydrate. He said it was a most potent soporific that was quite popular with members of the criminal underworld, who knew it colloquially under the title Mickey Finn. But that should not prejudice us against it, since such a potion would prove invaluable on a long arduous journey where sleep might sometimes prove elusive.

The ship's horn boomed from the lone funnel that towered above us like a gasometer. The SS *Pandora* was a splendid ship: 25,516 gross tons, with a length of 640 ft and beam of 85. She was built at Harland and Wolff in Belfast in 1935 to service the transatlantic route to Quebec.

We were not due to weigh anchor until gone midnight, and the ship was alive with folk wandering around, exploring. Some who had boarded earlier in the day were already straying further afield and reporting a swimming bath deep in the bowels of the ship filled with chlorinated water just like the ones in town.

'I wonder which of my trouser suits would be best for driving a steam engine,' mused Jenny.

'You still on about that, are you?'

'I thought we could use the time on the voyage for you to teach me.'

'Even if I were disposed to, I couldn't because there isn't time.'

'We have almost two weeks until Singapore.'

'Indeed we do, but in order to drive you first have to learn to fire the engine, and that art, I'm afraid, takes a lifetime to master.'

Jenny peered at me, looking for a clue as to whether I was joking. I wasn't. It really does take that long.

'I don't want to fire,' she said finally.

'Every man who ever drove a steam engine first spent many years on the footplate firing, it's integral to the process.'

'Very well, then, I shall learn to fire first. That can't be difficult, you just shovel coal into a hole.'

'Is that what you think?'

'It's what everybody thinks,' she said triumphantly.

'Well, they couldn't be more wrong if they tried. Driving the engine is not really all that complicated. You could learn that in a week. The real skill, the dark art, is building the fire.'

'So why is the driver the one everyone shakes hands with at the end of the journey?' She spoke with the air of one trying to catch me out.

'Because he is like the captain of a ship. He has the responsibility. If anything goes wrong it is his fault. He will have taken half a lifetime to work his way up to where he is. Shaking his hand is a form of recognition of these long years of service.'

'I think you are being unfair. I can't see what is so special about making a fire. You just light some coal and off you go.'

'No, you light some coal and off you jolly well don't go, at least not for eight hours. How long do you think it takes to boil a kettle that big? The fire will be lit in the firebox the night before, if it is a morning departure.'

'I am determined that you will teach me during our voyage,' she said, in a voice that suggested the matter was not up for debate.

———

On the dockside down below, the railway lines gleamed and tank engines shunted freight alongside our berth. A motor bus pulled up and seconds later a party of children disgorged and were assembled into a small platoon under the command of a lady with stern mien and sharp nose. They marched towards one of the gangways. The tank engine tooted its whistle, the ship's horn groaned again, and a spirit of exultancy arose in my chest.

'Someone must have a sweet tooth,' said Jenny.

I followed her gaze. Across the wharf, through derricks and cranes interlaced like branches in a forest, something glimmered in the sky. A cylinder around five foot high and three wide. It was being hoisted by crane from the dockside into the waiting hold of a cargo ship.

47

It twisted slowly, high above the gang of shouting steve-
dores below, and as it did some script on the cylinder
became discernible. Tate & Lyle Golden Syrup. The
biggest tin I had ever seen. The gleam from lights on
the deck of the freighter onto which it was being hoisted
caught the metal and made it appear brazen, like something stolen from a pagan temple and housed for years
in a museum. The outline of the lion could be faintly
discerned. I wondered what it was for, and recalled
Lady Seymour's account of the terrible boating accident that caused Curtis to take to his bed for many
weeks. Was this the sort of behaviour one would expect
from a young man? Or was he even then of a fragile
disposition?

———————

We shared our table at dinner during the voyage with a
couple, Mr and Mrs Carmichael, a chap called Charlie
Quinn, and a Miss Frobisher, who was travelling alone
to visit her brother in Adelaide.

Charlie Quinn was on board with a small circus travelling to Malaya and was both clown and tiger tamer. A
combination, he told us with evident pride, that was
unique. Mr and Mrs Carmichael had recently retired
after a lifetime as inspectors of Mission schools overseas. They had the air of people who had spent most of
their lives travelling.

As we sat down to dinner on the first night, Mr Carmichael reached over to shake my hand and make his introduction while Mrs Carmichael beamed at us. Mr Quinn, who was seated to my left, offered me his hand. Miss Frobisher was the last to arrive. The meal began with Brown Windsor soup and we made small talk about the way the world appeared to be going to the dogs. This I have noticed is a favourite topic wherever the English gather.

Mr Carmichael looked at me through half-narrowed eyes, nodded imperceptibly and said, 'First time out East, is it?' He continued without waiting for an answer. 'It can be confusing at first, but you won't go far wrong with the advice given to me by my grandfather who was a great traveller. East of Suez, he said, there are two types of country. Those where you should hit the taxi driver with your walking stick and those where you shouldn't.'

'I have a better tip,' said Mrs Carmichael. 'Would you like to hear it?'

'Very much,' I said.

'My tip is designed to keep you out of gaol, especially in countries where the guards spit in your soup. This is what you must do. On arrival in any foreign land, you must head straight away to the General Post Office and buy an envelope. All post offices sell stationery, but the quality varies greatly, and this is the point. You must lick the flap and seal the envelope. Then wait five minutes.'

She paused to make sure she had our interest, and indeed it appeared that she had.

'There are two types of country in this world, you see; I call them A class and B class. Most of Europe is A class, except the Mediterranean lands. Singapore is A class, and so is Hong Kong. Shanghai is B class. Almost everywhere else in Southeast Asia is B class, except for Tokyo, which I would go so far as to say is double A class in this respect.

'If you are in an A-class country your envelope flap will be still be stuck down five minutes later. If you are in a B-class country it will have come unstuck. You must not think the envelope test is trivial, because everything you need to know about the country can be worked out from it. It tells you, for example, about the state of the public buildings, the state of repair of the roads, the desirability of using publicly provided lavatories. The answer to the latter being absolutely *not* in B-class countries unless you want to contract cholera.

'It tells you whether the trains run on time, whether the banknotes will be grubby or pristine. It gives you precise insight into the insolence of public officials. It tells you how often you can expect to get food poisoning, how careful you must be in counting your change. And most importantly it tells you an essential piece of information about the police. In class A countries, if you get in trouble and try to bribe them you will go to jail. Whereas in class B countries you will go to jail if you do *not* bribe them. This simple fact alone is worth a king's ransom when travelling in those lands where you are advised to boil your drinking water.' During the course of this little speech, Miss Frobisher arrived and listened intently to it. 'Bravo!' she said when it was finished. 'Bravo! I'm going all the way to Sydney.'

'Definitely class A,' said Mrs Carmichael.

'Are you hoping to start a new life?' asked Mr Carmichael.

'Oh no, it's a return ticket. I'm going to visit my brother. He's been out there fifteen years and now, when we had finally given up all hope, he seems to have found himself a wife.'

'How lovely,' exclaimed Mrs Carmichael, as if few things were more dear to her than the welfare of this total stranger.

'Yes!' agreed Miss Frobisher. 'It's funny how these things turn out. We always thought he was forever destined to the disfavour of Fate. He bought a diamond mine there but it never produced much. Except this.' She opened her handbag and took out a diamond ring. Even to an untutored eye such as mine, it seemed an awfully big diamond. The Carmichaels made suitable expressions of surprise and delight.

'He brought the uncut stone over last year and left it with me, to get it cut and set in London. I won't be so vulgar as to tell you what it is worth, but when the jeweller told me, I almost fainted.' She paused and added, 'It's … it's the engagement ring …' Then she lowered her voice and leaned slightly forward as if public disclosure of the next revelation might scupper the whole thing. 'He hasn't asked her yet!'

Just then our attention was distracted by a troupe of children, the ones we had seen on the dockside, passing in a file two abreast, and led at the front by the lady with the sharp nose. The children, boys and girls of a variety of ages from around four or five to thirteen, looked cowed and lacked the exuberance one normally sees from children. They seemed to lack the excitement that infected even the adults on a big ship.

'Poor swine,' said Charlie Quinn softly.

'Why so?' asked Miss Frobisher.

'You probably don't think life could be much worse than the one they are leaving, but you'd be wrong. Orphans. Mother Britannia sends them out to Australia because it's cheaper than paying for their upkeep in Britain. Trouble is, once out there they have to work. Manual labour. Sleep outside. Skivvies. Some of them are treated brutally. And there's worse, too. Things it wouldn't do to mention in polite company.'

Miss Frobisher gasped.

'They say to the children, "Hands up all those who would like to ride to school every day on a kangaroo." All those who put up their hands get sent to Australia.'

'I can assure you, sir,' said Mr Carmichael, evidently affronted by Mr Quinn's remark, 'that no such iniquities will be visited upon these children. As a matter of fact they are very much to be envied.'

'Envied?' said Mr Quinn. 'I should be greatly surprised.'

'Then you are easily surprised,' said Mr Carmichael, his face turning red. 'I can assure you these children are very lucky.'

'You sound very certain of the fact,' said Mr Quinn.

'Indeed I am, since I am the superintendent of their fate. They are transiting to Australia under the golden auspices of the Saint Lucy the Remarkable Society, of which I happen to be an officer.'

'I can't believe they would lie to little orphans,' said Miss Frobisher in an attempt to defuse the situation, which had grown slightly uncomfortable.

'That's nothing,' said Mr Quinn. 'They tell them their mothers are dead, even though it is not true.'

'That strikes me as a most unlikely thing for a charity to do,' said Mr Carmichael in exasperation.

'In my experience,' said the clown, 'people who run charities often have very little of it in their own hearts.'

'We do not lie to the children,' insisted Mr Carmichael. 'Moreover, it seems to me not unreasonable to expect them to work in their new home, for the Lord has so ordained it that bringing a child into the world outside of wedlock is a sin that must be expiated, and if the mother is not in a position to do so, then the duty naturally falls to the child.'

I thought of my own mother, condemned by the heartless words of Mr Carmichael. It seemed to me he had inadvertently confirmed Mr Quinn's previous remark. My thoughts travelled back to my own childhood.

There had been twelve 'Gosling Class' special railway detectives created at the Weeping Cross Railway Servants' Orphanage between 1902 and 1914. All were named after railway stations. Cheadle Heath, Cadbury Holt and I were now the only ones left. I thought of all the ones who had perished. Lightcliffe, shot at dawn in 1917. Luton Hoo, stabbed in the eye with a swordstick in 1921. Tumby Woodside, stole money from a collecting tin attached to a dog, and was thrashed to death in 1921. Temple Combe, died in the electric chair at Sing Sing, 1925. Conway Marsh, crushed by an elephant in Indochina, 1926. Kipling Coates, lost in an opium den in Shanghai, 1927. Mickle Trafford, dragged from his ship by a giant squid, 1928. Hucknall Byron, sent to the Gulag on Kolyma River, 1935. Amber Gate, lost on the *Hindenburg*, 1937. We had always been discouraged from talking about our mothers. I don't think we were ever told they were dead, but we were given the impression that they might as well have been.

Jenny, sensing my disquiet, squeezed my hand. Then she said to Mr Carmichael, 'I don't agree with that at all.'

'You don't agree with what?' he asked.

'That the children should pay for their mother's … she did nothing wrong, a woman who gives up her child like that is … well … she must have very strong reasons, otherwise she wouldn't do it.'

'The Bible is quite clear on the issue.' He spoke in the icy tone of one unused to being defied, particularly by a woman.

'I don't believe God punishes poor women who are destitute and … and …'

'Perhaps you should be more prudent in your remarks.'

'Why?' she said with a challenge in her voice.

'Because He will be listening.'

'How do you know it's a He?'

Mrs Carmichael gasped, and one could sense eyebrows being raised around the rest of the table.

'I beg your pardon?' said Mr Carmichael.

'I read a book that said God was a She.' It was clear that Jenny had not taken kindly to Mr Carmichael's remarks about unmarried mothers. She really did have a feisty spirit on occasion, and from what I had seen of it, Mr Carmichael would have been well advised to exercise some caution.

Charlie Quinn laughed.

'What an avant-garde notion,' said Miss Frobisher, seemingly unsure whether to be delighted or appalled.

'Are you mocking your Maker?' said Mr Carmichael, who had now turned from red to plum.

'No, I greatly admire Her.'

Charlie Quinn laughed again.

Mr Carmichael recited: '*In the portion of Jezreel shall dogs eat the flesh of Jezebel: And the carcase of Jezebel shall be as dung upon the face of the field in the portion of Jezreel; so that they shall not say, This is Jezebel.* You should mark her fate carefully.'

'I can tell you,' Mr Quinn interrupted, 'from having seen with my own eyes, that the lives of these children being sent out to Australia would make even Oliver Twist wince.' He turned to me and, without missing a beat, said, 'I think I've seen you somewhere before. Have you ever been to Kuala Lumpur?'

'I'm afraid not,' I said, 'We're from—'

'Barmouth,' said Jenny.

'Where's that?' said Mr Quinn.

'In Wales,' she replied. 'Jack once drove a steam engine there.'

'How exciting!' said Mrs Frobisher.

'From Paddington.'

'I once caught that train,' said Mr Carmichael. 'Damn thing was late. You know what I did? I walked up to the engine at Reading and gave the driver a guinea to make up the lost time. It worked too. Bloody scoundrel!'

I laughed, relieved at the opportunity to lighten the atmosphere. 'I assure you, Mr Carmichael,' I said, 'he was nothing of the sort.'

'My bribe worked, didn't it?'

'It certainly must have appeared that way! In truth, it had no effect whatsoever. You can rest assured that both driver and his fireman would have strained every nerve and sinew to make up the lost time, no goal would have been dearer to their hearts. Your bribe had no more

56

effect than if you had bribed the sun to rise. Of course, drivers and their firemen are poor men. The driver would have accepted your kindness and used it to stand a round for his mates in the pub later.'

'You make him sound like a saint.'

'If you knew the dangers he braves—'

'Like what?'

'Like … fog for example. Some days it can be so thick you can't see your feet. You have no idea where you are, you drive blind, you peer out of the cab, straining to see the signals, if you miss one it could lead to disaster, but you *do* miss them. You drive at dead slow, sometimes the only way of knowing where you are is by sense of smell, you smell the gasworks, for example, and because you know the road so well you can work out your progress. Even if you spot a signal, you can't see what it shows, the signals are lost in the fog. Sometimes I have climbed the gantry and edged my way along like a sailor up in the rigging, and then felt the position of the signal by hand.'

'Jack, that sounds terrifying,' said Jenny.

'Yes! Down beneath me was the train, but I couldn't see it. Believe me, if passengers understood what goes on in fog they would never board a train.'

Mr Carmichael snorted dismissively.

Mrs Carmichael turned to Mr Quinn. 'It must be wonderful to be a clown.'

'Why must it?' he said.

'Well … I mean, isn't it? Everyone loves a clown.'

'I don't.'

'Oh!'

'Being a clown is a curse. I wouldn't wish it upon my worst enemy.'

Mrs Carmichael struggled not to let go of an axiom that had served her all her life. 'But clowns make everyone happy.'

'They don't make themselves happy. Clowns are the unhappiest creatures on God's earth, surely you knew that?'

'How could I possibly know that?'

'It's the one thing everyone knows about clowns. What sort of person has to paint a happy face on each morning? Did you never stop to think about that?'

'So why choose to become one?' she asked, puzzled.

'I didn't.'

'Now I'm really confused.'

'When you were in school, was there a little fat kid whom nobody loved?'

'I'm not sure if I remember …'

'Of course there was, there's one in every class. I was that kid. Nobody liked me, nobody talked to me. Of all the trials that afflict you in later life, none are as miserable as being the kid at school nobody likes. Then one day, I fell over, and the kids laughed. So I did it again, and again they laughed. Being laughed at is painful, but it is better than being ostracised, so I learned to act the fool. When I did, the kids wanted to have me around. Not because they liked me, they never liked me, but they liked having a fool around. I became the fool. The trouble is, once you put on the red nose you are never allowed to take it off.'

Mrs Carmichael was lost for words.

'Jack's going to teach me to drive a train,' said Jenny brightly.

'What on earth for?' said Mr Carmichael, rather loudly.

'He says it can be rather … rather wonderful …'

'Never!' said Mr Carmichael.

'Yes, yes, he said it was like the pleasure a man takes secretly with his wife.'

'Golly!' said Mrs Carmichael, 'I didn't know it was *that* bad.'

Jenny laughed and said, 'From what I've heard you might go so far as to say it was quite lalapaloosa.'

I stiffened. Jenny had confided to me that during the war a young American soldier had been billeted in the house she shared with her aunt. They had become quite thick, and in the course of their friendship he had taught her all manner of words I had never heard before. When she first told me this, I admit I had been quite out of sorts about it. Since then I had tried not to mind, but it was surprisingly difficult. Jenny shot me a glance and I forced a smile.

'What does that mean?' said Mrs Carmichael.

'It's Eskimo,' said Jenny. 'It means dreamy.'

We remained at the table long after the others had left. As we stood up to leave Jenny noticed Miss

59

Frobisher – who it had to be admitted had taken one or two more glasses of wine than was good for her – had left the engagement ring lying on the table. Jenny picked it up and said she would return it.

Later, on deck as we took the air, Jenny said, 'So am I not allowed to say lalapaloosa?'

'I didn't say you may not.'

'I know you didn't say it, perhaps I'm just imagining it. It feels awkward, but really it shouldn't be. Cooper is dead, along with lots of other young men. I can't unknow him or the funny words he taught me. They are all that's left of him, really.'

'Yes.'

'Just lalapaloosa, and Spoony, and calling a glass of water in a restaurant "dog soup".' She pressed her head against mine. 'I've got you now.'

'You must say lalapaloosa whenever the urge takes you,' I said tenderly.

'Thank you Jack. It would be difficult not to. Since we met, everything has been pretty lalapaloosa.'

She decided on an early night and I strolled to the bar for a nightcap. After a while, Charlie Quinn sidled up to me and said, 'I know your secret.'

My heart quickened.

'I saw your face in the paper in Southampton. You done a chap in.'

I forced a laugh.

'Welshman. A miner's son. Newspaper said you were wanted by the police under suspicion of pushing him into the path of the train. I knew I'd seen you some-where before, but couldn't place it. When your wife said you used to work on the railway, that's when I had it.'

'I'm afraid you are gravely mistaken, Mr Quinn.' I struggled hard to counterfeit an insouciance wildly at odds with the tumult in my breast. 'It's true I used to work on the railways, but so do lots of other people. And I've never once, at least as far as I can recall, pushed a chap under a train. I have cleaned plenty of such chaps off trains and know what a frightful mess it makes.'

'You're a cool customer, that's for sure. But you are beginning to sweat at the gills in a way that confirms my suspicion. Personally, I have no wish to be of assistance to the police, but it so happens that I am in a spot of trouble and urgently need two hundred guineas. I really didn't know where I was going to get it from, but now I do. If you see what I mean. If I mention this to the cap-tain, they will inform the authorities in Singapore, or maybe at Port Said. I'll see if I can find a copy of the newspaper, I expect someone on board will have one.'

He left without a backward glance and I considered this dark revelation. If the chap with the dead-fish eyes and the burned face was, as I supposed, an agent for Room 42, it would seem that not only did he push poor Ifan into the path of the train thinking it was me, but had then, upon discovering his error, arranged for an arrest warrant to be issued specifying me as the murderer. If Room 42 and its agents had the power to do that, then it was certain they would also have the power to fix the outcome of any trial.

As for the matter of 200 guineas, it was true that with the funds Lady Seymour had provided, I could perhaps pay Mr Quinn. But it was certain I could not satisfy him. As a former detective, I knew a thing or two about blackmail. It is a crime hallmarked by one implacable fact, namely this: it is impossible to buy what you are paying for. Even after the payment, the item which you sought to buy remains in the possession of the black-mailer. You stand exactly where you stood before you paid, only poorer. And having indicated once your willingness to pay, you are certain to be presented with a second demand, but this time at a higher price.

The pickle we were in had taken a distinctive turn for the worse. Things were now anything but lalapaloosa.

Chapter 5

TWO DAYS OUT FROM Southampton we entered the Bay of Biscay, where a storm was boiling. The winds screamed at us from the south-west, and buffeted the ship like a headmaster boxing a boy around the ears. The ship rolled like a drunk leaving a saloon bar and became a ghost town as passengers deserted the decks and corridors and kept to their cabins. The sharp smell of sick filled the air and the moaning of the wind was punctuated from time to time by the far-off sounds of crockery breaking. And always there was the squeaking, squeaking, squeaking of the ship's innards being twisted. From time to time we would crash head-on into a particularly big wave and the ship would shudder, and from deep in her belly there would come a boom as if a giant had struck a gong.

None of our dining companions turned up for breakfast during the next three days. Jenny and I had the ship to ourselves. I did not tell Jenny about Mr Quinn's remarks. He was one of those whom seasickness had banished to his cabin. I was aware that the matter needed to be resolved, but had no idea how to do it.

No one had ever blackmailed me before. Perhaps it would not have mattered so much if it were just my fate at stake, but I was greatly worried for Jenny. She, sensing nothing of this, gaily continued to interrogate me on the art of firing a train, oblivious to how far from my thoughts such a concern was.

'What do I do first?' she asked. The lounge had the slightly eerie quality of emptiness that one finds when one gets up in the night and walks about.

'What do you mean?'

'How do I start?'

'You start like every other fireman, you cook breakfast. You must learn to cook breakfast.'

'That's not firing!'

'Yes it is!'

'I already know how to cook breakfast.'

'But not on a footplate.'

'It can't be very different.'

'No, if you cook your breakfast at home on a shovel, it is not greatly different.'

Jenny laughed. 'Jack Wenlock, don't think I don't know what your game is!'

'I haven't got a game,' I said in a voice that betrayed the presence of the cloud hanging over me.

'Jack?' said Jenny. 'Are you all right? You seem a bit … subdued.'

'Do I?'

'You are not worried about me, are you?'

'No, of course not. To tell the truth, I'm … I'm a bit concerned about the coal.'

She looked puzzled. 'What coal?'

'The coal they are firing the ship with. If you look at the smoke coming out of the funnel it has a greenish tinge. I've seen it before, we used to call it "coal mange".'

Jenny peered at my face for a second to see whether I was serious. Having satisfied herself that I was, she stood up and walked out through the door that led to the deck. She came back a few minutes later. 'You are right,' she said with mock seriousness. 'Definitely green. You must tell the Captain.'

I laughed. 'I hardly think he will pay any attention to me!'

'We'll see about that,' she said. A ship's officer dressed in white, with gold trim, walked past and Jenny hailed him. 'There's a problem with the smoke,' she said.

'What smoke?' he asked, puzzled.

'Coming out of the funnel,' said Jenny. 'It's green. Although the problem is really with the coal. It's got mange.' I could tell she was enjoying herself enormously, but really there was nothing funny about coal mange.

'By Jove!' said the officer. 'Green, you say?' He seemed delighted by the revelation.

'Green*ish*,' I added, anxious not to overstate the matter.

'Haven't you seen?' asked Jenny.

'I must confess I haven't looked. Is green smoke so terribly bad?'

I joined in. 'I strongly suspect it is caused by a fungal bloom that is commonly called "coal mange". It means your coal will burn poorly, greatly reducing the efficiency of your engines, and the fumes produced are liable to make your stokers rather poorly.'

'Jack … er Mr Wenlock, my husband, used to drive a steam engine,' said Jenny with the air of one putting down a trump card.

'My word,' said the officer. 'Did he really? How splendid.' He seemed quite boyish for an officer, although I suspected this was a deceptive air conveyed by what appeared to be an affecting candour and the slightly inept cut to his blond hair.

'He used to fire them too, so he knows about coal.'

'Well, in that case,' said the officer, 'I will have to make the Chief Engineer aware of the predicament. He's quite a touchy fellow and I don't imagine he will take too kindly to being told there is a problem with his smoke, but it can't be helped. We can't have green smoke.' He thanked us and left.

'Now,' said Jenny. 'Tell me what is really wrong.'

I looked at her, and she peered at me with a look that combined both curiosity and concern.

'You are not persuaded by the smoke? It really is green.'

'I know, but that is not what is troubling you.'

A string quintet began playing 'Dance, Ballerina, Dance' at the far end of the empty lounge. Jenny took my hand and gently eased me to my feet. 'We'll dance first, and then you can tell me.' And this we duly did. Two lone figures in an empty lounge, dancing like drunkards on a deck that seemed to continually fall away from their feet.

'As I say,' said Jenny as we waltzed, 'you really need not worry about me, Jack. I can honestly say, I have never been so happy in my life. It feels like … like we are eloping or doing something equally naughty. I've never really had much opportunity to be disobedient before. I quite like it. It feels like … it feels like we are Bonnie and Clyde.'

'Does it really?'

'Yes! Yes, it does, it feels so … Jack I've never felt like this before.'

There came another gong boom from deep in the innards of the ship.

'Does the danger that we may be facing not trouble you?'

'Jack, the very reason we are in trouble is because of me. I'm the one who brought you the case.'

We continued to glide and occasionally stumble around an empty dance floor. The musicians were clearly used to the situation and played with aplomb, as if we were sailing over a mill pond.

'That moment in your office when the train passed beneath the window and without seeing it you diagnosed a fault because of the chuffs—'

'I didn't really diagnose anything, just observed that it was a 4–6–0 Castle class—'

Jenny interrupted me. 'I know! The one with a sloping throatplate in the firebox and the steam superheating that falls short, giving a characteristic double cough in the chuffs.'

I pulled back slightly to peer into Jenny's face. Was she teasing me for my obsession? It didn't seem so. She returned my gaze and said, 'That's when I fell in love with you.'

I blinked in surprised delight. 'Well, then I'm even luckier than I had supposed. Any number of men could have told you about the double cough in the chuffs.'

'That's partly what I love about you, Jack. There isn't another man alive who would say such a thing to a lady and you don't even know it.' We danced on in silence for a while. Then Jenny said, 'You mustn't worry about me, Jack. I'm sure we will be all right, I feel it. And … just think! Your mother! Wouldn't you be willing to fight a hundred tigers for a chance to discover her whereabouts?'

'I would, I would. But I couldn't expect you to.'

'But don't you see, Jack? Don't you see! Nothing could be dearer to me than this because I know nothing could be more dear to you.'

'Yes, but—'

'No buts, Jack! Since that moment we stood on the footplate and became man and wife, my fate and yours have been joined, indivisible. We will be happy together, or unhappy together.' And so we danced, and when the musicians took a break, we walked out onto the deck, and stood buffeted by the wind, pressed against each other and against the deck rail. Then I told her about Mr Quinn.

She listened to my words with a serious expression, nodded and said, 'There is only one thing to be done, we must push Mr Quinn over the side tonight.'

I was startled. 'Do you really ... I'm not sure I could ...'

Jenny giggled. 'I wasn't serious!'

'You weren't? Oh ... I see. I rather thought you might be, because I had already considered this remedy.'

'I have a better way,' she said. 'We'll frame him.'

'Frame him?'

'Implicate him in a crime. I saw it done in a film, *When Blackmail Turns Blue*, or something like that. I still have Miss Frobisher's ring, we'll frame him for stealing it. You must invite him for a drink to discuss the money, and when he is not looking put the Mickey Finn that Mr Jarley gave us into his drink. Then I'll take his key and conceal the ring in his cabin. Then later I will say to Miss Frobisher that if she needs to send people on errands to her room she would be better advised than to choose Mr Quinn, who did not strike me as honest. And she will ask what I'm talking about and I'll say I saw him coming out of her cabin just now. Naturally she will go and check her room and her belongings and discover the ring is missing. She will tell the ship's officers, and they will search his cabin and find the ring. Easy.'

'You certainly make it sound easy,' I laughed.

'If you can think of a better plan, let me know,' she said with a gleam in her eye that suggested she found the whole thing rather jolly. 'It worked in the film.'

On the fifth day, we awoke to find the day calm and the sea gentler than a pond. Passengers began to emerge, like hibernating animals in spring. Jenny had gone to the library to write some letters. Apparently if you gave them to the Purser you didn't have to put any stamps on and they would be posted in the next port of call.

I decided to explore the ship once more, and found a small gift shop next to the Purser's office. There was a display in the window about the future of transport; it included a toy – a small model, about 6 inches long, of an entirely new type of train. One powered by atomic energy. The engine was completely white, and stream-lined like the Mallard. I went inside to take a closer look and read the accompanying leaflet.

The exciting new force of atomic power will transform the railways of tomorrow. No more will steam be generated using coal – that one-time food of the dinosaurs. The hard, backbreaking job of fireman will be consigned to the museum, along with the filth and soot and ash. Gone too will be the conventional driver clad in oily rags. In his place will stand a pilot, his uniform a Prussian blue jacket with gold braid hoops on the cuffs, and a peaked captain's cap. No more the grime-besmeared face with a look of permanent exhaustion. The engine driver of tomorrow will stand tall and preside – proud heir to Professor

Einstein's glory — over a gleaming white cockpit of a type familiar to fans of the space-travelling hero Mr Flash Gordon.

It all sounded so utterly marvellous. I bought the atomic engine on impulse. Jenny, I knew, would be thrilled. The act of buying the toy felt mildly wicked, and I realised that I had never bought anything on impulse before. Visions of our son one day presiding over Einstein's glory swam up before me.

I returned to the deck and stood at the rail. Mr Quinn appeared between me and the sunlight.

'I've found it,' he said. He held out a copy of *The Times*, folded open to an inside page. 'You're in it, see? Man wanted for grisly murder. Your picture, too.' I gave the article a nonchalant look. The photograph was a few years old, from the Register of Goslings, but it certainly looked like me.

'I'm glad you are here, Mr Quinn, I've been looking for you.'

'You have?'

'Yes, I wonder if you would be kind enough to join me for a drink after dinner tonight. You see I have a proposition to put to you that could result in your acquiring considerably more than two hundred guineas.'

Mr Quinn's eyes lit up. 'Really?'

'As much as two thousand perhaps. But of course if you are not interested—'

'No, no,' he interrupted, attempting not to sound too keen. 'I don't mind listening to your proposition. I shall see you in the bar this evening.'

He walked off, and shortly after, Jenny arrived. The wind had dropped. Scraps of blue sky appeared, behind tattered rags of cloud. It was a cold blue, pure and deep. The tang of salt on the breeze was sharp. Jenny and I climbed to the funnel deck. We held on to the rail and leaned into the wind, which was fiercer up high. The funnel emitted a throb that we felt in our bellies, and a lovely scent of smoke hung on the air, supplemented every so often by gusts that blew the smoke downwards to the deck before whipping it away again.

'Who did you find to write to?' I asked.

'Cooper … Cooper's parents.'

'Oh, I see. How very nice.' This disclosure had a dampening effect on my spirits.

'You don't mind?' she said with concern.

'Mind? No, of course not. Why should I … Why … why did you write to them?'

'To see how they are. They were very kind to me when … their son died.'

'Kind in what way?'

'They sent money. My aunt and I really needed it.'

'I see.'

'Please don't mind.'

'I don't.' Jenny and I rarely fell out, but a tension had arisen between us that was hard to ignore.

'You should inform your voice then, Jack,' she said in a tone I had not heard before. It contained a hint of anguish.

'What does that mean?' My answer came out unintentionally sharp.

If it was possible to flinch imperceptibly, this is how Jenny received my remark. She was silent for a moment and then said, 'I was being silly, sorry. If you would prefer me not to write to them, then, of course, I won't. It doesn't matter.'

'You must write to whoever you please. Really, I don't mind.'

'How can I believe your words, Jack, when you say them in a voice I never hear from you?'

'No, really, perhaps this other matter has affected me. I don't mind you writing … I was just curious to know what on earth you would find to write about.'

'I told them we were on a ship heading to Singapore. I said it was our honeymoon.' She looked at me, eyes sparkling behind the windblown hair, with an expression of impish fun, as if the admission had been especially naughty. What heart could fail to be melted? Because it was in some strange way true. 'By Jove!' I said. 'By Jove!'

'I also read some of the book, *Trust in God, She Will provide*.'

'I have to say, I find that a very curious title.'

'So far it seems rather fun.'

Miss Frobisher joined us and greeted us gaily. An atmosphere of mild excitement seemed to have possessed the passengers, the same found on a morning when snow has fallen in the night for the first time in a winter, and folk emerge to leave the first footprints. Travelling by ship renders us all children again.

Miss Frobisher was visibly excited. 'You'll never guess what,' she said. 'I've found out we have a very important guest travelling with us.' We gave her a look of polite inquiry and she continued. 'Solveig Connemara! The film star!'

As if on cue, a regal lady appeared on the deck below us. She was holding the arm of a chap who was huddled against the wind. He wore a trench coat, with white spats, and had the unsteady air of one who has spent his twilight years in Florida and is now unused to inclement weather. He held a cane in a manner that suggested it was largely for show, but sometimes provided necessary support. Solveig Connemara wore a fur coat, a head scarf, and dark glasses that concealed most of her face.

Miss Frobisher nudged my arm sharply and hissed, 'There. See! I'm going to see if I can have a word with her.' She left once more, filled with excitement at the prospect of this new errand.

'Jenny,' I said. 'While you were writing your letters I happened to notice a rather fine souvenir on sale in the purser's office. It's a new type of train that runs by focusing the rays of the sun or something. It burns

74

atoms instead of coal.' I took it out of the paper bag and showed it to her. 'The beauty of it is, atoms are so small you could carry enough to fire you from Paddington to Penzance in a thimble. Isn't that wonderful! I thought we could keep this and give it to our son—'

I could sense rather than see Jenny stiffen. 'Our son?'

'Yes,' I continued excitedly. 'Imagine it! Wearing a pilot's uniform and standing at the helm like Flash Gordon.'

She said again, 'Our son?'

'Yes, I mean, of course when—'

'We don't have a son.' Her voice was a pained whisper, more pained than I think I had ever heard it before.

'No, no, you are quite right, but I thought—'

She moved away from me. 'Well, that's … that's really wonderful. Perhaps next time you will consult me before you go buying toys for *our* son.'

She strode off. This was so far from how I had pictured her response that I felt almost dizzy with shock.

I remained at the ship's rail for at least an hour before retiring to our cabin. Jenny was sitting on the lower bunk, staring at nothing. She did not turn as I entered.

'Jenny,' I said softly, 'I'm so very sorry.' I put the toy train in the rubbish bin just inside the door and sat down next to her. I spoke with head bowed to my lap. 'It seems without ever intending to I have grievously hurt you and said or done something inappropriate, and I can only—'

She placed her arm round my back and pressed her head down onto my shoulder, her words muffled slightly. 'No, Jack, it is me who should apologise. I ... I don't know what came over me.'

'I expect you are tired,' I said.

'Yes, I'm sure that is it. I'm sorry.' And then there was no sound bar the endless squeaking of the ship's innards and Jenny's silent weeping.

That evening, over dinner, Miss Frobisher told everyone of her discovery. 'Three Academy award nominations for best actress. What a voice! Started out in Vaudeville. It shows. Child star. In Larry Long's *Five Singing Popsicles*. Terrible what happened though ...'

Miss Frobisher let the words dangle in the air, like bait. Mrs Carmichael took it.

'She gave up singing, didn't she?'

'You mean you didn't hear?'

'No.'

'It was the talk of the town!'

'We've spent most of our life in the sort of town where the talk is of the price of goats,' said Mr Carmichael.

Miss Frobisher resumed her narrative: 'She was playing opposite Johnny Sorrento in *The Mule Comes Too*. They fell in love. Thick as thieves they were. Barely twenty she was.' She paused as if considering how best to broach what came next. She made an expression that suggested it was her painful duty to tell us. 'He got her in the family way. But she was under contract to star in *Oops, I Thought You Were Daisy* and two more films produced by Sam Flamenco. Story is' – she lowered her voice, and leaned slightly forward as if to stress that this particular piece of gossip should go no further – 'Sam Flamenco made her get rid of it.'

My ears pricked at the mention of that name. Sam Flamenco was the name of the producer whom Curtis had met on the boat to Borneo. I turned to Jenny, who was staring at me equally astonished.

'Get rid of what?' said Mr Carmichael, and then the realisation hit him like a blow. 'Oh! I see. Oh no, how … infamous!'

Miss Frobisher nodded. 'It was either that or her career was over. Never the same afterwards, though. *Oops, I Thought You Were Daisy* ran into financial problems. The production was abandoned after a month. After that, Solveig just disappeared. Never married. Took to drink. Fell quite low, they say. Poor thing.' She lowered her voice again. 'They say there was a spell in prison, too.'

Mr Carmichael nodded.

'After all that, I never expected to see her with *him*.'

'Who?' said Mrs Carmichael.

'That chap she's travelling with – it's Sam Flamenco.'

I had not seen any of his movies but knew the sort they were: tales of derring-do and high adventure, often featuring spies whose lives one suspected bore little resemblance to the lives of real spies. Tonight I felt as if I had fallen into one of his films. There were few more ordinary men in the world than me, and yet I found myself being pursued by an agent of a shadowy organisation called Room 42, intent on my murder. I in turn was in pursuit of a chap called Curtis, who, it seemed, was himself engaged on a quest to find my own mother, a woman I had never entertained the slightest hope of ever meeting. And now tonight on this very ship was a man who had recently gone into some sort of partnership with Mr Curtis. If this really were a film and I saw it at the cinema I should say it was far-fetched.

After dinner I set out to discover Mr Flamenco, who had dined in the First Class dining room aft. I found him in the bar, surrounded by a group of people, three ladies and two gentlemen, whom I took to be his dining companions. He was telling a story and they were hanging on to his every word.

'The ship eventually arrived on the shores of a mysterious island, marked on no maps or charts, and surrounded by a thick bank of fog with magical properties that made the compass go haywire. Captain Squideye had been searching all his life for this island. It was known by the name Shimushir and was said to contain a portal to another realm. In the land beyond the portal there grew a flower whose perfume had the power to mend a broken heart. But the portal was guarded by a huge monster, a giant ape called

Chomghuürgha. He lived on top of the mountain, and down below lived a tribe of islanders who would appease the monster with human sacrifices. They said the monster was particularly fond of white women.'

The three ladies squealed in feigned shock. He paused to enjoy the effect, like the showman that he clearly was. Then added, 'Miss Connemara will play the lead. It will be the glorious consummation of her stellar career.'

'The part calls for a virgin,' she said drily, 'but he couldn't find one in Hollywood.'

More shocked laughter erupted.

I stood, fidgeting nervously behind the backs of the group, unobserved, wondering how to interrupt and what on earth I would say.

'You probably think I'm a bit too old for the part, but Sam has a good make-up team, and he tells me if you drink the water on this island it restores you to the first bloom of youth. That's if the monster doesn't gobble you up first.'

'Is the monster real?' one of the men asked.

'Oh yes,' said Mr Flamenco. 'It has to be. We can't afford a model.'

The second man turned to Miss Connemara. 'But aren't you afraid?'

Miss Connemara laughed. It was clear she had been drinking quite a bit. 'Afraid, honey? Some hairy brute putting his beefy paws all over me and promising me the Gate to Paradise? It's the story of my life.'

They all laughed again, although the joke struck me as having a well-worn air to it. Mr Flamenco noticed me lurking, and said with undisguised irritation, 'Yes?'

'I'm awfully sorry, Mr Flamenco, I was … well … I was wondering …'

'Sure, buddy. Solvy!' Miss Connemara turned to me and said, 'What's your name, honey?'

'Er … Wenlock.'

She picked up a studio portrait of her looking much younger from a pile that lay on the table and scribbled 'Wenlock' on it. She thrust it at me. I took it dumbly. They all returned their attention to Mr Flamenco and his story.

Just then I saw Mr Quinn approaching. I put the photo in my jacket pocket and walked over to meet him.

I had already surveyed the bar so as to work out how best to put Jenny's scheme into practice. There were a few alcove tables along the perimeter wall in near-darkness that would do the trick. Mr Quinn made my task easier by first putting his cabin key down on the table and then ordering both a pint of beer and a single-malt Scotch. I was pretty sure he would not have placed such an order had he been paying for himself. He downed the pint quickly, with the happy result that he soon needed to visit the lavatory, leaving me free to pour the chloral hydrate into his whisky unobserved.

During the next hour he ordered three more whiskies, and made frequent trips to the lavatory in order, he said, to throw cold water onto his face. Apparently the sea air was making him drowsy. During one such trip, Jenny came and took his key, and also the copy of the newspaper he still carried. On another occasion Mr Carmichael strolled past and exchanged a few words with me.

'I'd be careful of that chap, if I were you,' he said. 'I don't trust him.'

'Really?' I said. 'I thought he had an honest face.'

'Honest? I hardly think so.'

'Well, let's hope he is.' I laughed. 'He just told me he used to be a locksmith and there wasn't a single door on this ship he couldn't open.'

Mr Carmichael's eyes started from their sockets. 'Just be careful. I have an instinct for these things, and it never lets me down. He's a queer fish.' He nodded solemnly and walked off.

Apart from the drowsiness, there seemed little evidence that the Mickey Finn was having much effect on Mr Quinn. I explained to him my plan. 'I've been observing you since Southampton,' I began. 'And you strike me as an honest man. I have an instinct for these things and it seldom lets me down.'

Mr Quinn looked quite surprised by this estimation of his character.

'Am I right, Mr Quinn?'

'Er … yes, of course. Honest … that's me. As the day is long.'

'That's what I thought. You can't imagine how pleased I was when I discovered you would be our table companion. I've been looking for a man I could trust for quite some time now. I have a job you see, one that requires a certain amount of ' – I paused to give the word a special meaning – 'discretion.'

Mr Quinn struggled to look suitably grave. 'Yes, indeed.'

'You strike me as a man who understands the need on occasion for discretion.'

'Of course!'

'Particularly in matters where large sums of money are concerned.'

Mr Quinn wore the expression of a boy from a family too poor to buy sweets who somehow inherits the sweet shop. Then a stray thought darkened his countenance. 'This … this undertaking … is it … is it …'

'It is entirely legal, Mr Quinn. On that you have my word. I want you to carry a suitcase from Singapore to Kuala Lumpur on the train. An act that is legal in the entire Malayan archipelago.'

'Good,' said Mr Quinn. 'Good. A suitcase?'

'Yes.'

'Is it particularly big?'

'Not at all, a very modest suitcase in size … about the size of six loaves of bread.'

'Six?'

'Maybe seven.'

He nodded. 'And for this you will—'

'Pay you two thousand pounds in cash. Half in Singapore, the rest at your journey's end.'

He now looked as if he had eaten half the sweet shop. 'My word!' He darted a glance to either side in a way that was sure to alert anyone watching that something nefarious was going on and said softly, 'I don't mean to pry, Mr Wenlock, but is there ... will there be anything in the suitcase?'

I too looked to either side before leaning in conspiratorially and whispering, 'Only some money.'

'Money. Yes, I see.'

'I need to move the funds between my casino in Singapore and the one in Kuala Lumpur.'

Mr Quinn's eyes widened. 'You own a casino!'

'More than one. Five actually. The story of how I came by them would make your hair stand on end, but the pleasure of telling it to you must wait for another day. The important thing to remember is this: it's totally above board, just a piece of accounting ... housekeeping. About twelve to fifteen thousand pounds. The case usually weighs about eight or nine imperial pounds. Will that be too heavy for you?'

Mr Quinn answered in a voice filled with wonder, the sort day trippers use when first catching sight of the giant stalactites of Cheddar Cave. 'Oh no,' he said, 'I should be able to manage that nicely.'

'I would do it myself, but I don't travel well by train—'

'I thought you used to be a train driver?'

I coughed to disguise the sharp pain in the heart his remark occasioned. 'I did! But then I went down with coal mange ... never been the same since. Can't go near a train. Broke my heart it did. Really, you will be doing me a great service. Will you help?'

'Of course I will,' he said.

'I'm so grateful. The last chap I hired to do it ran off with the money.'

Before Mr Quinn could reply, Miss Frobisher arrived in the company of the officer Jenny had reported the green smoke to. Alongside him were two rather burly men wearing uniforms that were too small for them.

The first officer nodded to me and said, 'Good evening, Mr Wenlock.' He seemed a touch disappointed to see me drinking with Mr Quinn, as if he expected better of me. 'Please excuse the interruption. Mr Quinn, I wonder if I might have a word with you in private? Over here, perhaps.' He pointed at a vacant booth. Mr Quinn frowned at the interruption, but stood up and walked to the booth with the officer. As I watched them I sizzled inside with nervous excitement.

The officer spoke to Quinn and then held out the ring. Quinn's eyes popped almost from their sockets. He looked at the ring, shot a glance to Miss Frobisher, who was standing nearby wearing an expression of icy hauteur, then he looked at me, and back at the ring. Then the penny dropped. In a rage, he strode towards me and shouted, 'You dirty, rotten, crooked swine, Wenlock!'

Conversations around the bar stopped, as everyone looked to see where the shouting came from.

The officer swiftly interposed himself between the two of us. 'Now see here, Mr Quinn. I would advise you not to add calumny to your list of crimes.'

'It's Wenlock you should be arresting, he's a bloody murderer!'

'Really, sir!' said the officer, appalled at Mr Quinn's loutish manners. 'I would firstly ask you not to use such language in the presence of ladies, and further advise you not to be objectionable to Mr Wenlock, whom I happen to know and admire. He is a champion fellow. We are all indebted to him for his sharp-eyed observation this morning.'

'He's a bloody lying, twisted son of a dog, that's what he is!' shouted Quinn. He pushed the officer aside and lunged at me. This was the cue for the two other chaps – who were tensed and ready – to play their part. They jumped forward and grabbed Quinn by both arms, pinioned them behind his back as easily as if he were a rag doll. I formed the impression that these two chaps were not really officers but stokers whose help was enlisted on occasions when chaps were disagreeable. I also got the impression they rather enjoyed the job but were anxious not to let any hint of that appear in their expressions. In this they only partially succeeded. They frogmarched Mr Quinn away and off to the ship's brig, where I later discovered he fell instantly asleep.

He spent the rest of the voyage locked in the brig, making so many wild accusations against me, I was told, that the Captain recommended the authorities in Singapore prepare a brain doctor to examine him. I did not get another chance to talk to Mr Flamenco, for he and Miss Connemara left the ship at Port Said. The ship tarried the better part of a day there, and I now received another fragment of the screenplay sent out from England by airmail, together with the news that Lady Seymour had arranged an interview for us in Singapore with Curtis's business partner, a Mr Simkins.

Jenny and I stood at the rail and watched Mr Flamenco and Miss Connemara depart in a white taxi. After it had gone we lingered for a while before moving to the starboard side to get a different view of the port, arriving at the rail in time to catch a glimpse of a freighter slowly steaming past. Lashed to the deck, aft, was the tin of Tate & Lyle Golden Syrup we had seen in Southampton.

'It's following us, Jack,' said Jenny.

'It certainly seems to be.'

'Where do you think it is going?'

'I really have no idea.'

Just then Miss Frobisher joined us and informed us with barely contained excitement that she had managed to speak with Mr Flamenco before he and Solveig left. 'He's working on a new movie,' she said. 'It's about a pirate who buys a white woman at a slave auction with the intention of sacrificing her to a giant ape! But then they fall in love.'

INT. SLOPPY JOE'S BAR, MACASSAR. NIGHT

The wildest seaman's bar east of Java. A slave auction is in progress. MILLIE TOOKEY stands at the front on a dais, with her suitcase. Next to her are three MALAY LADIES. A European man wearing a white linen suit officiates. Small round tables fill the rest of the space. A host of scoundrels and rapscallions of every stripe are drinking liquor and gambling. Malay pirates, US navy sailors, Chinamen, Arabs, demimondaines etc.

All eyes turn to the door as CAPTAIN SQUIDEYE enters. Handsome and fierce, like a seafaring Heathcliff, he wears a black patch over one eye and radiates an authority that causes lesser souls to quail.

                    AUCTIONEER

        What am I bid for this fine
              English rose?

He indicates MILLIE.

                   CAPT. SQUIDEYE

              One English pound.

CAPTAIN SQUIDEYE takes a seat at a
table where a CHINESE BUSINESSMAN in
a Western suit sits, seemingly about
to bid.

                    AUCTIONEER

             One pound! You joke!

The CHINESE BUSINESSMAN opens his
mouth to bid. CAPTAIN SQUIDEYE puts
his hand over the CHINESE BUSINESS-
MAN's mouth. His bid is muffled.
CAPTAIN SQUIDEYE puts the barrel of
a revolver to the CHINESE BUSINESS-
MAN's temple. His eyes almost jump
from their sockets in fear. Everyone
in the room watches and understands
the message.

                    AUCTIONEER

   Any advance on a pound? There must
         be! Gentlemen please!

The people in the room shift uncom-
fortably, and avoid the roving gaze
of the AUCTIONEER.

                    AUCTIONEER

   Very well, sold for one pound to the
      gentleman with the eyepatch!

FADE OUT

EXT. THE OCEAN. DAY

Wide shot of SQUIDEYE'S tramp steamer
sailing gently on a placid sea. Gulls
wheel over the ship. The ribbon of
smoke from the single funnel lies
across the sky like gauze.

EXT. DECK OF TRAMP STEAMER. DAY

SQUIDEYE is introducing MILLIE to the
crew: BIG JIM, MOWGLI, SCARFACE,
JAMIE SCAB, DICKIE SILVER, BONNY. CHO
LEE, a Chinaman in traditional Chinese costume and cue, holds her
suitcase.

                        89

SQUIDEYE

And this is Mowgli, the bo'sun.

MOWGLI

(Makes mock-gallant bow)

Charmed, I'm sure!

MILLIE

I want to go home.

SQUIDEYE

Home? What is that?

MILLIE

I want to go home to England.

SQUIDEYE

England! Men, hands up all those who
would like to sail for England …

(He waits for a reaction.)

… not one?

MOWGLI

Captain, if we go to England they
will hang us.

90

SQUIDEYE

Oh yes, I forgot. So they will. Well, my dear it looks like we can't go to England. And besides, if we do you will miss your wedding.

MILLIE

I'm not getting married!

SQUIDEYE

Oh yes you are.

MILLIE

Who to?

SQUIDEYE

It's a surprise.

MILLIE

I don't want to get married.

SQUIDEYE

You have no say in the matter.

MILLIE

I refuse.

SQUIDEYE

You will do as you are told! Cho
Lee, take her below to her quarters.

Chapter 6

IN SINGAPORE WE TOOK a taxi from the port, a cream Ford Anglia driven by an affable Chinese gentleman who spoke very good English. The weather as we crossed the Indian Ocean had grown increasingly warmer and muggy but had been partly alleviated by the perpetual breeze that merely moving through the water out at sea provides. On arrival in Singapore the breeze stopped and the sun took on the quality of a blowtorch in the sky, its effects intensified by humidity of a sort we had only ever experienced before in the Weeping Cross swimming baths.

A rainstorm accompanied our arrival, very intense but short-lived, and the rain clouds soon passed, but the clammy atmosphere did not. The streets were busy with cars, and men in shorts and vests threaded between them pushing handcarts. The air was warm as blood, and filled with a variety of unaccustomed scents, some rotten and putrescent and others sharp and sweet, laden with sugar and aniseed.

'Do you think it ever snows here?' said Jenny as we approached our hotel.

'I think it rather unlikely,' I said. 'We are almost bang on the equator I believe.'

'I will never complain about the weather again.'

'I don't think I've heard you complain about the weather in all the time I've known you!'

'I'm saving it all up for summer. Come June, you won't recognise me. You'll wish you'd never set eyes on me.'

We had arrangements to stay at the Oranje Hotel on Stamford Road, just down the street from the Raffles, both in proximity and in price. But since we had to assume that Mr Quinn might persuade the authorities in Singapore to look into his story, we took rooms in a different hotel opposite the Oranje. After we had unpacked we took an empty suitcase across the road, checked in and left the suitcase there. We then laid a false trail by asking the desk clerk to find us a berth on the next ship to Yokohama.

We then walked to the Raffles to find Mr Simkins. The white-shuttered hotel looked like a wedding cake. The doorman was a Sikh gentleman in a splendid suit and turban whiter than the building. He showed us to a set of rattan chairs arranged around a table inside the main building. We sat down beneath a slowly swirling fan high in the ceiling, and ordered tea from a waitress who, though Chinese, seemed dressed in a similar fashion to the girls in the Lyon's tea shop. Our table gave us a prospect of a reception desk across a tiled floor, and to our left a courtyard garden separated from us by a low wall.

Mr Simkins joined us after a while and ordered himself a ginger ale. He wore a cream linen suit and sighed a lot, though not I felt from the heat, but rather as a general comment on life. His hair was slicked smooth with pomade and in his eyes one saw a sadness, the melancholy of a man who has reached his middle years without adventure and misfortune and wonders perhaps whether he might have been too careful to avoid these things.

'Curtis became unreliable,' was his verdict. 'Went off the rails. Started wearing rouge and blacking his hair. Even had it set in a permanent wave. He looked like a tin soldier. Started talking some ballyhoo about the Graf von Scharnhorst, of all people. Claimed he met him before the Great War and that the whole thing was set up by the ruling families of Europe.'

'What whole thing?' I asked.

'The bloody war, of course. Don't ask me why they would do that. I took no notice of him.' He paused, as if a stray thought had crossed his mind, and his voice became slightly distant. 'We make but two boat trips in our lives. The one out, and the one back. If you find out you don't particularly like it out here, then you are in a bit of a fix. You can spend years denying it to yourself – after all the whole thing is quite irrevocable, so there isn't a lot of point moaning about it. All the same, the truth can never be denied, can it? Sooner or later it knocks on your door, usually when you get up to visit the lavatory at four a.m. The world looks different then, there is no room for artifice. That's when it strikes you: you only have one life to live and you've thrown it away.'

'Is that what happened to Curtis?' asked Jenny.

'I rather think so,' he said. He called the waitress over and ordered more tea. 'The question that keeps me awake is this: would any of it have happened if the Japs hadn't been such dirty swine? If they had possessed the decency to fight like honourable men perhaps things would have been different. We used to have our pictures taken once a year at Nakajima's studio in the arcade here.' He indicated the rough direction of the arcade with a twist of his head. 'We all liked Nakajima, he was a good Jap. Polite, friendly, quite funny, you couldn't not like him. That was what made the betrayal all the harder.'

'What did he do?' said Jenny.

'Nakajima took our pictures, that's what he did. Everyone who was anyone came to the Raffles. And he took their pictures and put them up in the arcade. A complete Who's Who of the expatriate community. You have to admire the chutzpah. It was the perfect job for a spy, wasn't it?

'I'll never forget the day the Japs turned up. The story went that they had deliberately avoided bombing the Raffles in order to use it as their Mess. I can believe it, too. They renamed it Syonan Ryokan and changed the clock to Tokyo time. General Yamashita installed himself in an entire wing, and then this bloody fellow Nakajima appears dressed as a general. Bloody scoundrel! He was quite cold about it too; all that yessir no-sir stuff was a thing of the past. We used to call him Nicky-nacky, well there was no more of that. Old Maynard said it once and got slapped in the face by him. By the damn photographer! It was like finding your wife in bed with the barber. He didn't hit back, though, which was just as well. Heaven knows what they would have done. Nailed him to the door I shouldn't wonder. This was at a time when they were machine-gunning the Chinese out at Changi.

'And then there was a massacre on the golf course. I think that's when we knew we were dealing with absolute beasts. The spat with Curtis started over the gun emplacements. They were on the golf course, two fifteen-inch guns, pointing right out across the Strait. We would have blown anyone in the Strait to Kingdom-come.' He laughed. 'We thought we were impregnable. But then the news came that the sly dogs were coming through the jungles of Malaya, through the back door. That was impossible, or so we had supposed. They rode through the jungle on bicycles. Contrary to all rules of civilised warfare. The brass hats wanted to turn the guns round, but that would have required bringing the next meeting of the Greens committee forward by six weeks. Mr Curtis was opposed to it, and quite rightly in my opinion. It would have set a terrible example. The rules and regulations were there for a purpose and oughtn't to be messed with except in an emergency.'

'Wouldn't the need to defend the island against the Japanese have counted as an emergency?' asked Jenny.

Mr Simkins peered at her through half-narrowed eyes as if wondering whose side she was on.

'I mean,' she added, 'some people might think so.'

'Oh they did,' he said. 'We were almost evenly split, and it was only the casting vote of the Chairman that determined the outcome. The guns remained where they were. There was quite a bit of rancour and feelings were running pretty high. Curtis was quite shaken by some of the things that were said. That was the beginning. A week later the chit system was abandoned.' He noted the questioning looks on our faces. 'A chap used to be able to procure a drink here at the bar by writing his name on a chit of paper, and settling up later. Some good-for-nothings ran up quite a tab over the months but generally it worked well. The locals were baffled by it of course.

'But then in the final weeks they abandoned the system. You had to pay for your drinks. We knew then it was only a matter of time. There was nothing for it but to stay on and dance. We sang "There'll always be an England" till our throats were hoarse. Not like those buggers in Penang. There the locals woke up one morning to find the British had scarpered in the night. All through 1941 you couldn't get a table without a reservation. Mr Applebaum and his band of Hungarian Emigrés carried on playing "If You Knew Susie" and "Bye Bye Blackbird" every night. The ladies still kept cards to schedule their dance partners. The blackout curtains lent the whole thing a certain … frisson of danger. We kept our pluck, that was the main thing. But Curtis really started to go downhill with the news of the sinking of the ships *Prince of Wales* and *Repulse*.'

Mr Simkins paused as if the memory of the two lost ships was especially painful. I let my gaze rise to the ceiling in which rows of fans quietly swirled. I wondered how it must have felt for the staff forced for a while to call this most emblematic symbol of British power by a Japanese name and adopt the strange contrivance of Tokyo time.

Our host continued. 'And then on the morning of 7 February a rumour swept through Singapore, about the silver roast beef trolley. I was out at Tanjong Pagar, but rushed back as soon as I heard. I knew it couldn't possibly be true, but it was. I saw Curtis just after lunch. He was ashen. He wasn't usually given to grand speeches, but he said to me then perhaps more in one sentence than he usually said in a month. His voice was quite strange. It was like the voice of an Englishman who had avoided excesses of emotion all his life and, now that his life had been utterly and irretrievably destroyed, everything he loved, cherished and worked for reduced to ash, tries to intimate that it is just an inconvenience and nothing to get worked up about. He said a group of chaps had approached him and told him the responsibility for the greatest defeat of British arms – which all knew now was unavoidable – along with the consequent total collapse of the British Empire in the East, rested on the shoulders of him and the rest of the Greens committee.'

'But what was the piece of news that brought you back to the hotel?' I said.

He looked me directly in the eye and said, 'The hotel management had taken the silver roast beef trolley from the Grill and buried it in the Palm Court.' He paused to let the implications of this sink in, and added, 'When *Prince of Wales* and *Repulse* went down, they were dark days but we could still hope. But when the silver roast beef trolley went down, there was a finality about it that really brooked no denial. I imagine the feeling would have been the same on the *Titanic* when you stood on deck, freezing in the winds coming from Newfoundland, and watched the last lifeboat be winched away, with still half the ship's complement on deck. Did you ever think about that?'

We said that we did not. For some reason I recalled a story I had heard about the hotel. It told how chaps would recline in their chairs for a nap after lunch and chalk the time they wished to be woken on the soles of their shoes. Did Curtis do that too?

Mr Simkins flicked some imaginary fluff from the knee of his trousers. 'Before the war Curtis was with the Colonial Service for a while. Then he came to work alongside me at Crayford & Crayford. We worked together in a small one-room office administering the smelting of tin golliwog badges in Malaya. After the

100

war we went back to work as we had before, but nothing was ever the same again, least of all Curtis.

'He looked similar, a bit thinner but who wasn't? There was a look in his eye, though, or perhaps there wasn't. It had gone. Only once did we speak of it. I told him one evening as we were finishing work, "You know Curtis, it really had nothing to do with the guns." I wanted him to understand, you see. It didn't matter which way they were facing, there was no way we could have stopped the Japs once they came through the back door. They didn't even have to invade, they could have cut the water supply and forced us to surrender without firing a shot. Losing the two capital ships was just a sign of the times. In the absence of air power, ships are sitting ducks. He said he knew that, but ...' Mr Simkins paused and a pained expression came into his eyes. 'You see, the Japs when they arrived ... they did things ... it was really very terrible. Curtis lived out on Alexandra Road, near the hospital. So he heard it. Heard what they did there, sat through the night listening to the screams of the nurses. It was the beginning of December when he told me he was leaving. He said he was going off on a hunt for the scattered fragments of a screenplay. I thought he was joking at first, but off he went. Last I heard, he'd turned up in Bangkok. He did something there that scandalised the British community. That alone is a most remarkable piece of news, for in the ten years I knew him I don't think I can remember him ever having caused a stir before.'

He took out a fountain pen and notebook. 'You need to speak to his priest. He'll tell you where to find him, if you can catch him sober.' He stopped and looked up. 'I use the term "priest" loosely. He *was* a priest, I'm not sure what word you would use to describe what he is now.' He tore out a page and scribbled down a name and address. Webster. Hotel Malabar, Malabar Street. 'It's a notorious neighbourhood and I recommend you do not take your wife there.' He glanced at Jenny and seeing the look on her face, added, 'Or at least make sure you leave before midnight. The British sailors are wont to put on a show at that hour that no decent man would want a lady to see. I don't understand why the shore patrol allow it. It reminds one of the final days of Rome. You could wish for no better indicator that we are all washed up.'

INT. SHIP'S HOLD. NIGHT

CHO LEE is holding a lantern, showing
MILLIE the cargo. The light gleams on
a giant tin of Tate & Lyle Golden
Syrup. He moves on to show rows of
glass flasks containing a colourless
liquid.

CHO LEE

Missy come see.

MILLIE

What is it? Liquor?

CHO LEE shakes his head and mimes a
patient being given ether and losing
consciousness.

MILLIE

Chloroform? What for? Why so much?

CHO LEE

Missy husband.

He carries the lantern further into
the hold and shines it on a plaster of
Paris cast of a giant ape's footprint.

MILLIE

I don't understand.

CHO LEE mimes a gorilla and then
points towards the roof and to the
plaster cast to indicate the gorilla
is very big. He acts out putting a
wedding ring on MILLIE'S finger.

CHO LEE

Sings the Wedding March

MILLIE

My God no!

INT. CAPTAIN'S CABIN. DAY
MILLIE stands in the doorway, SQUIDEYE
is reading his charts.

SQUIDEYE

I do not remember giving you
permission to visit the hold.

MILLIE

Is this true? Cho Lee says you have
promised me in marriage to a giant
ape?

SQUIDEYE

I will punish him for his loose
tongue.

MILLIE

What is the big tin of syrup for?

SQUIDEYE

Your betrothed has a sweet tooth.

MILLIE

I won't do it. You can't make me.

                    SQUIDEYE

You will do as you are told. I can do
what I damn well please. I bought you
fair and square.

                     MILLIE

There is no need for bad language.

                    SQUIDEYE

                     What?

                     MILLIE

You said 'damn'.

                    SQUIDEYE

This is a ship, not a church.

                     MILLIE

I'm not scared of you.

                    SQUIDEYE

Then you are the only one aboard who
                     isn't.

He moves towards her. MILLIE kicks him
in the shin and runs out of the cabin.

EXT. C/U OF PORTHOLE. DAY

MILLIE, nose pressed to the glass, stares out disconsolately.

INT. DARKENED ROOM. DAY

MILLIE is kneeling at the side of her bed in silent prayer. The Virgin Mary appears before her. She watches MILLIE for a while and then reaches out a gentle hand to stroke her cheek.

MILLIE

Holy Mother?

MARY

Child.

MILLIE

Oh Holy Mother, what should I do?

MARY

Do not fear. All will be well.

MILLIE

How can that be? I am promised in marriage to an ape.

106

MARY

You must work on the Captain's
heart.

MILLIE

How should I do that?

MARY

The same way you would catch a fish.

MILLIE

I've never caught a fish.

MARY

Child, men are easily beguiled. I
never met one yet who could resist
the chance to be a knight in shining
armour. What we need is a school of
dolphins.

Chapter 7

I WAITED IN THE LOBBY, soothed by the fan. The night was as hot as the footplate when the firebox door is opened. I must have dozed off for a few seconds, because I did not see Jenny descend the stairs. 'What do you think?' she said, rousing me from my reverie, and adding for dramatic effect, 'Ta da!' She was wearing one of the trouser suits in the collection. Cream linen, with a matching jacket belted at the waist. My face fell.

'I knew you wouldn't like it.'

'I didn't say that.'

'You didn't have to.'

'I think it's … it's … dashing.'

'I think it's swoony.'

'That too.'

'Why shouldn't I wear it?'

'No one has told you that you shouldn't. Perhaps it might be considered a touch too modern for … Singapore.'

'In lots of parts of the world it is considered totally normal for ladies to wear trousers.'

'Indeed it is. And in some it is considered totally normal for them to wear nothing.'

Jenny laughed. 'Jack, for you, that is surprisingly funny.'

'My tragedy is that I don't do it on purpose.'

She laughed again and took my hand. 'I bet Millie would have approved.'

I was quite startled by her casually referring to my mother. 'Do … do you really think so?'

'Don't you?'

'How can I possibly know? I know almost nothing about her.'

'Yes, but look at what you do know. What she did. That took real pluck, don't you think? Falsely accused of stealing money, thrown out onto the streets with no one to turn to … it must have been horrible. And then to think up a brilliant plan like that – to forge an invitation to the Gosling Programme. What amazing spirit that shows, and she was only sixteen. Don't you agree?'

'Yes, yes, I do!' For a brief moment I saw her vividly in my mind's eye, standing before an imposing house at the end of a dark street, looking up as if summoning the courage to ring the bell. I was pierced with anguish for her suffering. 'Yes,' I said now more softly. 'What an astonishing spirit she must have possessed.'

'In a way it was almost like getting one back on Her Ladyship.'

The image of long ago vanished, like a bubble pricked by the tone in Jenny's voice. 'I have noticed a number of times when you refer to Lady Seymour, there is a hint of disdain in your voice.'

'Is there?'

I did my best to mimic her tone. 'Her *Lady*ship.'

She gave me a butter-wouldn't-melt-in-her-mouth look.

'Don't you think it was generous of her to give me this information about my mother?'

'She could have sent you the photo years ago, Jack.'

'I suppose that is true, but I imagine … people like that are very busy.'

'I suspect the thought never crossed her mind.'

'I imagine sending chaps photographs of their mothers would have been forbidden by the rules of the Gosling Programme.'

'Yes, I expect it was, and yet she breaks those rules when it suits her purpose, such as when she needs you to do something for her.'

'Really, Jenny, that is a very harsh light in which to view her behaviour! Don't you recall she said she would have been willing to help my mother if she had made her circumstances known.'

'Yes, but Millie clearly didn't think so, did she?'

'B-but she was mistaken. We have Lady Seymour's word.'

Jenny gave me a look that defied precise classification but certainly held more than a hint of disbelief.

'Are you saying she behaved in bad faith?'

Jenny saw the consternation growing on my brow and looked conflicted herself. 'I don't know, Jack, but it does seem to me that these people … are very good at seeming to care for your welfare but really are only interested in themselves. She could have sent you the photo a long time ago, but obviously the thought never entered her head. What does that tell you?' She squeezed my hand. 'But what about Millie? What a plan! Aren't you proud of her? She must have been remarkable, Jack, really remarkable ...'

'Yes, yes!' I said, pride welling up, 'she really must have been.'

'And she would definitely have been the first to wear a trouser suit, mark my words.'

'Well, all I can say is, you seem to know my mother better than I do.'

Jenny smiled up at me, and then her countenance darkened slightly. She said softly words that would only later reveal their full meaning to me: 'I know how she felt, Jack.' And then she led me out through the hotel doors.

We hailed a cab in the street and handed the driver the slip of paper that Mr Simkins had given us with Webster's address. Considering the reputation of our intended destination, the taxi driver – a Sikh gentleman – seemed not greatly surprised by our request and drove off amicably.

'We're ... we're visiting a friend,' I explained.

He nodded. 'Don't buy any watches.' He told us the area to which we were headed was called Bugis Street and was named after the Buginese people from the island of Celebes in Indonesia. They were a seafaring race of traders and occasional pirates, who in former times had sailed up the river here to trade. The main thoroughfare we drove along was wide and lined with palm trees. Cars passed in either direction, mostly British marques as far as I could see, along with bicycles and Triumph motorcycles.

'Your friend, is he a frequent visitor to Singapore?' said the taxi driver.

'I'm afraid I couldn't say,' I answered. 'He's not really a close friend. We don't know much about him.'

'You don't know him?'

'Not very well,' I said.

The driver considered for a few seconds. 'In my experience you can tell a lot about a man from the sort of hotel he stays at. But in this case, it would depend on whether he knew what sort of hotel it was before he booked.'

'My feeling is he has been in Singapore a long time, so I imagine his choice was deliberate.'

'I'm not one to judge,' said the driver, in words that conveyed the opposite of their intended effect.

'Is it terribly dangerous?' said Jenny.

'Only to your soul,' said the driver. 'You will be in no physical danger, brawls are very rare and your Royal Navy Shore Patrol are quick to break them up. The greatest danger to you is of being cheated or scandalised. You should be aware that not everyone wearing a frock is a lady.' His eyes darted for the tiniest fraction of a second to Jenny and her attire.

'And tonight, not everyone wearing trousers will be a man,' said Jenny.

The driver smiled.

'In the war ladies wore trousers and no one minded.'

'So I understand.'

'They worked on the railways too, didn't they Jack?'

'Yes,' I said, 'they did.'

'They wore trousers for that. I'm going to be a train driver,' she said.

'I'm sure you will make a very good one,' said the driver. 'But why not become an actress? Katherine Hepburn also wears this style.'

The driver pulled up at the end of Malabar Street and apologised that he could take us no further, for reasons that were obvious. The street, which formed a crossroads with Malay Street, was clogged with tables and chairs at which the whole world seemed to be sitting and engaging in something of a bacchanal. The people who sat at the tables were mostly European, but all other races seemed to be present too. There were many sailors in white bell-bottomed trousers and the traditional blue sailor collar. The music from some unseen gramophone was Chinese and was amplified by the crowd who caroused and sang along. In among the throng waiters in vests and shorts threaded their way past boys with trays of cigarettes and trinkets hanging from their necks. But most striking were the ladies—assuming they *were* ladies—in bright gaudy frocks of all colours of the rainbow. They wore Western dress and cavorted with the sailors and other tourists in a most licentious manner.

The Hotel Malabar had seen better days. At least one hoped it had. The lobby had a red-tiled floor that was almost as black as dried blood with grime. The desk stood unmanned, stranded like a rotting ship. Even the fan forgot to swirl. There was no bell to ring, so we slapped the wooden counter and shouted out 'Hello.' After a while a boy appeared and answered our inquiry simply by pointing up. We climbed a staircase that gave one no confidence that it would support our weight and walked onto a small landing, containing four doors. One was half open and the sounds from within led us to believe that we had found our quarry.

'You know exactly what I mean!' said an American voice. 'Don't you play the innocent with me, with your holier-than-thou bullshit. I trusted you. All my life I looked up to you. I worshipped you, you know that? You little double-crossing jerk … I ought to break your legs, that would take the smile off your face, wouldn't it, eh? You goddam plaster saint. Well, I've got a better idea!' A gunshot rang out. I kicked the door open and beheld an amazing sight. The man was lying on the bed, holding a semi-automatic with an outstretched arm pointing ahead. The room was full of the sweet stench of cordite and swirling gun smoke. At the far

115

corner of the room a five-foot alabaster crucifix stood propped against the wall. The wall was pockmarked with bullet holes, but Jesus seemed to have escaped serious damage.

Sitting on the end of the bed was a young oriental lady in a scarlet satin cheongsam, nonchalantly filing her nails. She looked up. 'Don't worry,' she said, 'he lousy shot.' Then she put down her file, jumped up and held out a hand to shake. 'My name Zsa Zsa!'

We both shook hands solemnly. She was of the Malay complexion. She wore her hair coiffeured in the modern style, her lips were letterbox red, but it did little to conceal the jaw and throat of a boyish man.

Mr Webster, who wore stone-coloured trousers and an open shirt betraying no sign of a dog collar, apologised and explained that he and Jesus had fallen out over a girl. He proposed we repair to the street for a cooling beer, and this is what the four of us did.

We sat in the street at a metal fold-up table and Mr Webster ordered satay and beers, which soon arrived. I explained to him the purpose of our visit. He listened without interruption, and once I had finished allowed a second's pause before saying the name *Curtis* in a voice that combined laughter, disbelief and derision.

He didn't seem eager to expand on that single word, so we made small-talk for a while. I asked him about the need to leave before midnight and he laughed. 'It's just a show your Limey sailors put on when they've had too much to drink. I think you need to be born there to understand it.'

'What do they do?' said Jenny.

He pointed to the end of the street where an out-house stood against the end wall of a building. 'That building is the john. The sailors like to climb onto the roof and put on a show that Englishmen seem to find incredibly funny and the rest of us don't understand.'

'What sort of show?' I asked.

'They call it the Dance of the Flaming Ass— sorry, Arseholes. Your guys climb on the roof, pull down their pants and stick newspaper up their ass and set fire to it. The guys below egg them on with the song, "Haul 'em down you Zulu Warrior!"'

'Golly!' said Jenny. 'I hope they do it tonight.'

'Jenny!' I snapped, 'You can't seriously …' I turned to Mr Webster. 'Are you perhaps taking us for a ride, Mr Webster?'

'Webster, call me Webster. Everyone else does. If I understand your meaning, no I'm not.'

Zsa Zsa pointed at Jenny's jacket and said, 'I like your suit. Where you buy?'

'I bought it in England,' said Jenny. 'Do you like it?'

'Very beautiful. Would look good on Zsa Zsa.'

Webster leaned across and said into my ear, 'The way to tell them apart generally, is the prettier ones are the men.'

'If you like,' said Jenny, 'I could give you one. If you write down your address for me, I will send one to you.'

'Are you joking?' asked Zsa Zsa.

'I have a few in my luggage,' said Jenny. 'I'm sure I could spare one. Where should I send it?'

'Send to Webster,' said Zsa Zsa. And then having accepted that Jenny was in earnest, she squealed with disbelief and delight at the prospect of receiving a trouser suit.

'The chap we met at the Raffles gave us to understand you and Curtis were friends,' I said.

Webster considered for a moment. 'I guess you could say that, more on account of our living in the same flea-bitten hotel at the same time. If we had met in any other walk of life I don't suppose he would have given me the time of day.'

'Has he ... do you think he has suffered some form of nervous breakdown?'

Webster took a long drink from his beer and said with a chuckle, 'He might have done, but I've never really understood what that means, "nervous breakdown".'

'I thought it was when a chap can't take any more and goes off the rails,' I explained.

'The concierge at the Raffles called it late-flowering Bohemianism,' added Jenny.

Webster pulled a face that suggested he approved of the description. 'You heard about the screenplay, I suppose?'

We said that we had.

'That was pretty Bohemian for a man like Curtis. I never knew him before he came to live here, but we talked a lot and the impression I got was of a man who had lived a very quiet and timid life. But something had been undermining the respectable exterior for a while, like termites eating the wood of his soul. The Japs interned him out at Changi, so that must have been pretty hellish. The surrender of Singapore hit him hard. He was obsessed by the thought that the war might have been ... I don't know ... *engineered* somehow, deliberately started like the one in 1914. I asked him what made him think it had been engineered in 1914, and he said a German Count told him. Does that mean anything to you?'

'I can't say it does,' I replied. 'It seems a most extraordinary charge to make. But the chap we met at the Raffles said something similar.'

'Yup,' said Webster. 'It's a new one on me too. He also talked a lot about those badges made by the jam company.'

'They are called golliwogs,' explained Jenny.

'Yes,' said Webster, and added, 'He said to me, "You know I've suddenly realised what appalling things they are. And yet for most of my life I thought they were perfectly jolly. What have I done?"'

'Appalling? What a strange way to describe them!' I said.

'I agree with him,' said Jenny. 'They are sort of ... making fun of people, aren't they?'

119

'I've never thought so,' I said, slightly surprised.

'That's because it's not you on the badge. It's like when people pick on someone and the person is supposed to join in and laugh at himself because otherwise he would be a spoilsport, and they'd say, "Oh he can't take a joke."'

'You do see some things that never occur to me,' I said, and turned to Webster. 'My wife is reading a book with some very modern opinions in it.'

'It's called *Trust in God, She Will Provide*,' said Jenny.

Webster laughed and said, 'If God was a woman I wouldn't have fallen out with Her.'

'Mr Webster,' I said, 'what made you fall out with God?'

He took a long drink from his beer and said softly, 'I once had a girl ... and now I don't.' He did not expand upon that for a second or two. Jenny and I exchanged glances, neither of us sure whether to pursue the matter. But then he went on, 'Before the war I was posted to an American Mission at the Catholic Cathedral in Nagasaki.'

'Oh!' said Jenny.

'I didn't know there was a Catholic cathedral there,' I said.

'Well there isn't now.' He flinched. 'Sorry, that was a cheap shot. It was a beautiful town and so were the people. Then I went home on leave and the newspapers were full of a place I had never heard of in

Hawaii, called Pearl Harbor. Well, you can imagine the rest.'

'It does sound like a terribly cruel bomb,' said Jenny.

'I hear it works by focusing the rays of the sun,' I said.

'Actually, it creates a new sun, a mile above the city,' said Webster. 'Then there is no city.'

'Well, I suppose it won't be long before we have one,' I said.

'It sounds like the sort of bomb we would be better off without,' said Jenny.

'That's true,' said Webster, 'but you know how the military are when they get a new toy. This is one genie that won't be going back in the bottle.' He was silent for a while. It was clear the memory was very painful for him. Then he brightened and changed the subject.

'He's in Bangkok now. Staying at The Garden of Perfect Brightness. Everyone knows it.'

'What made him go there?' I asked.

'There's a firm there, import and export, called the Burma, Bangkok and North Borneo. They've got a flying boat to charter. Empire flying boat. Waiting for a new rudder or something. They are going to use it to fly to the island mentioned in the screenplay. Last I heard, Curtis had found himself a girl. Everyone finds a girl in Bangkok, but this one was European, blue eyes. Wouldn't have thought he had it in him.'

'Has he not been back here at all?' I asked.

'Only once as far as I am aware. Looking for an item in the post. I didn't see him. Why are you looking for him?'

Some instinct told me to just tell the truth. 'I have reason to believe the girl mentioned in the screenplay was my mother.'

Mr Webster's eyes widened. He gave the sort of look one wears when told the price of an item and it is unexpectedly high.

'And yet you seem to have about you both an air of desperation,' he commented.

'Yes. You see we had to leave England hurriedly, we are in a bit of a pickle.'

'What's a pickle?'

'A disagreeable situation. A man tried to kill me.'

Webster said, 'Hmm. That's a pickle. Can't you kill him back?'

'I would prefer not to.'

'Sometimes it's the only way.'

There was a pause as we watched the carousing. The atmosphere, though drunken, seemed most cordial, and had the feel of a carnival. It was still too early to see the show on the lavatory roof, and I had no desire to, but I knew if I tried to leave before it began Jenny's beautiful eyes would flash with impish scorn and she'd call me a stuffed shirt. The truth was, I *was* a stuffed shirt, and did not greatly mind. The behaviour of the sailors Mr Webster described is not new to me, I have seen drunken men scandalise other passengers in this manner on the trains. I have to confess, I have not the faintest idea what is funny about it.

'I tell you what,' Webster suggested, 'why don't we go and look in his room? Come with me.'

We followed him back into the lobby of the hotel. The boy was no longer behind the counter, and, without pausing to consider, Webster walked behind it and retrieved one of the keys. He beckoned and we followed him up the stairs to a room on the floor above his that he unlocked for us. It was dark inside, with a faint glow discernible through the louvred shutters from the street outside. The air was rank and stale. Webster flicked the switch and the fan in the ceiling inched feebly into motion. His fingers scratched at the wall until a thin yellow ghost glimmered from a single bulb that hung from the ceiling. The room was bare and largely empty. Just a single bed, a bedside cabinet and a wardrobe. On the floor at our feet were two letters that had been slipped under the door. Webster bent and picked them up, opened them and began to read. He passed them to me. The first letter was an invoice from a firm in London that supplied circus ringmaster's outfits. It was a demand for payment, seemingly the fourth of its kind. The second letter contained another tranche of the screenplay.

A photograph lay on the desk, and beside it a newspaper cutting. Having satisfied ourselves that there was nothing else of interest in the room, we returned downstairs to the table outside where we could take a better look at what we had found.

The newspaper cutting was yellowed and bore the headline: 'Five die in boating tragedy'. There was no photograph and only a few lines in the accompanying story.

Less than ten years after a terrible fire engulfed the west wing, tragedy has struck again at Wisskirriel Hall. Five servants, including the butler Mr Jarvis and head housekeeper Mrs Bainbridge, have been lost in a tragic boating accident off Puffin Rock. The boat foundered off the island shortly before noon on Saturday. There were reports of an explosion, but since the Cormorant was a sailing vessel confusion reigns as to what could have caused it. The police are working on the theory that they may have hit a stray mine. There will be a memorial service in the Wisskirriel Hall chapel on Sunday 16th at 11 a.m.

The photo showed a water buffalo standing next to the ruins of a temple. The stone head of a god, broken off from its torso, lay entwined in the roots of a tree, in a way that suggested the head was already lying there in the grass when the tree was a mere sapling, and had continued to lie there undisturbed as the tree grew around the head. Now it was encased by the tree like a knot in the wood. The stone head was round, exaggeratedly so, like a Halloween pumpkin. The face had a flat, wide nose, wide fleshy lips and blank, almond-shaped eyes. Its expression seemed to float between malevolence and a mocking smile. I turned the card over. It bore the marque of the photographic studio, 'Finky's Fotographic, Bangkok', and was scrawled with the words: *The horror! The horror!*

EXT. DECK OF SHIP. DAY

MILLIE has climbed onto the rail, threatening to jump into the sea. The CREW watch in amusement.

> MILLIE
>
> Don't come any closer!

> SQUIDEYE
>
> You really going to jump?

> MILLIE
>
> Yes. Rather be eaten than sharks than suffer this fate.

MILLIE looks over her shoulder: the dorsal fins betray the presence of a school of dolphins in the water. She jumps. The men cheer.

EXT. IN THE SEA. DAY

MILLIE surrounded by dolphins. They playfully nuzzle her.

MILLIE

(Fake screams)

Sharks!

Squideye dives in to save her. He swims
up to her and takes her in his arms. She
holds on tight. Their faces draw close
and they peer into each other's eyes.

MILLIE

You saved me!

SQUIDEYE

How did you know they were dolphins?

MILLIE

I didn't. Are they not sharks?

SQUIDEYE

(Staring at her as one smitten.)

Yes. Of course they are sharks.

MILLIE

My saviour!

126

EXT. DECK OF TRAMP STEAMER. DAY

The ship's CREW are cheering, MILLIE
climbs slowly and precariously up the
ladder attached to the ship's funnel.
Her TEDDY BEAR has been tied to the
top of the funnel. Alerted by the
cheering, SQUIDEYE rushes out on deck.
The ship yaws and thick black smoke
envelops MILLIE. She coughs and falls
to the deck, landing on a pile of
coiled ropes. SQUIDEYE rushes to her
aid, picks her gently up in his arms.

SQUIDEYE

My sweet!

MILLIE

(Groans)

SQUIDEYE is smitten. The ship's CREW
see this and smirk amongst themselves
like schoolboys.

SQUIDEYE

You wretched dogs! Mowgli, find the man
who did this and tie him to the wheel
with back bare.

MOWGLI

Aye, aye, Sir!

SQUIDEYE carries her below.

INT. MILLIE'S CABIN. DAY

MILLIE is lying on her bunk. SQUIDEYE
is tenderly ministering to her.

SQUIDEYE

I will introduce that wretch to
the cat.

MILLIE

You have a cat?

SQUIDEYE

Yes, with nine tails. And the man who
did this will feel them all lick his
back.

MILLIE

Please do not hurt anyone because of
me. I know it was just a joke.

SQUIDEYE

I have no choice. If I show even a
hint of mercy it will be the end of

us all. I rule by fear alone, nothing
else.

MILLIE

Why do you want to marry me to this
ape?

SQUIDEYE

He guards the portal to a valley
where, they say, grows a flower with
the power to mend a broken heart.

MILLIE

Is your heart so very broken?

SQUIDEYE

There is a wound on my soul that no
physician can heal. For once, long
ago, I did a terrible thing.

MILLIE

Captain, what did you do?

SQUIDEYE

I killed a child.

MILLIE

(Gasps)

Goodness, no! Who was this child?

SQUIDEYE

It was my own little boy. He had
tuberculosis of the spine. He writhed
in pain so much he broke his own ribs.
So I took a rope and tied him to his
bed, then smothered him for love.

MILLIE

Smothered?

SQUIDEYE

(Weeps)

Smothered with a pillow on his angel
face.

MILLIE

Poor Captain!

SQUIDEYE

I pray you never know what it is to
lose a son.

MILLIE

Oh but I *do* know. I once had a son. A
lovely boy. He did not die, but he is
dead to me.

SQUIDEYE

A son?!

MILLIE

His name was Jack. There is not a
moment in the day when my heart does
not break for him.

TRANSCRIBER'S NOTE: THE NEXT FOUR
PAGES HAVE BEEN RENDERED ILLEGIBLE BY
SALT WATER DAMAGE.

Chapter 8

MR WEBSTER INFORMED US there was a train for Kuala Lumpur that left each night at seven minutes to midnight, and that would arrive just before dawn. From there we would be able to travel on to Bangkok. The journey would take three days in all.

We returned to our hotel and had the clerk make up our bill. I walked across the road to the hotel we had originally booked. The man behind the desk told me the ship for Yokohama departed the day after tomorrow and our tickets would arrive next morning. He also said a man with a burned face had been inquiring after us. I thanked him and told him that should the man with the burned face return he was to be sure to tell him about the boat we were catching to Yokohama.

We left that night on the train. There were very few lights to be seen after we left the brightly illuminated station. We sensed the waters of the causeway more than we saw them. There is a stillness to water at night which one feels in one's heart, and the smooth gliding of a railway carriage magnifies this tranquillity most agreeably. Even the chuffs from the engine were slow and muted. But this tranquillity was disturbed by the thoughts racing in my mind. What on earth had Curtis discovered during his quest?

'I'm scared,' said Jenny.

I nodded. 'Yes, we are in a bit of a pickle, I'm afraid.'

'This man with the burned face seems to know exactly where we are going.'

'Yes, it does rather appear that way.'

'Do you think Lady Seymour has told him?'

'I can't see why she would. I believe her desire to discover the fate of her son is genuine. And even she doesn't know we are going to Bangkok now.'

'Does he know we are looking for Curtis, do you think?'

'I'm not sure, but if he makes inquiries about us at the Raffles, he will soon learn about it.'

'And then he will discover Curtis is in Bangkok, so the tickets to Yokohama won't fool him for long.'

'I'm rather afraid, they won't.'

'What will we do, Jack?' Jenny stared at me with a look that suggested for the first time, perhaps, that the gravity of our situation had sunk in. In the gloom of the carriage her eyes glistened with soft fear.

'We don't have to go to Bangkok,' I said. 'With the money Lady Seymour has given us we could go just about anywhere.'

'But wouldn't he find us wherever we went?'

'I believe if we took more care about covering our tracks we might escape him.'

'But what about your mother?'

I was silent for a while as I reflected on how to say something that I knew Jenny would dislike intensely but

134

which it behoved me to say. 'I cannot turn back, but you can.'

The pause that followed was no longer than a musical beat, and then, 'What do you mean?'

'I think you know what I mean.'

'Are you sending me away?' she asked in a shocked whisper.

'I think it's for the best, don't you?' I tried to sound matter-of-fact, as if we were discussing some trivial matter of housekeeping. Jenny did not answer but stared at me, searching for some sign that I was not serious. In truth, I knew if she left me I should not have the strength to continue. I knew with a certainty beyond words that I could not live without her. 'Yes, Jenny,' I said. 'I really think it would be safest and for the best if you returned to England.'

I stared into her eyes, straining every nerve and sinew to counterfeit in my gaze a conviction that I did not possess. Jenny opened her mouth to speak and all I heard was a strangled whisper, 'Yes.'

'Definitely the most sensible thing. There really is no need for you to be put in danger on my behalf. You are not wanted by Room 42, you could travel back to England and await word from me.'

Her voice was barely audible, a hoarse whisper. 'Yes, of course. I mean … if you send me away … I will go.'

'There! You see? You'd be much safer in England, and in a few weeks I would—'

'Not England.' Her voice was soft, and distant, as a voice in a dream.

'Not?'

'No. Not anywhere. If you send me away, I will go there.'

'How can you go "not anywhere"?'

'It's where we all go one day, isn't it? It's where Cooper went.'

I flinched at the mention of his name. I understood she had not said it with an intention to wound, but simply because to mention this dead American soldier at this moment was the closest she could come to a blasphemy that might express the agony in her heart. 'Jenny, you … you surely do not mean—'

As the train chugged softly on, the already dim lamp in the ceiling grew dimmer. The glistening in Jenny's eyes became more acute, gilding the edge of her cheek, and then I saw she was crying, silently.

'I promised to love, honour and obey you, Jack. It wasn't hard, no one needed to make me promise. But if you send me away, I will obey you though it will be the hardest thing I have ever done. But I can't promise to go back to my life in England, the very thought is hateful to me.' The word 'hateful' was barely recognisable as she convulsed and then she sobbed. I took her in my arms and squeezed her tightly. 'Please don't send me away,' she whispered.

I rocked her gently as the train in turn rocked us. 'I won't.'

'If you ask me, I will kill the man with the burned face,' she said.

I froze, shocked by her simple words. Jenny was capable of saying such a thing in jest, but I knew she was not joking.

'You will not.'

'Wouldn't it be for the best?'

'It might. But if anyone should kill him it should be me, and yet I do not think I ever could.'

'Wouldn't it ... wouldn't we be happy?'

'I don't know. According to my understanding, desperate folk who resort to such deeds never resolve their problem but set in train a cycle of events beyond their control and which inexorably lead to their doom. We are not such people, Jenny, or if we could be I do not think we have reached the point of desperation. It strikes me as being some way off.'

Jenny listened, and nodded. 'In a way we passed it five months ago now, I think. Ever since we met we have been fugitives of a sort, and yet I have never been so happy, even when afraid. In fact, those words don't even come close ... it is not about being happy or not ... it's ... it's, oh I don't know. Have you ever watched a heron catch a fish, Jack?'

'I think I may have but without paying attention.'

'I saw one once. He stood on a branch at the pool's edge and watched the water. Half an hour he stood unmoving, and then flash! His head dipped into the water and was out again before you knew it and in his

137

beak was a fish. He paused before swallowing it, almost as if wanting to show it off. And for a second, there was a look in his eye. That look, Jack, that is how I feel all the time with you, and running in fear for our lives is a small price to pay for it.'

'That is rather a splendid way of putting it, Jenny. I hope you won't find me unoriginal if I say I feel the same.'

'You won't send me away?'

'No. I could more easily take out my heart and post it to England.'

'In a parcel wrapped up with brown paper and white string?'

'Of course, how else?'

'When you said … to go away … for a moment I believed you.'

'Well, then you are a bloody fool.'

She paused and then giggled. I had never before used such language to her, least of all in jest.

'We'll find a way, Jack. I know it. After all, Princess Elizabeth is on our side.'

'I am determined that we should find a way, Jenny, but I have to say I don't set much store by the possibility of an intervention in our fate by Buckingham Palace.'

She giggled again in a way that made plain she didn't set much store by it either. 'I'm sure there is nothing Her Majesty wouldn't do for a Gosling's Friend badge.'

I was about to reply when she raised her face to me and I noticed her grin. 'Yes,' I said, 'it's probably the only thing in all the world that a queen can't buy. Have you still got yours?'

'No, I threw it away the day after you gave it to me.'

I laughed. 'It really is jolly sporting of you to joke at such a dark time. But you are right. We have plenty of fight in us yet, for all the pickle we are in.'

'I can't imagine where I would rather be than in a pickle with you, Jack.'

We listened as if in a dream to the soft melancholic chuffing. When the causeway reached the mainland we passed through a station called Johor Bahru and glided slowly past a goods train held up in a sidings. The wagons were empty but for one, on which was lashed the giant tin of Tate & Lyle Golden Syrup. What did it mean? Was it following us? Or showing us the way?

INT. LOWER DECK. NIGHT

MILLIE, BIG JIM, MOWGLI, SCARFACE stand before a cupboard.

SCARFACE

Did you get the key as I told
you to?

MILLIE hands over a key to SCARFACE, who puts it in the cupboard lock and turns.

MILLIE

It's very strange for him to lock
away the fancy dress.

SCARFACE

The Captain is a strange man. He locks
the joy away from his own heart.

MILLIE

Yes, I have seen it.

SCARFACE

But on his own birthday we must
force the gates of his heart open to
admit our joy.

MILLIE

Yes, yes we must!

MILLIE

(Sings)

Long ago when I was a little girl

I dreamed of a dance where my heart
would whirl

And a man riding in on a sugar-white
charger

140

A duke or a lord or maybe an earl.

I grew up and my dreams got larger.

BIG JIM, MOWGLI, SCARFACE

(Sing)

Long ago when she was a little tot

She dreamed about the world as the
world is not.

Now she's promised in marriage to a
big brown bear,

No princes or dukes or similar rot.

Throw away your dreams because the
world don't care.

SCARFACE opens the cupboard. It is
filled with firearms. He hands them out.

SCARFACE

Happy birthday, Captain Squideye!

EXT. DECK. DAY.

Two sailors pinion the arms of SQUID-
EYE, who has been badly beaten.
Another sailor holds the struggling
MILLIE. Other sailors, openly drink-
ing from flagons of liquor, look on.

141

SQUIDEYE

I'll have your heart for this, you
snake!

SCARFACE

I do not doubt it, but first you will
have to find me. And how will you do that
when you are blind?

SQUIDEYE

I still have one good eye.

SCARFACE

I fear the prospects for that eye
are rather dim.

SQUIDEYE

No!

BIG JIM brings out a flask of
chloroform.

SCARFACE

Hold him fast now, boys!

More sailors take hold of SQUIDEYE.

SCARFACE

What shall we do, boys, has he seen
enough of this wretched world?

SAILORS

(Sing)

Aye, aye Captain!

No eye captain!

If you ever need a gaoler

Don't have a drunken sailor.

They prise open his 'good' eye. SCAR-
FACE pours on the chloroform.

MILLIE

Please don't!

SQUIDEYE

No! Damn you!

(Laughter)

SCARFACE

Throw him in the drink!

                    SQUIDEYE

          No!

The sailors throw SQUIDEYE over the
side. SCARFACE grabs MILLIE by the
arm.

                    SCARFACE

          I claim my prize!

(Laughter)

Chapter 9

THE ARRIVAL OF THE overnight train from Hat Yai at Hualamphong Station in Bangkok occasioned a bustling frenzy. People who arrived to greet and receive vied with shoeless porters in vest and shorts. They thronged to the doors, luggage was passed out over the heads through windows, while girls walked with trays for hats from which grilled chicken and fried insects were offered for sale. We followed, or were swept along with the throng as it surged towards the main building, a vast, high-ceilinged space filled with travellers, many of them sitting on the floor.

All railway stations are noisy cathedrals in which life's sacred rituals are enacted. No one would build a vast public space at great cost to house those departing at a bus station, and yet it is regarded as a necessity for trains. The gathering of so many people filled the building with a buzz like a hive. High up a clock presided. We picked our way through the groups seated on the floor. It was hot, but outside the heat hit us like a blow.

'Poo!' laughed Jenny. 'What a pong! Where's it coming from?'

I looked around and said, 'Do you know, I think it's coming from ... everywhere.'

'What is it?'

'Lots of things, I believe. Rotting vegetables, stagnant water …'

'Flowers.'

'Yes.'

'Jasmine,' said Jenny, 'medicine, ointment, lavatories, grease … and things I'm not sure I want to find out about.'

We found a taxi and showed the driver a brochure for our hotel. He drove out of the station into a broad and modern thoroughfare. It was clogged with dusty Fords and some cars that I fancied must have been made in Japan before the war. Men pushed carts. Passing between them and the cars were rickshaw drivers, skinny and gnarled and barefoot. We also saw two elephants amid the traffic.

Along either side of the road ran canals. From time to time, thin boats passed down these, overloaded with people. The waters were the colour of cocoa. Other, smaller canals, more like drainage culverts, lay stagnant, filled with junk and emitting a mouldy stench.

We passed a grand building that stood out amid the rather shabby architecture that lined the street.

'General Post Office,' read out Jenny.

'It's a shame Mrs Carmichael is not here to try her envelope test,' I answered.

'Definitely what she would have called a Type-B country,' she said. She gave me an impish look. 'Bear that in mind if you have to bribe a policeman.'

We turned right into a side road and entered a narrower, more congested district. Chinese script began to predominate. Glimpses of brown river flashed intermittently to our left as we drove further into the neighbourhood. The road narrowed but filled with more and more people. There were more rickshaws and fewer cars, until soon we were the only car, pushing slowly like a snowplough through the throng. Wheeled food stalls lined the road now. Men scooped up tentacles of noodles and strained them through giant colanders, steam enveloping them, while other stalls were hung with the innards of unknown animals, bits the butcher normally throws to the dog.

Along the ground stood rows of baskets, from which you found cockerels' beady eyes observing you. The smell had intensified and grown sweeter, with the putrescence now mingling with liquorice and aniseed, burning charcoal, steam, jasmine. We passed a temple with a lurid green- and red-glazed roof, and smelled the heady scent of incense. From the gloom came glimpses of shimmering gold, jade and dragon faces. The driver hit his horn and turned left into a lane barely wide enough to fit the car, and up before us, fronting the river, rose a building of yellow stone five storeys high and lined with balconies. It was our hotel, The Garden of Perfect Brightness.

The building was painted the same yellow ochre as Colman's mustard. The windows were faced with louvred shutters, each painted the shade of dark green that is common for the railings and benches of municipal parks in England. The upper windows had small balconies and wrought-iron railings. The building was in a compound surrounded by a wall that had once been plastered and painted cream. There was a gate wide enough to admit a car, and the driver drove through and up a small drive to stone steps and a portico. Two boys dressed in off-white trousers and short-sleeved shirts with epaulettes opened the car doors and organised the retrieval of the travelling cases. To the left through a small gate in another wall we could see a lawn, and beyond that the river.

We climbed the steps and walked into an airy lobby that took up most of the ground floor. The floor was dark polished teak and studded here and there with potted plants and large empty jars. Ceiling fans swirled high above our heads. Immediately to the right was a reception desk with three liveried officers in attendance. Despite the slightly run-down exterior of the hotel, the desk seemed very efficient. A manager calling himself Mr John strode forward to greet us, and conducted us to some lounge chairs in the centre of the lobby, set around a table strewn with issues of the international press. Orange juice was brought for us and Mr John took our passports away to finish the formalities. Jenny gave me a look of approval and I had to admit it was rather grand.

The centre of the lobby was dominated by a grand staircase that rose with unusual steepness because it omitted the first floor, ascending instead to a landing on the second floor. On the landing there was a table and glass case containing a rattan ball about four feet across.

A boy showed us to a room on the third floor, opening the door with a brass fob the size of a shoehorn. The bathrooms were shared with two other rooms on the floor, but the boy assured us these were currently vacant. The room was very pleasant, filled with bright dappled light of the sort that you find in rooms overlooking water. It had a teak floor, a big slow ceiling fan, some rattan furniture and a bed enveloped in a mosquito net. We both strode over and threw open the doors to the balcony. 'Chaopraya River,' said the boy proudly. The lawn below looked very beguiling, leading directly to the river, which was quite a bit wider than the Thames. The lawn was strewn with chairs and tables under wide parasols. We could see a young girl seated at one table, and beyond, in the river, a most remarkable sight: a flying boat floating on her belly like a swan, bobbing gently in the river swell.

Instead of unpacking we returned to the lobby and walked outside onto a small terrace set with reclining chairs, before following a path across the grass towards the river. The girl we had seen from the window sat in a bath chair, loosely wrapped in blankets despite the oppressive heat. With an air of great absorption she picked up a piece of paper and began folding it carefully, into the shape of a little bird. We stood and watched, and it was some time before the girl became aware of our presence. She looked up at us and smiled.

'Good afternoon,' said Jenny. 'I hope we are not disturbing you.'

'Hello,' said the girl. 'Have you just arrived? You are English. My name is Hoshimi. It's Japanese, but I am a great admirer of England.'

'How wonderful,' said Jenny. 'We are Jack and Jenny Wenlock.'

'How did you learn such excellent English?' I asked.

'Mr Wenlock, you are very kind, but I know my English is … perfectly awful! The scraps I have managed to learn are from my father, who for many years taught English at the Technical High School.'

'How interesting!'

'In Nagasaki my father used to take me every Saturday to visit Marmaduke's Emporium on Tenjimbashisuji street. The most wonderful English merchandise could be obtained there. Pears soap, Robertson's jam, Tate and Lyle Golden Syrup, "Out of the strength came forth sweetness". Heinz ketchup, tennis balls, Winsor and Newton watercolours. It was such a marvellous place. They also had the most beautiful model railway that ran round the perimeter of the shop. A 4–6-0 Great Western Railway 'Castle' class, engine number 4070 Godstow Castle. It was painted in shiny apple-green livery, and pulled six coaches painted chocolate and cream.'

'We got married on that train,' said Jenny.

Hoshimi's face lit up with delight and surprise. 'My word! Did you really? How spiffing!'

'The ceremony took place on the footplate,' I added.

'The footplate? I never knew such things were possible.'

'Oh yes,' I continued. 'It used to be the case. The driver of a mainline steam locomotive on the Great Western Region was permitted under certain circumstances to perform the marriage ceremony.'

'I have heard that the GWR is … sadly no more.'

'That's right,' I replied. 'Sadly.'

'Such a shame. The model in Marmaduke's Emporium had a sleeping carriage attached. Have you ever been in one? I can't imagine anything more wonderful than sleeping in a train.'

'Yes,' I said. 'And I can assure you, there is nothing more wonderful.'

'I didn't think there could be. Mr Marmaduke also had every edition of the Railway Gosling Annuals. Except the 1931 one. For some reason we were not able to procure it in Japan.'

'You weren't alone,' I said. 'They only printed one copy and then destroyed the printing plates.'

'Surely not!' said Hoshimi, her face flushed with concern. 'Why on earth would they do that?'

'It contained some unflattering remarks about His Majesty King George the Fifth.'

'Was he not a splendid fellow?'

'Not everyone thought so,' I told her.

'Dear me,' she said. 'It sounds like I had a lucky escape. I can recite all the names of the kings of England. I should not like to read unkind remarks about them.'

We left her once more to her origami and walked down to the river. It felt more like an inland sea than a river, with a succession of tiny wavelets lapping rhythmically against the bank. Boats plied the river in all directions. Thin motorised ones carrying people sped past in the centre of the stream, overtaking giant barges laden with stone, moving with glacial slowness seawards. At other places we could see ferries criss-crossing from side to side, stopping at jetties and disgorging hundreds of people before resuming their journeys.

The floating plane was a Short 'C' class Empire Flying Boat. She was moored quite far out in the stream, at the end of a wooden jetty some 20 yards long. I was struck by her size, more like a double-decker bus than a plane.

I had known from my reading that there were twin decks inside, but had never quite pictured what that entailed in terms of size. And when you see a photo of one sitting out in a tropical lagoon, you get very little idea of scale. Standing this close gave one to understand why they talked of casting off when travelling in a flying boat. The fact that there were multiple decks could be gathered from the siting of the cockpit, which sat very high on the front, like a pince-nez perched on someone's nose. The letters beneath the cockpit windows gave her name, *Connemara*. The paintwork here did not quite match the rest of the fuselage, suggesting that her name had recently been changed.

A chap in a linen suit stood to our left, staring at the water and smoking a cigarette. On noticing us he sauntered over. 'Are you the pilot?' he asked. He was short, probably no more than five foot five, and had a nose that had been broken long ago and set slightly to the left of the centre of his face. He smiled amiably.

'I'm afraid not,' I said.

'Jack's more of a steam-train man,' said Jenny brightly.

'I was joking,' the man said. 'You look far too sane to be the pilot.'

'Oh,' I said, rather shocked by the bitter edge to his voice. 'Is the pilot insane?'

'He will need to be, won't he? At the moment we don't have one.'

I remembered the hot sticky night in Singapore when we drank beer with Webster.

He had talked of the flying boat, but his words at that time conjured in my mind an image that existed only in the realm of fantasy, the idea seemed so wildly improbable. And yet here she was, and the very matter-of-factness of that name change – Connemara after the love of Sam Flamenco's life, Solveig Connemara – gave the mad enterprise a solidity that could not be denied. And yet, it could not be doubted that to set off with a film crew and a troupe of actors in search of an island marked on no maps and home to a mythical monster was indeed an adventure for which the pilot would need to be insane.

The man spoke again, this time more softly, as if a more pleasant thought had emerged. 'Hard to believe such a magnificent bird could come out of such a rotten egg, isn't it?'

'I'm afraid I don't understand your meaning,' I said.

'Sorry, I didn't mean to be enigmatic. I meant the Empire Air Mail Service for which she was originally built. Such a lovely bird, is she not?'

'Indeed she is, really quite splendid.'

'And yet she came into being born of the conviction that every Englishman should as by birthright be able to send a letter to anywhere in the Empire for the price of a cup of tea. It's the cup of tea part that gets me.' He paused and reflected for a second. 'That's the beauty of a sea plane, it means the postman can get to places that don't have runways. The last one got eaten, apparently. All that survived was his hat.' He walked over to a table and stubbed his cigarette out in the ashtray there. Then he walked back towards the hotel without another word to us.

We returned to our room to fetch the postcard we had taken from Curtis's room in Singapore. Shortly after we got back there was a knock on the door. I opened it to find a pudgy man in a grey suit. His collar button was undone, his tie skew-whiff. He was short with a sad face and dome-shaped head that lent his countenance the aspect of a mole.

'I say,' he said, 'I don't suppose you have any paper? I wouldn't normally ask, but the local paper is filthy stuff, she refuses to use it.'

'Who does?' I said.

'The Japanese girl, she uses it to fold cranes.'

'I expect they will have some in the writing room,' I said.

'The hotel won't let her have any more paper – they think it's bad luck or something. These bloody people are the limit, most superstitious race on God's earth. They think everything is bad luck. It's just an excuse if they don't want to do something.'

Jenny, who had been listening, joined me at the door and placed her hand on my back. 'I don't think we have any,' she said.

He became visibly alarmed. 'But you must have! Everyone has writing paper, dammit!' He stood up on his toes and tried to peer over us into the room.

'Well we don't,' said Jenny. 'We hate writing, don't we Jack? We'd rather get squiffy instead.'

Frustration creased his brow. 'Look, I know this is … but don't you see? The bloody dance is tomorrow. St George's Day. We're running a tote on how many she folds. I've got her down for six hundred and sixty-seven. She's slowed down a lot recently … her strength, it's failing. To tell the truth, I'm quite worried. I told her father to get a new doctor, but he refused. Bloody Jap.'

'How inconsiderate of him,' said Jenny. 'Maybe he doesn't know who St George was.'

'That's hardly the point.'

'What is the point?' said Jenny, with a chill in her voice that suggested the chap had better watch his step.

'I've got a lot riding on this.'

'Maybe you should offer her a commission.' She smiled as she said it, but the smile did not reach her eyes and even this boorish chap noticed. He blinked and said as if it were hardly to be credited, 'Are you being flippant?'

'Look here, Mr … ?' I gave him a stern look.

'Earwig. They call me Earwig.'

'Well, Mr Earwig, let me be candid with you. We don't have any writing paper to spare and, if we did, I rather doubt we would give you any in view of your manner—'

'What do you mean?'

'You knock on our door without introduction, use vulgar language in front of my wife—'

Another guest had appeared from one of the rooms and paused in the corridor to listen.

'OK, OK,' he said, dismissing the quest. 'I only asked for paper, not a bag of bloody Spanish doubloons.' He walked off in exasperation, shoving rudely past the other man, who had the relaxed air of someone who would be unperturbed if the building was on fire. His hair was cropped short in a style that suggested he was or had been in the military, but one got the impression that it was not the ordinary sort of military. More the sort of chap who carries a cyanide pill secreted in a shirt button in case things get dicey.

'See what true love can do to a man,' he said with a smile. 'If he wins the tote he's hoping to take Sugarpie out.'

'Who's Sugarpie?' said Jenny.

'A rather attractive Siamese lady.' He sauntered off.

Some time later, Jenny took the writing paper which she had saved from the SS *Pandora* library and gave it to Hoshimi.

———

We returned to the lobby with the postcard and showed it to the man at the desk, inquiring about Finky's Foto-graphic. We were directed to an arcade of shops across from the hotel. A small crowd of dozing rickshaw drivers sprang to attention on seeing us leave the hotel and we wended our way through them and across the street.

The studio stood in a row of shops, which included tailoring services, travel goods, temple artefacts. There was also a darkened shop with a 'Closed' sign on the door, called Burma, Bangkok and North Borneo. Import & Export. In the window there was a model of an Empire Flying Boat, and a dusty globe with a length of red string pinned across its surface linking Rangoon to Bangkok, Georgetown, Singapore and Kuching in Borneo. It was too dark to see further into the shop.

Next door, the window of Finky's Fotographic featured a display of framed photographs arranged around an antique bellows camera. The name 'Fink' was written in gold cursive letters across the glass and this was repeated on the front door. There seemed little sign of life and, not sure of the protocol, we knocked, waited for a brief moment and then entered. A bell rang. The shop smelled strongly of cigarette smoke. It was lined on either side with shelves laden with photographic supplies, and at the far end was a desk and a chair. A chap in a linen suit sat at the desk in the gloom, smoking a cigarette.

'We meet again,' he said. It was the man we had seen earlier by the river.

'Are you Mr Fink?' asked Jenny.

'Yes.' He reached out his hand and I shook it, saying, 'Jack and Jenny Wenlock.'

He shook Jenny's hand as well and said, 'Welcome to The Garden of Perfect Brightness. This your first time in Bangkok?'

We said that it was, and he told us he had been here eight years. 'Whereabouts in England are you from, Mr Fink?' Jenny asked.

'Brighton. I used to be the Brighton Biffer.' Seeing the look of polite puzzlement on our faces, he continued, 'Boxing. Middleweight.'

We looked appropriately surprised.

He opened a drawer and took out a tin that once had contained throat lozenges. 'Excuse me while I take my medicine.' He removed the lid to reveal the contents: a collection of dried grubs. He popped one in his mouth.

'Caterpillars of the Swallowtail, they feed them on rue.

Here did she fall a tear, here in this place
I'll set a bank of rue, sour herb of grace.

'Shakespeare. They are said to be good for the particular form of epilepsy I suffer from. Reduces the severity of the seizures, the frightening clarity of the auras.'

'Do they work?' I asked.

He paused to consider. 'I'm not sure they do. But rue is a versatile plant. Gulliver, after returning from his sojourn in the land of the Houyhnhnms, used to stuff his nose with it because he couldn't bear the stink of English people. Not that I mean to suggest that you—'

We laughed. 'Do you dislike England so terribly?' I said.

'Is that why you don't go back?' asked Jenny.

He laughed. 'No! No, I love the old place. I love the grime and soot and brown skies filled with choking smoke, dreary grey clouds, and rainslicked streets where armies of miserable blighters crowd the pavement and say nothing more adventurous in their lives than,' he tilted his head back and scrunched his lips up towards

159

his nose as if balancing something on his top lip and said in a comic voice, 'Cheerio!'

We laughed.

'Yes, how can you not love dear old Blighty? I would go back, but I'm afraid it might be rather difficult on account of a misunderstanding I have with the Royal Military Police. Besides, I seem to have mislaid a vital piece of equipment here in Bangkok.'

'Perhaps we could help you find it,' said Jenny. 'Jack is a detective.'

Mr Fink looked aghast, 'Oh God, is he?'

'Not that sort, Mr Fink,' I hastened to reassure him. 'Whatever the nature of your misunderstanding with the police, it is no concern of mine. I used to work on the railways.'

'What is it you have mislaid in Bangkok?' said Jenny.

'My heart, of course. What does any chap lose here?'

'Oh I see,' she said. 'You poor thing.'

'*My pen ry*,' he said.

'Beg your pardon?'

'*My pen ry*, it means never mind. You'll hear it a lot. Besides, losing one's heart is not so very terrible, that's what the heart is for. It's easily done. Especially here. It's some kind of sorcery, I'm sure of it. If you let her into your heart, your ruin is assured.' There was a pause that turned slightly awkward. Mr Fink's disclosure seemed a touch too intimate for a first acquaintance and it was difficult to know what to say now. He took out another cigarette and lit it without offering us one. 'Railwayman, you say?'

'He's teaching me to fire a steam engine,' she said proudly.

'What's there to teach?' he replied in a dismissive tone. 'You just throw in some coal and wait, don't you?'

'You couldn't be more wrong if you tried,' she admonished.

'A fire is a fire.'

'No it jolly well isn't!' Jenny contradicted him with the zeal of the newly converted. 'There are all sorts of fires, and you have to match your fire to suit the terrain. If you are going uphill—'

'That's easy, I throw in more coal.'

'Well I'm afraid you are too late if you do,' said Jenny with the air of one who has just clinched the argument. 'You should have thrown the coal in fifteen minutes ago, it won't help you now. You'll just end up at the station with too much steam and have to blow it off. Thirty gallons of your hard shovelling blown off in a minute.'

Mr Fink seemed to quail. 'I never knew it could be so complicated.'

'Oh yes,' said Jenny. 'There are so many things you have to take into account, even the phase of the moon. Did you know that?'

'Of course,' said Fink. 'I knew that.'

Jenny shot me a glance and said nothing.

I put the postcard down on the table. 'We were rather hoping you could tell us something about this photograph. It was sent by a friend of ours. This would appear to have your shop's marque on it.'

Upon seeing the card all the colour drained from his face and he froze. Into his eyes came the desperate look of a man who beholds the ghost of a man he once slew.

'Mr Fink, are you all right, sir?' I said. 'Mr Fink?'

He sat not moving, like one carved from stone.

'Mr Fink,' said Jenny, 'would you like some water?'

He gave his head a barely perceptible shake and said in a pained whisper, 'I am having a seizure. You must wait.'

We stood there awkwardly. Slowly his fainting fit passed and his features shed whatever force had locked them.

'I do apologise,' he said. 'It happens from time to time.' He looked down at the card, the way a dog looks at the stick that has beaten it.

'Can you tell us anything about this picture?' I said. 'Is it one you remember taking?'

'I take lots of pictures,' he said in a voice suddenly cold.

'It was sent by Mr Curtis,' said Jenny. 'Do you know him?'

'Name rings a bell, I suppose.'

'Was he a customer here?' I asked with mounting frustration.

He made no answer. All the warmth had evaporated.

'Do you recognise the location?' Jenny persisted.

He shrugged. 'Not really.'

My voice rose a register in exasperation. 'If you don't mind me saying, Mr Fink, I find it rather hard to believe you would not remember the location of this scene. It is quite extraordinary, the way the tree has grown around the stone head. I don't believe I could ever forget seeing such a wonder. If it were in England the roads to it would be clogged with the traffic from sightseers.'

He looked me in the eye, wearing an expression that suggested this new topic of conversation was very painful for him. 'Actually, I do mind you saying. And we are not in England. Sights like this might strike you as marvellous, but they are ten a penny here. If you want to see some ruins, you should visit Ayutthaya, the old capital, about thirty miles north. Then you'll see. There's a trip there tomorrow, as it happens, taking Hoshimi. I expect you saw her on the lawn.'

'Yes, we did,' said Jenny.

'From Nagasaki. She's got the atom-bomb disease, whatever that is. Something to do with the blood. No one seems to know much about it.'

'Oh dear,' said Jenny. 'Poor thing.'

'She's folding origami cranes. There is a children's legend in Japan, apparently, that says if you fold a thousand origami cranes you get your dearest wish answered. Don't ask me what number she is on now, Earwig will tell you. He'll ask you for paper, if he hasn't already. Has he? He's running a tote, you see. The swine.' He stopped, and looked at me.

'We're sorry if we are importuning,' I said with forced patience, 'but to be perfectly frank, we are very worried about our friend.'

'Are you now? Well, I shouldn't be. If he's gone missing in Bangkok, there will be a woman involved somewhere, there always is.'

'There was talk of a girl with blue eyes,' I said.

He looked even more uncomfortable. 'Was there? I wouldn't know.' The look in his eyes suggested that he did. 'European girls are not easy to find in Bangkok, Malaya is better. Most chaps here are more than satisfied with the local girls. Or you could try the cemetery – a lot of chaps who go missing end up there.'

I found the facetiousness of Mr Fink's last remark tiresome and contrived. It was clearly designed to avoid giving a straight answer. 'Mr Fink, I will ask you directly: is it your opinion that Mr Curtis is dead?'

'Well, we're all dead in a way here, aren't we? I know I am.'

'Please don't play games with me.'

'Tell me, Mr Wenlock, are you familiar with the cliffs at Beachy Head?'

'I have heard them spoken of.'

'People often go there to throw themselves off, people for whom the pleasures of this world have lost their savour. It takes a few seconds to complete the drop, considerably longer than a man being hanged. Have you ever wondered what passes through the mind of a chap as he falls?'

'I am pretty sure I never have, but I suspect two seconds or whatever it is are not really sufficient to have thoughts of any great consequence.'

Mr Fink's last few comments had been delivered in a deadpan voice, contrived to give us the impression that he was world-weary and did not care very much. But with the talk of jumping off Beachy Head he now became animated, as if this was his true passion. 'Yes, that is the fly in the ointment when it comes to Beachy Head. But here in Bangkok it is different. We too are all falling to our death, but the Siamese have contrived to slow time down so that we can better enjoy the sensation.'

'If you feel you are dying,' I said with mounting impatience, 'then perhaps you ought to visit a doctor.'

'Ah yes, but what if he cured me?'

'What about the buffalo?' Jenny said with feigned sweetness, trying to approach him from a different angle. 'Could it be significant?'

'Don't be bloody stupid,' he said, 'it's just a buffalo.' The anguish in his voice suggested it might be more than just a buffalo. 'If it was a picture of a cow in a field in England, would you ask if it were significant?'

'The message written on the back suggests something rather more serious than a girl,' Jenny retorted.

He turned it over and read it. 'Look, Mr Wenlock, if you are going to start looking for Curtis, might I suggest you send your wife out of the country first?'

'No you may not!' cried Jenny.

165

'Well that would be my advice,' he said quietly.

'Is it terribly unsafe here?' I said. 'So far everyone has been most pleasant.'

'Everyone smiles,' added Jenny.

'Yes, don't they?' said Mr Fink. 'The Siamese smile is a strange beast. Often it can mean the opposite of what you suppose. If your mother just died, for example, and you told a chap about it, in all likelihood he would smile. If a man was about to cheat you, he would smile. Or if you embarrassed him. Or if a chap was standing before you plotting your murder, he would give you the most beatific smile of all.'

He paused and his eyes narrowed as if recalling a particularly painful memory.

'Nothing is as it seems here … nothing.'

I retrieved the postcard. 'If you should think of anything that might help us in our—'

He cut me off. 'Mr Wenlock, don't be such a bloody fool! Look, you both seem like very nice people, but if you don't mind me being frank, you seem a bit wet.'

'Wet?' I said.

'Behind the ears! This isn't the Home Counties. Take my advice and bugger off while you still can.'

'Look, Mr Fink,' I began. He cut me off.

'No, *you* look, Mr Wenlock! I've tried being reasonable but … really! I mean you barge in here, asking all sorts of impertinent questions about … buffaloes and goodness knows what else … I mean, it really is too much … asking things.'

We thanked him for his advice and returned to the hotel. As we did we discussed what had just taken place.

'What do you make of him?' asked Jenny.

'I must say,' I replied, 'I find him a mess of contradictions. On the hotel lawn earlier, he struck me as quite pleasant, affable. Partly it was an act, I believe. The account of the postman being eaten sounded a bit too glib, well-rehearsed. But here just now I found him a bit slippery, and quite clearly host to a secret that gives him great pain. His reaction to the image on the card was startling.'

Jenny nodded. 'Yes, and when he turned it over and read the back, did you notice how … how he didn't seem to think much of it?'

'Yes, he did not remark on it even though it was a most remarkable thing to read.'

'Do you think he was right about what he said? That we are a bit wet?'

I laughed. 'I'm quite sure we must appear that way, but we mustn't worry. I have every confidence we will turn out better than his unflattering estimation of us.'

167

Chapter 10

As we descended to dinner that evening we stopped on the first-floor landing where the two bifurcating stairways met. We examined the glass case containing the rattan ball. It comprised interweaving slats of rattan similar to the cages we had seen in the street outside containing live cockerels, but this was entirely spherical. Spikes had been driven through the outer shell and faced inwards, a bit like the instrument of torture known as the Spanish Maiden.

'I don't think I'd like to descend these stairs while merry,' said Jenny. I looked down and understood. They were rather steep. She turned her attention to the ball. 'What do you think it is?'

Before I could answer, a voice intruded. 'If you're hoping for a game, you'll have to bring your own elephant.'

We turned to see two men: one short and stocky, the other quite tall and athletic, both in their forties. They were dressed similarly to Earwig, with the same tie, although theirs were fastidiously knotted. The taller of the two held out a hand, 'Spaulding,' he said, 'and this is Roger.' The shorter one didn't offer his hand but gave his head a slight upward jerk and said, 'Rather!' His face was ruddy with health and his hair was brilliantined in such a way that it resembled the outline of a 'Q' on its side, like a comic-book hero.

'I expect you are wondering what it is,' said Spaulding, nodding towards the rattan ball.

'Is it some sort of cage?' I said.

'It's a metaphor,' he said, 'for the Oriental heart.'

I looked to Roger. He smiled and said, 'Rather!'

'Sorry, I'm being facetious, a vice I abhor,' said Spaulding. 'It's a football for elephants to play with. Rather grand, wouldn't you say? What could be more fun than a kick-around on the park after work, eh?'

'What are the spikes for?' said Jenny.

'They used to stuff a chap inside the ball,' said Spaulding. 'Some miserable convict sentenced to death. This was a hundred years or so ago. Nowadays they just machine-gun them.'

'You mean the elephant kicked the ball with a man inside?' said Jenny in disbelief.

'Oh yes!'

Earwig appeared and joined us.

'I believe you have already met Earwig,' said Spaulding. 'He has something to say to you, don't you, Earwig?'

Earwig shifted his weight awkwardly and said, 'Yes, er, I ... I owe you both an apology for the scene earlier. I was not myself.'

'It's the heat,' said Spaulding.

'Oh it's quite all right,' I said. 'I was perhaps a touch—'

'It wasn't *that* hot,' interrupted Jenny.

'Well, all the same,' said Earwig, 'I'm sorry.'

The three turned to descend the stairs. As they did, Spaulding added, 'I hear you are looking for Curtis.'

I forced a laugh. 'Whoever told you that?'

'The Chief of Police. Well, he's not really the Chief, he just thinks he is.'

'How does he know?'

'You'll have to ask him that. But you don't need a chief of police to find Curtis. It's the same anywhere, but even more so out here. When a chap goes off the rails, there is usually a very simple explanation. *Cherchez la femme.*'

———

At the entrance to the restaurant we bumped into the American we had seen earlier when Earwig knocked on our door asking for paper. He introduced himself as Kilmer and then, with that unaffected familiarity that characterises Americans, invited us to join him for dinner. We accepted. He looked even more relaxed than the last time we had seen him, and wore an expression that suggested he had access to privileged truths about the world which permitted him not to care too much about the everyday concerns that troubled the rest of us.

The room was furnished in dark rosewood furniture that gave it a heavy and sombre aspect. It must have been gay in the morning, though, since the windows – now shuttered – gave way on to the lawn. The waitresses wore pencil skirts in dark silk and tight peach and apricot silk bodices cinched at the waist with belts of gold braid that glittered in the dim light. Their hair was gathered in an immaculate bun behind the crown of the head, while the waists of these ladies were narrow as children's back home, and their shoulders were bare. Bracelets of gold jingled softly at their wrists and others enclosed thin biceps. Their skin had the colour and smoothness of honey. They moved between the table as quiet as dormice, scooping rice from silver urns held in the crook of the arm.

They were very elegant, but what struck me most particularly was their carriage. They walked as if balancing an invisible earthenware jar upon their heads. But so little did one see of their feet moving that it might be more accurate to say they glided as if on wheels.

I happen to believe that posture and carriage are windows onto a chap's character. There is a good reason the armies of the world set so much store by a straight back and upright stance. The outward form is the container for a man's spunk. On the battlefield, or more usually during the long oppressive spells leading up to the battlefield, it is the inner man that holds things together. A man can endure any number of hardships if the pilot light inside is still burning. The first indicator that things are amiss is the head: it drops. Everything follows from that.

There were two menus, an à la carte featuring a selection of Siamese and Chinese dishes and a European table d'hôte. As we read the menus, other diners were admitted. Hoshimi was wheeled in, this time accompanied by what we took to be her mother, and smiled and waved to us. Her father was dressed as if for a wedding, in a dark frock coat and dark tie. He held himself with that same concern for outward form that I alluded to. His face was severe and shone as if polished rather than scrubbed. The three chaps, Earwig, Roger and Spaulding, dined together at a table. There were two other couples dining.

After some polite small-talk I decided to broach the subject of our visit to Mr Kilmer. Did he by chance know of Mr Curtis?

He laughed, 'Oh yes, I met him. He arrived somewhere mid-March, and went missing just after Spaulding's birthday, which was the first week of April. I've met plenty of unusual people, but he would have won a prize.'

'Unusual in what way?' I said. Mr Kilmer gave me a noncommittal stare. 'I don't mean to pry, but we are most anxious to find him, we … we know him from long ago and are very worried.'

It was evident from the look of solemn acceptance he wore that Mr Kilmer plainly saw through that lie, but did not seem to care very much. 'I guess it all depends on what folk consider unusual, but turning up at Spaulding's birthday celebration wearing a necklace of human ears would probably qualify, wouldn't it?'

'Goodness gracious!' I said. 'Where on earth did he get the ears from?'

'Stole them from me,' said Kilmer. 'I made the mistake of showing them to him, I should have guessed he would pull a trick like that.'

'Would it be impertinent to ask how you came by a collection of ears?' I said.

Kilmer raised a glass to us and said over the rim, 'During the war I was in Indochina, training partisans to fight the Japanese. I worked with the Hmong people, from the mountains. Wonderful folk, some of the finest people I've ever met. I paid them a dollar for every Japanese ear they brought me. I acquired quite a bagful.'

'Oh I say!' I said, somewhat taken aback by his shocking revelation.

'Really!' said Jenny in an excited tone.

'We used to interrogate the captured Japanese soldiers in a plane, and when my men had finished with them, we would throw them out.' He paused and narrowed his eyes as if troubled by that vision of the past. 'Now I see them in my dreams, falling, or before the war, taking their children to the zoo.' He picked up a napkin to wipe his mouth, held it for a long while, lost in thought, before throwing it down. He insisted on paying the bill and invited us to join him downstairs in the nightclub for a whisky.

The muffled sound of a jazz band playing enticed us as we descended the stairs to the basement. A neon sign advertised the Bolero Club. It looked very much like any such place back in England. There was a small stage and dance floor with tables and chairs set around it. Further back there were booths, and to the right of the stage a separate seated area, surrounding a central desk that looked oddly out of place in this environment. Three young Siamese ladies in Western frocks sat at these seats and spent their time scanning the room discreetly. An older woman sat behind the desk with a ledger in front of her, and stared into space.

We were shown to a table near the dance floor and ordered drinks. After a while, Roger, Spaulding and Earwig arrived and were shown to another table. Earwig threw Mr Kilmer a black look in passing. He smiled back, and said to me, 'Have you met the three musketeers yet?'

'Yes, briefly. They seemed a little odd. Who are they?'

'Do you mean who are they really, or who do they say they are?'

'I don't know. Is there a difference?'

'I don't know either. They say they are here to wind up the affairs of the Burma, Bangkok and North Borneo Company, but they don't seem to do much winding up, the office is always closed. If you ask them they will tell you they are awaiting the arrival of a giant tin of syrup.'

'That's interesting. I think we passed it a number of times on our way here.'

'It must be true then. It's going to Shimushir. It's a movie prop.'

'Is it empty?' said Jenny. 'I don't suppose the monster will like that.'

'No, I don't suppose he would.'

'Do they have a pilot?' I said. 'Mr Fink told me the pilot would need to be insane.'

'Did he? Well of all the … actually, I'm the pilot.'

'No, really?' cried Jenny. 'For Sam Flamenco and Solveig Connemara? You are flying to Shimushir?'

He nodded.

'How extraordinary,' I said. 'What an adventure! Is Mr Flamenco paying you handsomely?'

'He's not paying me at all. Who needs money?'

'Plenty of people as far as I can see.'

'Not me.'

'I do hope that didn't appear rude, I just assumed it was an offer of employment.'

'No need to apologise. He offered and I'm going, for the same reason most folk are going, to mend a broken heart.'

'Oh I see!' I said. 'These Siamese girls can be devilishly pretty, can't they?'

'Yes they sure can, but it wasn't a girl who broke my heart, it was a man.'

'From what we saw in Singapore,' Jenny said, showing clear signs of becoming merry, 'the men are even prettier!'

Kilmer laughed. 'That's for sure. The man who broke my heart was not pretty in the conventional way. His name was Ho Chi Minh.'

'I'm afraid it doesn't ring a bell,' I said.

'A great man. He was a great admirer of the United States. I helped him write the new Vietnamese constitution, which was based on the US constitution. He could have been a good friend of ours, but I was told that wasn't possible. The next wars had been planned for Vietnam and Korea and they didn't really care whether Ho Chi Minh was an admirer of George Washington. They are running out of places to have their wars, Europe won't be ready again for many years. It's going to be against communism this time. So, he's doomed. The new enemy will be Russia.'

'But the Russians were our allies,' I cried, greatly surprised by his revelation.

'Yes, I know, but it's been decided so there isn't much we can do about it. The Germans and Japs will be our friends and our former allies the Russians will be the new enemy.'

'But you'll never get the people to accept that,' Jenny said in bewilderment.

'Oh yes, give them ten years and they will have forgotten it had ever been different.' He raised his glass. 'Chin, Chin!'

'Here's mud in your eye,' Jenny said. 'Let's get blotto!'

'Jenny!' I said. She grinned and drank more.

'Good plan,' said Kilmer. 'Let's get canned.'

'Embalmed,' said Jenny.

'Owled.'

'Ossified.'

'Scrooched.'

'Spifflicated.'

'Blitzed.'

'Bombed.'

'Juiced.'

'Pickled.'

'Shucked.'

'Snockered.'

'You win,' said Kilmer. 'Where did you learn all that?'

'A friend,' said Jenny.

'She used to know a GI during the war,' I explained.

'Yeah? What else did he teach you?'

'Poker.'

'You play poker? We'll have to have a game.'

'You'll lose your shirt,' said Jenny with a sly grin.

Kilmer laughed. 'You know what? I believe you.'

———

Further conversation was stopped by a new event. The door opened and a ripple of tension seemed to pass through the room. A Siamese lady in a Western frock and with her hair styled in a permanent wave entered. She did not so much walk as sail into the room. All eyes were drawn to her and, though seemingly barely more than twenty, she carried herself in a manner that suggested she knew the effect her entrance was having.

She walked with her nose slightly tilted up, with a regal bearing that the Queen of Sheba would have envied. There seemed to be a half-sneer on her mouth, but one got the impression that this too was partly deliberate, a form of acting. As she walked she would occasionally catch the eye of someone she knew and a grin would break out, rearranging her imperious features into what no doubt was her true disposition of girlish fun.

She sauntered up to the desk, signed the book, then sat down with the other ladies, but did not speak to them. In turn they affected not to have noticed her arrival. A drink was placed before her and she raised it to her lips and slowly scanned the room over the top of it. Her gaze swept like a slow searchlight across the table of the three chaps. As it reached Earwig he waved at her. She paused for a tiny fraction of a second, her face betraying no sign that she had seen the wave, before moving on. Earwig stood up and began to walk across the room. Her gaze came to rest on Kilmer, where it lingered. It was enough.

He stood up and said, 'This is my cue.' He walked to the desk, and such was the timing that his path intersected with Earwig's and they almost bumped into each other. The issue of who was to pass first hung in the air for a fraction of a second, but then the American drew himself up to his full height and brushed past Earwig. He strode up to the girl and exchanged a few words. Earwig followed close behind and said something that made Kilmer turn sharply and give him a look of challenge. The girl wore a butter-wouldn't-melt expression. Earwig spoke to her and she gave him a look of wide-eyed innocent inquiry. She turned her eyes back to Kilmer, who passed a remark that made them both laugh and made Earwig turn red. Kilmer walked up to the desk and handed over some money and then the girl intertwined her arm with his and led him on to the dance floor. Earwig simmered for a second and then turned sharply away, knocking into a table before leaving the room in a temper.

Jenny squeezed my hand, and said, 'Bet you half-a-crown *that* is Sugarpie.'

———

Later, in the lobby, Earwig sidled up to me. 'Wenlock,' he said, in a manner that struck me as rather impertinent, 'you don't want to get too thick with that Yank.'

'He seems nice enough to me.'

'Of course he does, but I wouldn't be taken in, that's all.' I said nothing, so after a while he added, 'The chaps were wondering if you were free tonight ... for a while. Not your wife, just you.'

I looked at him.

'We … we want to show you something … about Curtis. Take you somewhere. We think it might help you understand. We'll meet you in the lobby at eleven.'

He left without waiting for a response, assuming no doubt it was a given. I felt sure the purpose of the invitation was to find out about me rather than help me. Everyone seemed to know we were looking for Curtis, even the chief of police   if what Mr Spaulding said could be believed.

For a man who had spent his life largely as a wallflower, Curtis seemed to have caused quite a stir since his arrival in Bangkok. Mr Fink's reaction to the buffalo photograph had been extraordinary. I couldn't fathom the meaning behind it but was fairly sure he had not been straight with us.

Chapter 11

OUTSIDE THE HOTEL THAT evening Earwig hailed two tricycle rickshaws – 'samlors' he called them. 'It translates as three-wheeler,' he explained with an expansive air. We got in the first, while Spaulding and Roger climbed into the second. The sun had set, but this had seemed only to intensify the hot muggy air, which was as steamy and warm as one's own breath exhaled into a cupped hand.

Our driver was a scrawny man, a scarecrow of sinew the colour of deep wood stain. He stood upright on the pedals to gain the necessary force to overcome the inertia, the muscles in his legs strained like hawsers, but once we were under way he sat back down and pedalled with more ease.

We ploughed slowly through the sea of oncoming people like a fish going the wrong way through a shoal. The narrow thoroughfare forced the people to jostle together and proceed like toothpaste squeezed from a tube. The whole world had come out to play, and one supposed this was largely because the intensifying heat of the dying day rendered whatever hovels they lived in unbearably hot. Neither did it seem that great store was set by leaving babies behind to stew; the tiniest of children, sometimes already wearing their pyjamas, walked along with the adults. The night air was a riot of noises: car horns, electronic music, a girl singing, shouts, and rising and falling with uncanny synchronicity, a chorus of cicadas, as if somewhere in this neighbourhood tonight a giant was frying bacon.

'We'll have fun tonight,' said Earwig.

I said nothing, wondering what the word 'fun' conveyed to him.

'You a bit of a sportsman, are you, Jack?'

'Can't really say I am, although I did play football at school.'

He laughed. 'Football! That's a good one. Well, even if you are not, you soon will be. You'll start off saying, "Oh no, I could never do anything like that!", and then you will. I did. Everyone does. Except Spaulding. You should have seen Curtis when he first came.' He laughed again and the driver lurched without warning into an alley to our right, one darker and less congested, the gloom pricked by the licking orange tongues of cooking fires in stoves on stalls that lined the way.

Behind the stalls a wide expanse of seating stood in the darkness under awnings strung up without much planning and festooned with lights. One got the impression that these dark canvas caverns continued for miles, like mine workings, into the heart of Bangkok. From time to time Chinamen ambled across our path swinging upside-down cockerels in one hand and long curved knives in the other. Along the floor, under the tables, other captive birds stared out from wicker baskets.

Some stalls had tanks of live fish and crustacea, and from time to time one would be fished out with a net and deposited straight into a sizzling wok.

'They'll eat anything, these people. You wouldn't believe,' said Earwig. 'Dogs, rats, bats, frogs, hornets, snakes ... anything with four legs except a table.' On saying that he dug me sharply in the ribs to alert me to the fact, lest I hadn't been aware, that this was a joke. I formed the impression that it wasn't originally his joke but that he used it often.

'How amusing,' I said. 'Do they really eat those things?'

'Those are quite tame. Live monkey brains, ever hear of that?'

'Really?'

'I've seen it. They have a special table with a hole in the middle. The monkey's head sticks up and they take the top off like a boiled egg. Then they stick their spoons in.'

'That really does sound quite appalling. Are you having a joke at my expense?'

'I swear to you it's true, Jack.'

———————

We pulled up at one of the restaurants and pushed through to a vacant table where we were waited on at once by a boy in short trousers and grubby vest. Spaulding took command and spoke to the boy in Siamese in a manner that suggested he was quite comfortable in that language. Earwig nodded to me with a gleam of proprietorial admiration in his eye, as if to say with regard to his proficiency, 'Look at that!' It was clear there were many things that Spaulding could do that Earwig admired.

Beers quickly arrived and we chinked the chipped glasses and drank each other's health. The beer was called Singha and came in a brown bottle wrapped in a label featuring the image of a golden lion. The beer tasted unlike any beer I had tasted before: it had a cloying sweetness that contrasted with a slight medicinal flavour. Although unusual, I did not find it unpleasant. The heat was even stronger here in the airless covered restaurant, almost as hot as when one opened the firebox door, but much more humid. In such an atmosphere there are few things more welcome than a cold beer.

We did not have to wait long for the food. Spaulding had ordered both Siamese and Chinese dishes and explained what they were when they arrived. Grilled chicken feet, roasted sparrow, fried grasshopper, fried beetle, cobra soup and a green curry. And rice. And more beers. The other diners ate with chopsticks, but without being asked the serving staff placed a fork and spoon down for each of us. 'Tuck in,' said Spaulding, reaching over with his spoon and scooping up some grasshoppers. Not wishing to be considered a wet blanket, which I suspected was the secret object of this escapade, I followed suit and crunched them thoughtfully. They were not unpleasant. They weren't really anything.

My thoughts turned to Jenny. She had been quite amused when I told her the chaps wanted to take me out, predicting all manner of lurid itineraries, only half in jest. The truth was, I would much rather be with her. The juvenile misbehaviour that men are traditionally expected to view as entertaining has always struck me as tedious. I was afraid if this was what they had in mind, the chaps were going to find me a terrible disappointment.

'Good source of protein,' said Spaulding, and looked at Roger, who raised a hand to minutely adjust his question-mark-shaped quiff and said, 'Rather!' He wore a permanent smile, slightly supercilious, as if life for him were a puzzling joke, and yet in his eyes there was a vacancy that suggested there was no one there doing the smiling.

A stallholder to my left fished his hand into an Ali Baba basket and drew out a cobra, head held at the throat between two practised fingers. With his other hand he sliced the snake open with a razor, then reached in and pulled a throbbing bit of flesh and handed it to a customer who swallowed it.

'Gall bladder,' Spaulding explained. 'You might want to try some yourself, it helps a man ... remain alert. Curtis went wild for it.'

'Curtis liked to remain alert,' said Earwig. 'There are better ways, though.' He drew what looked like a packet of sweets from his pocket and showed me. 'This is what you need, keeps you going. I can let you have some if you like.'

'What is it?' I asked.

'Panzer-Schokolade,' he replied unhelpfully.

'Tank chocolate?' I translated.

'It's what they used, isn't it? The German panzer crews. And our boys too, the pilots.'

'Benzedrine,' said Spaulding. 'Filthy stuff if you ask me.'

'Each to his own,' said Earwig. 'You know, you can get anything you desire here, in Bangkok. Anything.'

'I rather fancy I will disappoint you,' I said warily, anxious not to encourage them. 'I consider myself for the most part a contented man.'

'Have you ever been out East before?' said Spaulding.

'No,' I replied.

'You may struggle to hold on to that air of contentment,' he said. 'It's easy being content in a shop selling orthopaedic shoes, but what about in a sweet shop?'

The smallholder fished out a plateful of live shrimp. They danced and jumped and tickled the empty air crazily with legs like broken cocktail sticks. He threw them into a wok of boiling fat that exploded into clouds of steam that quickly disappeared. Then he poured in liquor of some description that sent the whole mess bursting into flames, and filling the air with the most intoxicating reek of charcoal, charred fish and alcohol.

'There are the girls, of course,' said Earwig, 'but that's just the start. Guns, drugs, gems …'

'Or if you want to hurt someone,' said Roger, 'that can be arranged.' I looked at him, aware that this was the first time he had spoken this evening.

'Or adventure,' said Earwig. 'Fancy yourself as a soldier of fortune? You can find an agent who will find you a war.'

'That's if your tastes are conventional,' said Spaulding. 'Contented men usually have tastes that are less obvious. Back home there is no way they can easily be accommodated, so they linger, they grow like a monster living in the sewer fed on the scraps that fall down the drains.'

I looked him in the eye. 'Was Curtis a contented man?'

He held his glass an inch below his chin and considered. 'I would say he was most discontented.'

'That surprises me. The information that I have is that he was one of those men in life who lack the imagination to be particularly discontented.'

'People like that are always the ones who surprise you. Some of them go a whole life without ever once revealing the monster – it lies dormant till the day they die. With others it breaks free late on in life, and wreaks havoc. They are the ones who surprise you. It is always the quiet, spectacled librarian who turns out to be the best torturer.

'Earwig talks about girls. Yes, you can get girls here, you can buy them for an hour or a lifetime for very little money. You can use them as your slave and subject them to the most vile degradations if that is what you like. Whatever it is … whatever terrible dream that nestles in the hidden cellar of your heart, the dream so dark and appalling you dare not even acknowledge it … here you will find the one opportunity in this world to assuage it. Here you will find people more depraved than you who will not blink to supply for money the corruption your heart dares not even name to itself.' He took a violent swallow of his beer and said, 'I have to tell you plainly, Mr Wenlock, your Mr Curtis was a most terrible rotten egg.'

We returned to the samlors and continued through the dark, sweaty, perfumed night to another assignation. As we rode I considered the strange narrative of Curtis that was being presented to me. The tale of a man who for years harbours some unnameable vice in the cellar of his heart, whose will finally crumbles and unleashes the forces of doom that he willingly embraces. It was a story violently at odds with the image of the human wallflower I had received so far. I thought of the Countess in Cornwall, telling his story through tendrils of mauve, late afternoon cigarette smoke. Could she have been so wrong about her son? Her own flesh and blood? Or was Mr Spaulding a man utterly without scruple?

Along the road urchins sold necklaces of flowers, and the perfume intermingled with the cooking smells and sweetened the reek of stagnation. Amid the crowds there was the occasional flash of amber, like fireworks, as groups of monks passed barefoot, shaven-headed and clad in saffron robes. Although I had no idea where we were, we seemed to be moving ever deeper into the labyrinth of alleys and small lanes, into the dark heart of this town.

The closeness of the houses made me think of images that I had once seen in a book of the poorer districts of London in the times of Dickens. Like those times, this felt like a human stew. The air and ground throbbed with the energy of so many people going and coming, never still, incessantly about some business like bees in a hive or at the calyx of a flower. You can get anything you want here, Earwig had said. Was that not true of all great cities where not far from beautiful houses lay districts where people lived in poverty too abject to contemplate? Or was there something here that other cities did not possess?

I lacked the imagination to picture to myself the desires of desperate men. My life had been spent in service of the railway and my wants had been small and not greatly difficult to gratify. At the Weeping Cross Railway Servants' Orphanage the food was, I can see looking back, spartan. But at the time I had nothing to compare it with, and thus did not hunger or crave things I had no knowledge of.

It is only since the war ended and my employment with the railway terminated that I have known

191

hardship, but I know that such hardship is soft com-pared with the agonies of those – and there are so many – who are truly destitute. And though I cannot imagine the tastes of those whom Earwig refers to when he says you can get anything you want, I have still frequently encountered men driven to desperation by the prompt-ings of these tastes, men who destroy themselves like moths consumed in a candle flame.

I have seen, many times, ladies with bruised faces who have assured me all was well, and seen the terrible remains of ladies caught in trees who leapt to their deaths from speeding trains. I have caught men accom-panying young children who were not their own, and I have read with grisly bafflement the scant details of the subsequent court cases. A man can get anything he wants here, but is that why Curtis came? From what little I knew of him I had formed the impression of a wallflower who went through life causing as little fuss as possible, and then one day some strange upset caused him to go off the rails.

His mother had said his recent letters contained evi-dence of a man growing more and more unwell. The concierge at the Raffles spoke of a nervous breakdown occasioned by the Fall of Singapore, and in particular the symbolic interment of the silver roast beef trolley. If this was true, then his quest around the shores of Borneo in search of my mother had accelerated a process that was already in train, the way a volcano can rumble gently for many years, the pressure inside slowly building, until one day the plug of solidified lava that fills the throat blows clear like a champagne cork and the surrounding countryside catches fire beneath a rain of burning rock.

Why did he come here? Was his quest at an end? Did he perhaps have a hankering – part of his inner moral collapse – to star in a film? Or was it merely for a reunion with Sam Flamenco, with whom he had formed that unlikely partnership?

But would going off the rails for him involve what was, to all extents and purposes, a form of pilgrimage to the stews of licentiousness? It seemed to me that this was the version one would find in an adventure novel, and it was from this that the chaps were drawing their inspiration. I felt that this evening was really a pantomime arranged to give me the impression that Curtis had done what many men who come to these strange and unfamiliar climes do. It did not ring true for me.

I turned to Spaulding. 'Why do you say Curtis was a rotten egg?'

'I didn't like the cut of his jib.'

'In Singapore they told me he did something that scandalised the British community here.'

'It's true. On my birthday. Frankly it nauseated me.'

'I heard he turned up wearing a necklace of human ears.'

'He did, but it wasn't that, it was the rest of the outfit that I objected to.'

'I see,' I said although I did no such thing. 'What was he wearing?'

'It hardly matters. I shouldn't worry about him, though. If he's gone off with a tart it won't last long. He didn't strike me as having a lot of money. Once it runs out, the love will be over. He's probably down at the coast somewhere, right now. Pattaya or Hua Hin, or one of the islands. You see them sitting outside their rented villas, staring into the evening sky. If you catch him early, he'll be in a sort of delirium of joy. Later on, you'll find him sitting on a chair staring out to sea looking crushed by the utter boredom of it all. That's when they start to quarrel.'

The beer must have been much stronger than I had imagined, because I seemed to have fallen asleep for a part of the journey. I awoke midway through some speech Spaulding was giving about a banquet once given by the old Manchu emperors.

'… three hundred courses, six days to eat. Frog's belly, carp tongue, leopard foetus, rhinoceros tails and deer tendons, elephant trunk, gorilla lip, monkey brain and camel hump, and to finish it off, egg tart.'

I nodded, my mind bleary.

'The best bit is this: bear's left paw. But specifically the left one, because that is the one it licks and is therefore considered more tender. Thing is, how did they know which one it licked? Do all bears lick the left paw? What do you think?'

We pulled up outside what appeared to be a down-at-heel hotel. A group of blind musicians played next to the entrance. One of them, a girl, raised a tin cup at the sound of our arrival and said, 'You good heart, sir.' It was unclear whether it was a statement or a question. Or perhaps just an expression of hope. A camera flashed in our faces – it belonged to a man wearing a dark suit and an inexpertly knotted tie. Spaulding shooed him away impatiently.

We entered a dimly lit passage. To the right was a small hotel desk, unmanned, with wooden pigeonholes behind containing keys. A telephone sitting to one side was the only sign of hotel life. To the left was a door leading into a bare tiled room in which some people were playing cards at a table. A fat lady with her back to us looked round with great effort. On seeing us, she stood up with even greater effort, and shuffled forward. She wore a dark skirt that rippled on her like the skin of a caterpillar. Her arms and shoulders were bare, and gleamed with gold bangles. Her face was thickly powdered white, like a ping-pong ball, and her dark thin eyes glittered.

'Here we are,' said Spaulding. 'Paradise.'

We followed the lady upstairs. I tripped on the step and had to be helped by Spaulding. I was aware of feeling increasingly out of sorts. I wondered what Jenny was doing and longed to be with her.

At the top of the stairs was a busy Chinese restaurant. The waiters wore jackets and ties, the waitresses cheongsams in midnight-blue silk.

We moved to the next room, a private room. I was finding it difficult to walk, but had enough presence of mind to refuse the offered opium. I ordered a cup of tea instead, which came without milk and tasted like the water one boils sprouts in. A girl brought a pipe about 18 inches long with a porcelain bowl at one end, and put it down next to a lamp on the table.

'It's the breath of God,' said Spaulding. 'Ethereal, celestial, it's like the world becomes a flower, did you know that? There's nothing like it.'

The girl unwrapped a piece of opium the size of a gobstopper, like a ball of dough. She divided it into smaller balls the size of peas, then put one on a small piece of wood and held it over the lamp, while shaping it with a spindle held in the other hand. It began to sizzle. Once satisfied she put it in the pipe and handed it to Roger, who sucked on it greedily, his face becoming for a second a gargoyle of longing: cheeks gaunt, eyes almost popping. He leaned back, eyes closed in some unimaginable delirium, and said softly, 'Rather!'

'These are called flower smoke rooms,' Spaulding continued. 'The girls are the flowers. Curtis thought you could get to Elysium by boat, that was his mistake; the gateway is a simple pipe. Hard to believe we had to force the Chinese to take the stuff at gunpoint – usually you need a gun to take it off people. What you have to understand is, it's not good for you to go looking for him. There are issues of … well, the security of England, do you see what I mean?'

'Not really,' I said.

'He probably isn't here anyway. Malaya's your best bet.'

'Funny, you are the second person to tell me that. The second in the space of a day to recommend I leave Bangkok straight away.'

'Who was the first?'

'Mr Fink.'

'Oh was he indeed? Did he tell you he and Curtis used to be very thick?'

'No, he didn't.'

'Until they fell out. Had a blazing row the night of my party. A real fireworks show it was. At one point Fink threatened to kill Curtis, and we had to restrain him. We never saw Curtis again after that night. Perhaps Mr Fink has good reason to direct you somewhere else.'

I pondered his words. Had Mr Fink been a touch disingenuous with us?

'What did they fall out over?'

'A girl I believe. With blue eyes. That's why I suggested you go to Malaya. You get more European girls there, hoping to find a husband among the lonely ranks of exiled plantation owners.'

'I see.'

'I suppose,' continued Spaulding, 'the real question is why you are looking for him. Why are you?'

'He's a friend of mine.' I became aware of a growing sleepiness. My voice no longer sounded like it was mine, as if it came from the cellar or somewhere far away.

197

'Really? How long have you known him?'

'Quite a long time.'

'What does he look like?'

I paused. I had no idea. Spaulding let out a laugh that was partly a sneer. 'You're a lousy liar, Wenlock. You are not a friend of Curtis. If you ask me, you are a detective sent to investigate his disappearance. Am I right?'

I forced a merry laugh. 'You couldn't be more wrong if you tried.'

'You think so? I'm pretty sure I've got you down right. I've met a lot of detectives, they all have a similar smell. You've got that smell, Wenlock. It's that sour, slightly cheesy odour you get behind the ears of boys who don't wash very often. All cops have it. You strike me as being a former police detective, dismissed for impropriety and now scraping a grubby living working privately. If we were in England it would be unmistakable because you would be wearing the trademark of all cheap gumshoes, a shabby mackintosh that has acquired a sheen from the grease of years – grease accumulated from many nights sleeping on the back seat of a car. Am I right, Mr Wenlock? I'm seldom wrong about these matters.'

I said nothing, my mind too preoccupied with the task of preventing my eyelids from closing.

'Am I right? Eh? Is that how you spend your life, sleeping in cars outside grand town mansions, spying on chaps committing adultery? That's what you do, isn't it? I know your sort. Vermin, that's what you are.

The first thing you say is, "I don't do divorce," but of course your sort would starve if you didn't, in truth it's all you do, isn't it?'

For a brief second, perhaps triggered by the increasingly bitter tone in his voice, a clear patch emerged in the fog of my mind. 'You sound awfully familiar with it,' I said in a groggy voice. 'Did something similar happen to you?'

I sensed rather than observed Mr Spaulding flush in a manner that suggested my words had struck home.

'You bloody little cad,' he said in a harsh whisper. 'Carry on like that and you'll get a bunch of fives. Enough of the phoney war, let me ask you straight. If you don't answer, it will be the worse for you. Who are you working for?'

I was having extreme difficulty focusing. 'I ... I ... me? Working for who?'

'Whatever Curtis was mixed up in is none of your bloody business, do you see? Nor of the man who hired you. I'm not the sort of chap to issue threats twice, so mark my words carefully, Wenlock. You keep out of this or you will get what for.'

Some time later I opened my eyes. I was lying on a bed in a darkened room. Downstairs I could still hear the muted sound of the nightclub singer. I dimly remember searching the corridor for a washroom. When I eventually found one, the door opened and a man walked out carrying a chamber pot. He wore a dressing gown over pyjamas. The chamber pot was full of yellow liquid in which floated with obscene simplicity, a stool. He looked at me and with that unerring air of Englishmen abroad who spot one another and crown the recognition with a banality said, 'I see it's turned out fine again.'

Much later I awoke in the hotel, in my bed, with a terrible headache. Jenny was sitting in a chair staring at me.

Chapter 12

JENNY BROUGHT ME A glass of water and said, 'Golly!'

I drank.

'I can't believe you went to a real opium den and had a cup of tea. Well, actually I can.'

'It's the cup that refreshes but not inebriates.'

'You really are a flat tyre.'

'Yes, I rather suppose I am.' I added with a grin, 'You would be better off with the sort of chap who enjoys that sort of thing.'

She lay down beside me and rested her head against my ear. 'Yes, I think you might be right. Were the girls very pretty?'

'Yes, I suppose you could say they were.'

'I'm asking you if you would say they were.'

'I find them quite austere, rather cool. It's disconcerting actually. One gets the impression that they do not think much of one.'

'I'm not surprised, ordering a cup of tea in an opium den.'

I laughed. 'It was clearly very strong tea judging by the way I'm feeling now.'

'Do you think they slipped something ... opium even, in your drink?'

'It would certainly explain a lot.'

'What did they want? I mean, *really*. They didn't show you very much.'

'I think they had three aims. First to warn me off. More particularly to accuse me of being a detective and gauge my reaction. I mean, really, to find out who or what I was. And third to give a spurious impression – that Curtis was some sort of licentious rake.'

'From what we know, he doesn't sound like one.'

'It didn't ring at all true to me. At one point Spaulding said something about national security being involved.'

'That's interesting.'

'He also told me Curtis and Mr Fink had a blazing row the night Curtis disappeared.'

'I was speaking about that with the hotel manager,' said Jenny. 'Apparently there was a break-in at the hotel that same night. An earthenware jar and a rug were taken.'

'Is that all?'

'So he said. You'd expect burglars to be interested in more than that, wouldn't you? The guests' jewellery, for a start.'

'Or the hotel safe.'

'Perhaps they had a fight and broke the vase and blamed it on intruders. Isn't it odd that Mr Fink forgot to tell us about his row?'

'Very odd. We must confront him about it. Apparently the argument had something to do with a girl.'

'The manager also talked about his bill. It hasn't been settled. He suggested that as old friends of Curtis we might like to protect his honour by settling his account. He said there was some uncollected mail for him that he would be happy to pass on to us.'

'You mean he will give us Curtis's mail if we pay his bill?'

'He didn't put it quite as bluntly as that.'

I laughed. 'He must suspect us of being detectives too! The sly old fox.'

'We could tell him to go jump in the lake.'

'No, I think we should settle Curtis's bill. We are after all representing the family here, in a way, and have substantial funds from Lady Seymour.'

There was a knock on the door and the boy outside handed me a note saying that Lieutenant Colonel Nopsansuwong of the Royal Siamese Police, Foreigner Division, would like to see me in the lobby at 9 a.m. This news set me on edge slightly. Even in England such a request would stir up the heart: one assumes the worst and wonders, 'What have I done?'

There were still fifteen minutes before the appointed time, so we went down and strolled out on to the lawn. A marquee was being erected in preparation for the St George's Day party. Hoshimi was seated at a side table folding her cranes. She smiled, and pointed out three cranes that had already been folded from the writing paper Jenny had given her. A boy in a blazing white jacket with a mandarin collar and silk jodhpurs brought us a tray of fresh orange juice. Earwig appeared, looked at Jenny, and said, 'That Yank spent the night with Sugarpie, the damn swine.' He walked off.

As if on cue, Kilmer and Sugarpie joined us. Kilmer made the introductions. Sugarpie wore a bright flashing grin that seemed to be both genuine and an impudent smirk.

'Madam first time Bangkok?' she said.

'Yes,' said Jenny. 'It's … it's very nice.'

'I no like so much. Why you come Siam? If Sugarpie have money, she go to Europe.'

'Is Sugarpie a Siamese name?' I asked stupidly.

'It America name,' she replied. 'My name Namwaan. It mean sugar water.'

'Honey,' said Kilmer. 'Sugarpie is an approximation.'

'Europe beautiful, see picture.'

Earwig returned. He stared hard at Sugarpie, who responded with a look of aristocratic disdain.

'I'll be having a word with you, later,' he said.

'I no speak.'

'I'll be the judge of that. We had an understanding.'

'Hey, buddy, relax,' said Kilmer, in a voice that managed to combine affability with a hint that it would be a very good idea to heed his instruction.

'When I want your opinion I'll ask for it,' Earwig said coldly.

'If I want to give it, you'll get it. Now quit bellyaching. The girl doesn't belong to you.'

'I don't see what business it is of yours, this is a private matter.'

'Don't be boring, Earwig, or I'll throw you in the drink.'

Earwig sniffed disapproval, but did not take Kilmer up on the offer.

I left Jenny and returned to the lobby to meet Lieutenant Colonel Nopsansuwong. He was seated reading at one of the rattan chairs. There was a fat leather book resting on the table. The policeman wore a chocolate-brown uniform that bore numerous insignia, braid and epaulettes, in a style that looked distinctly military. He stood up at my approach, put the newspaper down, and reached out to shake my hand.

'Mr Wenlock,' he said. 'Welcome to Siam. And thank you for taking the time to see me this morning.' His face was soft and round, like a moon, and his hair glistened with pomade, but what struck me most was the quality of his voice. His English was almost entirely accent-free, and suggested an intelligence at odds with the slight music-hall quality of the braid, epaulettes and other finery. He smiled.

'That's quite all right,' I said, knowing as well as he did that I could hardly have declined the request to meet him.

'I am afraid I have never heard of Weeping Cross,' he said, 'but I know Cheltenham well, I went to school there. Please, follow me, I wish to show you something.' He picked up the book and nestled it under his arm, and then beckoned for me to go before him.

We went out through the main entrance, to a waiting car – a shiny black foreign make that I did not recognise.

'Am I under arrest?' I asked only half in jest.

He laughed with a slightly exaggerated air. 'Not at all. I want to show you something that may help you enjoy your stay in Siam.'

We both sat in the back, the policeman uttered a few words to the driver, who drove us off.

'Good book?' I asked. Lieutenant Colonel Nopsansuwong tapped the spine of the book. 'It's my favourite book. Written seven hundred years ago in China by a man called Song Ci. It's called *Washing Away of Wrongs*, a handbook for coroners. Long before your Sherlock Holmes, he solved crimes using his brain. The book tells the tale of a murder in which a peasant was killed with a sickle. So the magistrate ordered all the peasants locally to bring along their sickles to the village square. He told them to put the sickles on the ground, and then they waited. Well, what do you know? Before long the blade of one of the sickles began to attract flies. Soon it was covered in them, and all there knew whose sickle had recently been covered in blood, and so the murderer confessed.'

I expressed approval and he continued, 'Yes, it is a clever story, and the whole book is filled with similar stories. I greatly admire it. Who knows, maybe we will find something in here to help us find your Mr Curtis.'

I flinched slightly at the suddenness of that comment, sure that was his intent. He smiled at me as if he had just passed a remark about the weather. Then he added, 'This is our Chinatown, much bigger than yours in London.' The road was clogged with cars, the pavements overflowing with people all seemingly bent on errands of great urgency.

'Tell me, Mr Wenlock, are you familiar with the Norwegian painter Edvard Munch?'

'No, I'm afraid I'm not.'

'He paints very gloomy things, like a child standing at the bedside of her dead mother. We Siamese are not Norwegians, we do not like to mope and be gloomy, we do not regard suffering as ennobling. We prefer something we call *sanuk*. This word is usually translated as "fun", but it has a deeper significance than that, it reflects our desire at all times to get enjoyment out of whatever it is we do.'

'I see,' I said, although I didn't. It seemed to me the policeman liked to give the impression of spontaneity to his remarks, but really they were most craftily chosen. 'How did you know I was interested in Mr Curtis?'

He tapped the book again. 'From reading this.'

I looked surprised and he laughed. 'No, I'm joking. Mr Earwig told me. He has a loose tongue. You

207

understand, of course, that we cannot permit private detectives to investigate our missing persons cases.'

'I can assure you I am nothing of the sort!'

'Mr Earwig said you were.'

'Oh did he? Well, he couldn't be more wrong if he tried. I'm here on behalf of Mr Curtis's mother, who is worried about him.'

Lieutenant Colonel Nopsansuwong nodded. 'It is the same the world over, mothers were born to worry. We Siamese venerate our mothers.'

'Where are we going?'

'To the other side of the river, a part of Bangkok little visited by tourists. It's called Thonburi.'

As if on cue the car left the thoroughfare and drove over a three-lane metal bridge. A latticework of girders rose like walls on either side of us, and through them glimmered the river.

'This bridge was named in honour of the first king of the present dynasty,' said the policeman. 'His title is Phra Bat Somdet Phra Paramoruracha Mahachakkri-borommanat Phra Phutthayotfa Chulalok. But you can call it Memorial Bridge. It was built by the Norman Long Company of Middlesbrough. They also built the Sydney Harbour Bridge.'

'By Jove! I believe they may also have built the Des-souk Railway Bridge over the Nile.'

The skyline of Bangkok flickered through the steel frame. A temple glittered in the hot sun. It had a bright orange-tiled roof, with elaborate swooping curves like the rails of a sleigh beset by golden towers like giant upturned ear trumpets. Down below, the riverbank was lined with slums of wooden houses built on stilts in the water. The pavements were just planks and boards, seemingly frozen in the moment just before collapse. Boys dived like gleaming seals into the water and waved; women bathed in the brown soup wearing sarongs knotted under their armpits.

In the district of Bangkok we had just left the streets were bedecked with signs and advertisements, neon scribbles recommending Dunlop, Horlicks and The British Overseas Airways Corporation. These familiar words felt comforting in so exotic a locale, reminding one of home and providing reassurance that there were people near at hand who spoke the same language and drank Horlicks. But all that vanished once we crossed the bridge. The locale grew more obviously alien. If I had been sitting in a private car, a taxi perhaps, I would have registered mild alarm. Sitting with a policeman I wasn't sure what I was to make of it. He seemed very refined in his manners, the reverse of domineering. What was he playing at?

Eventually we arrived at a small square before a toy-sized railway station. On the right side was a shabby hotel, the same one the chaps had brought me to the night before. In the light of day I noticed a broken sign saying *H tel 90*.

It appeared, however, that the policeman took more interest in another building on the other side of the railway station. It stood in a walled compound, and set in the wall was a rather ornate gate that might have adorned the palace of a maharaja. This fairy-tale quality was contradicted by the walls of the building that rose above it: the windows were barred and beyond, to the left, the corner was topped by a watchtower. It too had an ornate roof that made it look like a pagoda. Two chaps stood sentinel, and it looked to me as if they were armed. It was clearly a prison.

'Don't worry,' said the policeman. 'We are not going in. You wouldn't like the smell. I wanted to show you, that's all. Inside there somewhere lives the world's lone-liest man.'

'You are not telling me Curtis is in there?'

'His name is not important. He is a metaphorical man. A European man, from a land where the consular officials do not care to intercede on his behalf.

'Imagine it: you sleep on the stone floor with no bed nor blankets. Thirty men to a room, many of them the most desperate of men imaginable. Your food is a bowl of rotten rice, with the occasional fish head, once a day. You never wash. The stink is enough to knock a man unconscious the first time he encounters it. Outside these walls you will, as a European man, be treated with great respect and deference, but inside – ah! There you have no such luck. Outside those walls your status as a white man will be so high, and within them it would be correspondingly low.

'You remember me telling you about *sanuk*? You cannot have *sanuk* in such a place. Inside this prison a European man is more alone than Robinson Crusoe. It is not a fate I would wish upon anybody, and I mention it to you now for one reason. So that you do not take any action that might impose on me the sad obligation to put you in there. Do you see?'

'Is looking for a man so very wrong?'

'Never wrong, perhaps, but on occasion certainly unwise. You can imagine that I have looked high and low for Mr Curtis, explored every avenue, turned over every stone.'

'Yes, I'm sure. I didn't mean to imply—'

'But if you do imagine that then you would be wrong. I haven't done any of those things. I have spent no time looking for him. Why? Because it has been made clear to me that he is not to be found. Your British authorities, for reasons known only to themselves, have no desire to see him found, indeed they have a desire to see him *not found*. If the British do not wish Mr Curtis to be found and, despite my best efforts not to find him, he should turn up, I can assure you it would not be *sanuk* for me either. Do you understand?'

I assured Lieutenant Colonel Nopsansuwong that his meaning was most plain. We drove back to the hotel in silence and parked. The policeman turned to me.

'When we are young, Mr Wenlock, the monks tell us a story about a monkey who found a jar with a banana inside. The monkey reached in to take the banana, but the jar had a narrow neck, and this prevented him from getting his hand out. If he let go of the banana he would be able to free himself, but he just couldn't bear to let go of the banana, and carried on struggling and struggling in vain. And so he remained trapped until the hunters caught him.' He paused, and stared at me to gauge whether the story had achieved the desired effect. 'When we are young it is a story about a monkey, but when we grow older it becomes the story of our life. The thing we cling to most stubbornly is the one that undoes us. It could be money or ambition or hatred … all manner of things that take a grip on our hearts. The banana takes many forms. For some men – such as Mr Curtis – it could be the love of a blue-eyed girl. Most of the people in the prison are like that monkey.' He reached over and shook me cordially by the hand. He said, 'I do hope you enjoy your stay in Bangkok.'

I found Jenny waiting in the lobby, with a look of mild concern on her face. She scrutinised my expression as I approached as if to divine the seriousness or otherwise of my meeting with the policeman.

'Are we in trouble?'

'Who with?'

'I don't know. The authorities in Singapore … or from England.'

'I don't think so,' I said. 'He took me to see the prison and said how much he would regret it if I ended up there.'

'Oh, Jack!'

I smiled at her to offer the encouragement I did not feel in my own heart. 'Yes, I think he genuinely meant it. He really would regret to see me in there. He was warning us in the most gentle and courteous fashion to mind our own business.'

Chapter 13

WE DECIDED TO CONFRONT Mr Fink about the information I had received the night before. We were saved a trip to the arcade because we discovered him on the lawn smoking a cigarette, just as on the previous day.

He greeted us in a most genial fashion, as if he had forgotten the heated nature of our discussion yesterday. So genial and open, in fact, that it pained me to hold a suspicion of him, but the matter could not be avoided.

'Mr Fink,' I began, 'you will recall saying that a picture of an English cow in a meadow would not be of significance, and in that you are quite right. But I am troubled because no one would ever think to take a posed photograph of a cow, and yet here we have a man on his first visit to Siam enlisting the services of a professional photographic studio to take a picture of a buffalo. Is that not remarkable?'

He smiled and a distant gaze filled his eyes. 'Ah yes, but this was his first. You never forget your first.'

'First what?' said Jenny.

'First buffalo.'

We looked at him with puzzled faces, and he slipped into an explanation that was half-reverie.

'All chaps succumb. For the lucky ones, it's really just like a bout of measles. You recover, none the worse for wear, the scales fall away and you begin to acquire a sort of understanding. You look back at yourself the previous year when you arrived and you feel a bit sheepish. Back home a chap would laugh if a tart told him he was handsome. He knows he's nothing of the sort. But here it's somehow different, you believe it.

'It's no good getting on your high horse about it, every chap is the same. Well, most of them. It really is only a short step from that to falling in love. Then you are doomed. But she won't leave while there is still money, a commodity which she will spend with gay abandon until it has all gone. And then her love will turn to scorn, because in her eyes nothing is more contemptible than a man without money. And it will not make the slightest difference to her that you used to have money, or that the fact of your no longer having any money is entirely down to her.' He paused and seemed to have forgotten that we were there.

'You sound awfully cynical about it,' said Jenny.

Mr Fink laughed. 'Yes, but I don't mean to. I know it sounds absurd, but I don't mean to suggest the girl's love isn't real. That's the very devil of it: in many ways it is superior to the familiar variety. As long as the money lasts it is the genuine article, but how can a girl love a man with no money?'

'Very easily, I should say,' Jenny said a touch indignantly.

'Yes, in Europe perhaps, but that's because you have never known real poverty. Romantic love is a luxury the poor people of this world are not in a position to afford.'

'You sound like a man talking from experience,' I said.

Mr Fink looked wistful, almost sheepish. 'Oh yes,' he agreed in a soft voice. 'My trouble is, I have always found ways to get more money. I've lost count of the buffalo I've bought.'

'What has that to do with it?' said Jenny.

'Oh everything. You see, when you meet a girl here, the first thing that happens is the family buffalo dies.'

'That sounds very strange,' said Jenny.

'Yes, it's a disease common to the water buffalo of Southeast Asia, you see. As soon as the girl meets a foreign man the buffalo takes sick and dies. Without the buffalo they can't farm, so of course someone has to replace it, but who has the means? The chap, of course.

'The first time it happens, he's quite chuffed. He feels rather grand to be helping out, and he will talk about it in the bar. "I bought her a buffalo, don't you know! It's the least I could do, really. Poor thing, she deserves it. She hasn't had much luck in life, but her heart ... if you could see what I have seen ... her heart is so ... is so ..." At this point one or two chaps in the bar will leave, the

217

others will bury their heads in their copies of their newspaper, just wishing he would shut up, because there isn't a man in the bar who hasn't bought his fair share of buffaloes. Eventually, if he doesn't stop someone will crack and walk up to him, and cry, "Just put a bloody sock in it, will you?!"

'The chap doesn't understand. He thinks the bloke is suffering from the heat or something. And for a while he continues to enjoy that most perilous of feelings: being Sir Galahad. The girl feeds it of course. It's quite remarkable how skilfully a poor, uneducated, barely literate girl from the rice-farming districts can manipulate a chap who considers himself a man of the world.'

'Where's the harm in buying the odd buffalo?' I asked. 'I presume they are not expensive.'

'Oh no, they are not. But that is just the beginning. Not long after the buffalo goes down, so does poor Mama. She has to go to hospital for an operation that is only ever described in the vaguest terms. "Operation", the girl will say and rub her tummy or her kidneys, and quite often the source of the problem travels around the body from one meeting to the next. One day it will be her spleen and the next it will be something to do with her head. Well, what's a chap to do? Let Mama die? So of course he pays for the operation.

'For a while everything is wonderful and then another tragedy strikes. The girl shares a room with a friend she trusts like a sister. Then one day the friend discovers the secret place where she hides her money and off she goes with your girl's savings. How she cries, how the tears stream down her smooth lovely cheeks, how shattering is the wet look of heartbreak in those dark eyes. She faces destitution, and all for sums that are so pitiful ... All her hard work, so painstakingly saved, or so she claims, going without food so she can save enough to be a good girl. What's a chap to do? He would need a heart of stone not to help her. So he gives her some money out of pity, but then on her way home she gets robbed. So he gives her more, and this time she gets arrested by the police and they search her. They find the money and say, "What's a poor girl like you doing with all this money? You must have stolen it!" So they take that too.

'The poor chap can't help but feel sorry for her, this poor poor girl whose life seems to be one endless series of calamities, so he gives her some more money. As for the friend who ran off with the money, your girl hates her and vows to kill her if she ever sees her again, but then one day in the market you see them together seemingly getting along famously. Then her brother gets in trouble with the money lender. If he doesn't cough up a thousand tics, they will break his legs. What can you do?

'Then Dad is arrested and they need to bribe the policeman to get him released or they will all starve. And then the little sister needs to go to school to get an education so she doesn't have to do what her big sister does for a living, but there is no money to pay the fees because they used it to buy medicine for grandmother. What could be more noble than paying for a poor child's education? So of course a chap will give money to send little sister to school so she doesn't have to do what big sister does, even though in truth she won't go anywhere near a school and is almost guaranteed to end up doing what big sister does.

'And so it goes on. Each time he gives to the girl she is so overjoyed and tells him what a good heart he has. She assures him he's not like other men, and of course the one thing all men have in common, the one respect in which all men definitely are alike, is the secret conviction that they are not like other men. That's why they fall for it, you see, why they go with the girls. Back home, a chap rarely does such a thing. He wouldn't know how to, or where. And it would all be so terribly awful, so grubby that he would be repelled ...'

'Of all the buffaloes you have bought, Mr Fink,' said Jenny, 'was there ever a special one?'

He considered the question. Hoshimi's nurse wheeled her past us and placed her under a large parasol a few yards from us. She sat there staring at her cranes, but not folding anything. She looked at us and forced a smile, but today she looked drawn and gaunt.

'They were all special in a way,' continued Mr Fink. 'But, as I said, you never forget the first.'

Earwig strode past us and out into the garden, and towards Hoshimi. He looked down at the lack of activity on the table and said something to her and did a little mime of paper folding. The girl ignored him, still staring unhappily into space. Earwig quickly lost the jovial demeanour. He turned sharply and strode back wearing a face of thunder. 'It really is too much,' he said as he passed, without looking at us. We all turned our heads and watched him walk into the lobby and through to the bar where he could be seen chalking a zero on the blackboard.

Fink rose to leave.

'You're not going?' I said.

'Yes, I'm afraid I must.'

Jenny caught his hand as he left. 'What became of her,' said Jenny. 'The first buffalo?'

A sadness came into his eyes. 'After she had had every illness in the medical encyclopedia and suffered a series of misfortunes beyond the imagining of even the biblical Job, she started bumping into things. You see with the passage of time I lost my naivety, most chaps do. I started to understand that all these misfortunes that seemed to befall her every day, it was not done out of … I mean, I think she loved me and you will wonder how can a girl who loves a chap cheat him so, but I understood she didn't see it that way, that she was brought up to regard it in completely different terms.

'She did it for her family because it was expected of her, her upbringing demanded it and, frankly, if she hadn't done these things she would have been considered a heartless and selfish girl. A girl who did not take care of Mama. It's difficult for us to understand how sacred that duty is. It hurt sometimes, but I tried to accept it for what it was, and I did, I could. But when she started bumping into things and claiming there was a problem with her eyes ... I thought, no! I didn't believe her. So I left some money out, and she saw that well enough. That was the end of it. I sent her away with a flea in her ear. Her name was Choo Choo.'

'Is that Siamese?' asked Jenny.

'Yes. Sort of. Her real name was Jujit, with a low tone on the first syllable and a high tone on the last.' He demonstrated in what to our untutored ears sounded a most authentic way. 'Trouble is, most foreigners have problems with the tones, so if a girl has met a few she doesn't bother with the correct name, just an approximation that we fools can pronounce. It is not of my invention.'

Our attention was drawn to the landing stage, where a barge was in the process of tying up. Strapped to the deck was a strange cargo: the oversized tin of Tate & Lyle Golden Syrup. A group of men began to manhandle it from the deck onto a ramp and then onto the jetty. We all watched transfixed.

'By Jove,' I said.

Hoshimi's father hurried out onto the lawn, clearly excited, down onto the jetty. As he passed us he said, 'Tate and Lyle Golden Syrup. Out of the strong came forth sweetness. Hurrah for the King!'

'Hurrah,' echoed Jenny. We began to stroll towards the water.

'I imagine it's some sort of prop,' said Fink. He turned to go.

'Mr Fink,' I said, 'is it true that shortly before Curtis went missing, you and he had a violent disagreement?'

He flinched. 'Of course it isn't, what on earth makes you think that?'

'Something I heard.'

'Who from? Spaulding? I would advise you not to believe a word any of them say.'

'Even so—'

'I'm sorry Jack, but that really is none of your damn business.' He walked off, back to the hotel. I strode after him and caught his forearm as it swung back. 'I'm sorry, too, Mr Fink, but I really must press you. They said you threatened to kill him.'

He turned to look at me, his face filled with thunder. 'You are a bloody fool, Wenlock, if you believe anything they tell you. A bloody fool.' Then he violently shrugged away from my hand, and strode off, bumping against Hoshimi's table as he passed. It tipped over and the cranes fell onto the lawn. He did not stop and so it was left to me to put the table back upright and apologise to Hoshimi as I replaced the cranes. After I had finished I walked back to Jenny, passing Sugarpie, who had come to sit with Hoshimi. Sugarpie was wearing a tartan trouser suit, and waved at Jenny.

'How did she get the trouser suit?' I asked Jenny.

'Poker. We played last night while you were out with the chaps. I let her win. Apparently, it's her birthday. I thought we could use that information to worm our way into Earwig's confidence.'

223

'That sounds like an interesting plan.'

'I told him earlier and suggested he buy her a birth-day present. I said, I'm sure if you did that she would look very favourably upon you. He seemed quite taken aback, as if the simple idea of giving a girl a gift had never occurred to him before. He said, "Do you really think it will make her like me?" And I told him that I had it on the best authority that all girls like to be spoiled. He got quite excited and said, "I know just the thing," and with that he was off.'

'I don't think I've ever bought you a gift, have I?'

'Every day is a gift with you, Jack.' Her voice had a playful tone that allowed me to infer she was speaking only half in jest.

We sat for a while staring at the river, wider than the Mersey and brown as gravy. There was a strange and palpable majesty given off by the mighty flow, which rippled with wavelets and shimmered in the intense heat. A foot ferry plied back and forth from a jetty fifty or so yards upriver from ours. The Empire Flying Boat bobbed languidly, like a snow goose, the hull incandescent in the glare, so much that it hurt to look at her. The tin of syrup glimmered like a bronze Buddha. Roger strode across the lawn, placed a chair in front of the tin and sat down in the manner of someone guarding a prize.

Jenny slid her hand in mine. 'Would you like to win me in a tote?'

'I rather think I did after a fashion, I certainly won top prize in something.'

'Don't you think it wrong of Earwig to bet on something like that?'

'Yes, I think the chap's a scoundrel.'

We said no more for a while; enjoying the silence was pleasant. Hoshimi sat still as a statue, the only movement was the shimmering air and the rhythmic bobbing of the plane, which made one drowsy the way a hypnotist's fob watch is reputed to. After a while we went to the front desk and settled Curtis's bill. In return, the manager gave us an envelope. It was another tranche of the screenplay.

INT. CAPTAIN'S CABIN. DAY

SCARFACE enters dragging the protesting MILLIE. He throws her onto the bed, laughing.

SCARFACE

So, my pretty!

MILLIE

No, please have mercy!

SCARFACE

Mercy? What's that? How about a little kiss instead?

The faces of SCARFACE and MILLIE fill the frame. Their mouths inch closer as SCARFACE forces himself on MILLIE. When SCARFACE's lips are almost touching MILLIE'S, a knife appears at his throat and cuts. He falls. We see the holder of the knife. It is Cho Lee.

                    CHO LEE

          Missy good?

EXT. THE SHIP AND OCEAN. NIGHT

SQUIDEYE clings desperately to the anchor lashed to the hull. He slowly begins to climb the chain.

INT. SHIP'S CORRIDOR. NIGHT

CHO LEE turns to MILLIE and presses his index finger to his lips, as if to say, Shhh! They creep along the corridor. MILLIE is clutching a flask of the chloroform. SOUND of raucous drunken singing from the men's quarters. CHO LEE and MILLIE reach the open door from which the singing is coming. MILLIE hands the chloroform to CHO LEE, who breaks the seal, removes the stopper and rolls the flask into the cabin, quickly closing the door afterwards and locking it with a key.

They wait and listen to the singing. It quickly dies down to be replaced by LOUD SNORING.

EXT. THE SHIP AND SEA. NIGHT

A giant monster of the deep watches the ship with one cold gleaming eye. It is a giant squid, the biggest ever known.

INT. CAPTAIN'S CABIN. DAWN

MILLIE lies sleeping in the arms of SQUIDEYE. CHO LEE bursts into the cabin in distress.

CHO LEE

Captain, Missy! Come quick!
Big squid!

EXT. SHIP'S DECK. DAY

The entire front portion of the ship is entwined with the coiling tentacles of the LEVIATHAN. The metal of

227

the deck buckles as the monster begins to squeeze. His single implacable eye is the size of a cartwheel.

The LEVIATHAN squeezes harder, the metal plates in the hull shear and squeal, rivets pop out.

EXT. LIFEBOAT. DAY

SQUIDEYE, CHOO LEE and MILLIE sit in the lifeboat and watch the giant squid wrestle the tramp steamer down to the ocean floor.

Apparition of the VIRGIN MARY, wearing a sou'wester, appears in the lifeboat, sitting next to MILLIE. The LEVIATHAN turns his attention to the escaping lifeboat. He spots SQUID-EYE and emits a squeak of recognition.

VIRGIN MARY (voiceover)

It was as if two ancient warriors, battered by life and worn out by their years of combat, met for one final time on the world's edge. Captain Squideye, the most fearsome sea dog who ever set sail, here again facing his old foe, the Squid who took his

eye off Valparaiso. It was as if a
look of mutual recognition passed
between them. The giant squid, recog-
nising his old foe, raised a tentacle
gently and gave our boat a shove and
pushed us clear as the old tramp
steamer sank to the bottom of the
sea.

LEVIATHAN

SQUEAK, SQUEAK

Chapter 14

THE ARRIVAL OF TWO new guests, Sam Flamenco and Solveig Connemara, occasioned much fuss in the lobby. They had travelled with so much luggage they had to engage a room simply to keep it in. It was piled up in reception the way the belongings of folk moving house are piled up awaiting the removal firm. It did not appear that the hotel staff recognised them, or at least that they especially revered them. The two conducted themselves with the air of royalty travelling incognito but secretly hoping to be recognised all the same. We stood to one side and watched the bustle.

Mr Earwig joined us and wished us a good morning. 'St George's Day,' he said. 'The tote ends today. She's a long way short. To be honest, I've given up hope.'

'I have a mind to box your ears,' said Jenny.

'Oh really?' he said, surprised.

'Yes, it seems you took my husband to a house of ill repute.'

'Oh,' said Earwig, relaxing as he perceived Jenny was being playful, 'I shouldn't worry about that too much, he fell asleep.'

'So you both say,' said Jenny, 'but I would expect you to agree on a story between you. Chaps are like that.'

'Yes, they are, but in this case there really was no need. It was a filthy place, we went there only to show Jack the sort of thing that scoundrel Curtis got up to. Their mothers sell them, you know. Damnable thing to do.'

'You mean the girls are sold to … to … the …'

'Yes. When they get to fourteen or fifteen. At that age everyone has to earn a living, you see. They don't greatly mind in the way we would, they regard it as a duty to do whatever they can to help the family.' A thought creased his brow and he turned to me. 'I should imagine you can't conceive of your own mother doing such a thing?'

'I never met my mother,' I said. 'I was brought up in a railway servants' orphanage.'

'That's a shame,' he said. 'Although to be honest, I seldom met my mother, she was always ill. It was Wang Amah who looked after me.'

'Who was that?' said Jenny.

'I suppose you would call her a nanny. We were in China. My father was a missionary, in Tsingkiangpu.'

'My knowledge of the geography of China,' I began apologetically, 'is a bit—'

'I shouldn't worry, you won't have heard of it. No one has. We were the only Europeans for hundreds of miles. Father got some sort of thrill out of that. We moved there in 1904. It was a walled town. The first thing you saw when you approached on the main road was heads of criminals on sticks above the gate, and there were plenty of occasions when it looked like our heads might join them.

'Father would set off for days at a time with a knapsack containing a Bible and food, and off he would walk. A week later he could come back with bruises on his face and spittle on his clothes. Dog bites too. In ten years he made less than ten converts. It didn't deter him, though, he was doing the Lord's work and didn't expect the Lord to make things easy. The Chinese were mystified by him. They had no idea of sin, the notion that they were sin-blackened because of the actions of Adam and Eve was incomprehensible, and as for Jesus, they couldn't understand why they should care about him, or he about them.

'I had two brothers and a sister, they all died – two in quick succession from cholera. It came every year and swept hordes of people away. In summer there were mosquitoes and flies filling the sky – they used human ordure to fertilise the fields, you see, it was everywhere. In 1906 there was famine in the north and even Father wouldn't dare go out then. Have you ever seen those films on the Pathé Gazette showing armies of ants on the march, eating everything in their path? It was like that. Armies of emaciated people marching south, clogging the roads. They were so hungry they ate everything – cats, dogs, the bark from trees, even each other. Sometimes they would curl up on our doorstep just for somewhere to die.'

'That all sounds rather dramatic,' I said.

'And you were brought up by your nanny?' said Jenny kindly.

'Mother was always sick, so Wang Amah looked after me. She did everything for me.' He stopped and thought. 'Wang Amah had led a hard life and I suppose she … she treated me as her own. Then, when mother died of tropical sprue, I was sent to school in England. That's where I met Spaulding and Roger. They gave me an awful beasting when they found my photo of Wang Amah.' He laughed but his eyes misted with pained bewilderment. 'They called her rude names.' He took out his wallet and pulled out a badly creased black and white photo. He handed it to Jenny. The photo showed an old Chinese lady, very short and almost bald, smiling with one tooth. It was held together with Sellotape. She posed with two young European boys, one a year or two older, with his arm on the shoulder of the smaller boy.

'That's me.' He pointed at the taller boy.

'Who is the other chap?' I said.

'My brother Ben. He died. He had a weak heart.'

'Looks like your photo has been in the wars,' said Jenny.

'That was Roger, he tore it up. I was blubbing, you see. All the new boys did, of course, but Spaulding said it brought shame on Elgin House.'

'That was very mean, to tear your photo up,' said Jenny, visibly shocked.

'Oh, it was just horseplay. They were always playing tricks on me and things. Spaulding was captain of the rugger team and he was quite intolerant of boys who weren't ... I was always sick. The food was worse than in China. It came in boxes marked *Unfit for Human Consumption*, it was just ghastly. If you were sick they made you eat it up again.'

'Oh dear!' said Jenny.

Earwig turned to me, hoping for an ally. 'I expect that happened at your school?'

'No,' I said, 'there was never anything like that.' I stared at him, suddenly seeing him in a different light. Up until now I had found his company most uncongenial, but the sad story of his childhood made me think I ought to revise that judgment.

He took the photo back and stared at it. 'In her youth she had been a great beauty, so they had to hide her in the well when the soldiers came. She had bound feet. When she was little she had to sleep in the outhouse because her crying at night was keeping everyone awake. Imagine that!' He put the photo back into his wallet.

There was an awkward silence, which Jenny broke by changing the subject. 'Did you get a present for Sugarpie?'

He brightened instantly. 'Yes, yes, I did. Something rather rare, I think she'll like it. I really am most grateful to you for suggesting it.' He walked back to the hotel.

Later we were invited into the reading room for a small ceremony. Sugarpie was about to open her present. She sat in a rattan chair, a gift-wrapped parcel on her knee. Her eyes glittered with excitement, and Earwig stood before her, shifting his weight awkwardly from leg to leg. The expression on his face was a war between bubbling anticipation and an attempt to appear cool and uninterested. Sugarpie tore at the wrapping paper the way a child would. The paper was silver and reflective and looked rather expensive. Inside, the present was wrapped in tissue, a further obstacle to discovery that managed to raise Sugarpie's expectations to fever pitch. Finally, she unveiled the gift. It was a book, *The House at Pooh Corner*. Second-hand by the looks of it, with a paper dust cover that was torn and distressed at the edges.

'It's a first edition,' said Earwig proudly. 'Jolly difficult to get hold of. They only printed a thousand.' Two or three other guests had stopped to watch. 'Cost a packet, I can tell you.' Sugarpie was looking as if she had just unwrapped a lizard. 'Why give me book?' she said in voice filled with bewilderment. 'Why not buy gold? Must buy lady gold! Book is stupid.'

'One does not give money as a gift, it is vulgar.'

'What does that mean?'

'Vulgar? An offence against good breeding.'

'I no understand. Good man must give gold to lady.'

'Gold is nothing to the artistic treasures contained in that book.'

Sugarpie placed the book, unexamined, on the occasional table next to her chair. 'I think you make fun of Sugarpie.'

Earwig looked thunderstruck. He reached down for the book, retrieved it and thrust it back at her. 'Now look here you, I went to a lot of trouble to get you this. You'll have it and like it. I expect a handwritten note of thanks, too.'

Sugarpie twisted her head pointedly away so that she was staring at the ceiling, glowering. Her eyes were aflame and it was evident that a fury was brewing within her.

'Take it,' hissed Earwig.

'*My aow!*' she said.

'Take it!'

'*My!*'

'Take it, I say!'

She turned furiously at Earwig. '*My aow, na!*'

'Yes!'

'*My! My! My! My aaaaaaooooow loei! Nangseu arn len my aow ny loei. Yu tong hy gold dee gwa!*'

Before Earwig could reply someone clapped loudly in the manner of one asking for silence at a toast. We all turned. It was Kilmer.

'Quiet, everyone, please, I have a very important announcement. As you may know, today is Sugarpie's birthday, and I've got rather a special present for her. Sugarpie, how would you like to take a little trip on the plane?' He pointed out towards the flying boat moored in the river. 'We are going to test her out and I thought it might make a rather special birthday present, we could have a picnic.'

Sugarpie's face lit up as if a flashbulb had exploded under her chin. 'Go on plane?' she said. 'Go plane?'

'Sure, if you want.'

It was evident to all that she did. She squealed, jumped up and threw herself at Kilmer and hugged him.

'You are all invited,' he said over her shoulder. 'We are going to stop and have a picnic at Mueang Samut. We leave at eleven. Bring a sun hat.'

A man appeared in the doorway.

'And let me introduce, fresh arrived from Singapore, our co-pilot, an old friend of mine: Joe Webster.' There was a smattering of polite applause.

Webster spotted us and made a mock salute.

———

The flying boat was bobbing serenely on the waters, resting on her belly and supported by a float on each wing. Also on each wing were two propellers. The day was already hot; staff from the hotel were ferrying our picnic into the plane. We followed, walking down the jetty and entering by the forward door, which was situated at the bottom of the fuselage, on the port side. The area immediately inside was curtained off, with a smoking lounge to the left that also contained a metal ladder up to the bridge immediately above. A corridor, slightly offset to the port side, ran the length of the craft, passing the galley and two toilets, and opening into a cabin amidships that provided seating for three.

The impression the whole gave me, surprisingly perhaps, was that of a railway carriage in which a corridor ran the length of the left-hand side, with a series of compartments to the right. The effect was heightened by the rectangular windows on the port side, which had an elbow rail beneath to hold on to while admiring the view, and above it a small rack for luggage, just as in a train. Unlike a train, however, the seats allowed reclining the back.

I had decided to approach Mr Flamenco about Curtis at the earliest possible occasion. It seemed likely that if anyone knew of his whereabouts then Mr Flamenco, as his informal business partner, would know. I was also aware that the arrival of Flamenco and Connemara, along with Webster as co-pilot, made it likely that they would set off on their expedition imminently. Perhaps even tomorrow. Time was slipping through our hands. If my understanding was correct, the three chaps would leave shortly after the plane took off, leaving Jenny and me alone in the hotel, with the trail gone cold.

Sam Flamenco and Solveig Connemara commandeered the smoking saloon in a manner that suggested it was a private berth, and so we took our seats in the forward promenade lounge. The ladder to the upper deck was accessed via the galley and I climbed up for a quick peek. Kilmer and Webster were manning the controls, and Sugarpie sat in the wireless operator's seat with her back to them, looking as pleased as it is possible to imagine anyone could possibly be. The walls were bare, and curved above our heads like the walls of an Anderson air-raid shelter, a lattice of metal struts and reinforcing bars. The floor was wooden, but stained with oil that had leaked from the Exactor hydraulic controls. The anchor was housed in a stowage compartment immediately beneath the captain and his first officer. The engines were Bristol Pegasus 9-cylinder air-cooled radials.

Mr and Mrs Kuribayashi arrived with three Siamese men carrying Hoshimi and her chair. They walked past us to the rear saloon cabin.

'Where are we going?' I asked Fink.

'Meuang Samut,' he said. 'The hotel owns a beach house there.'

Kilmer passed down a request that we take our seats, and as we did a boy from the front desk arrived to inform me that they had an urgent phone call for me. I made my apologies and was assured they would be happy to wait. I followed the boy back up the lawn. At the desk, the receiver was lying off the hook on the counter top, waiting for me. The man behind the desk picked it up and held it out.

'Hello,' I said. 'This is Mr Wenlock.'

The line crackled, and there seemed to be no one on the other end of the line, just the hiss of static that waxed and waned. But as my ears grew used to it I detected amid the crackling another sound: a man weeping.

'Who is this, please?' I said.

More weeping, soft and whimpering. 'Curtis.' Then he hung up.

Chapter 15

A S WE APPROACHED THE town we spotted a little train puffing dreamily across a flat landscape below. From aloft it looked like a child's wooden toy engine. We overshot the town and landed just off a beautiful crescent of beach further south that ran for about six miles between two promontories.

A collapsible dinghy was produced from the rear cargo hold to ferry us ashore. There was little to see in the way of human habitation – a few fishermen's shacks, no more. The rest was an expanse of white sandy beach stretching in either direction for as far as the eye could see. It was so bright it hurt to look.

We walked across sand hot enough to fry eggs to a grove of palm trees beyond, in which stood a bungalow. The boys from the hotel set up deckchairs and parasols on tall poles, and erected two three-sided tents. Hoshimi was installed in one, and here she sat staring out at the glittering ocean, her paper flat on the table before her. A steward served us orange juice to which both salt and sugar had been added, but it tasted refreshing nonetheless. On the beach some way away they built a fire upon which it seemed they intended cooking fish procured from some local men who had appeared out of nowhere.

Jenny and I watched them from afar, clutching our orange juice.

'He didn't say anything else?' asked Jenny. 'Just said, "Curtis" and wept?'

'That's all.'

'What sort of weeping was it?'

I laughed softy at her determination to make something of such poor materials. 'What sorts are there?'

'I don't know … was it a sort of agony of heart, utter despair and hopelessness, regret, madness …'

'I think it was utter dejection, a man so consumed by despair that he no longer has the strength of heart to weep loudly.'

Jenny nodded as if this told us something, which of course it didn't. But at least we had learned one thing: he was alive. Instinct told me he was calling from Bangkok.

We returned to the main company and watched the lone figure of Earwig, a man who could appear solitary in a crowd, walk along the beach and stop outside the tent where Hoshimi sat, still as a statue. He spoke a few words, which she did not appear to register, and did a little encouraging mime of someone folding, but this too had no effect. He walked on in exasperation and then retraced his steps and this time went into the tent. He took something from his pocket and put it down on Hoshimi's table. He walked out, with more of a spring in his step, but was felled by a crunching rugger tackle from Roger, who flew at him with the speed and ferocity of a charging bull. It was as if a giant had reached down from the sky and plucked up Earwig like a doll and dashed him to the floor.

Roger roared with laughter and Spaulding cried out, 'Good tackle!' Earwig, clearly in pain, made no attempt to rise. Roger sat down on his victim's back, forcing his face into the sand with one hand and using the other to scoop sand on it. Spaulding joined in piling sand on Earwig's head until it was covered by a small mound. His legs and arms flailed in protest, but Roger was a powerful, stocky man. They were both laughing, Roger and Spaulding, laughing at their cruel sport.

Eventually Roger climbed off and Earwig raised himself onto all fours, and spat out sand, then started to get to his feet. Roger offered him a hand, but he looked at it the way a dog looks at the stick that beats him. He rose unaided and Roger took up the stance of a boxer and made a couple of token jabs at Earwig. He refused and tried to turn away. Roger ran round to confront him again and made two more jabs and an uppercut, terminating inches from Earwig's face. Spaulding laughed.

'Come on,' repeated Roger, 'see if you can hit me.' He danced and feinted to the left and right, ducking imaginary blows. Earwig tried again to escape. 'Go on, I won't hit back, promise!' They stood facing each other, Roger beckoning and cajoling Earwig to throw a punch. He did a curious mime in which he held an imaginary piece of paper before his nose and tore it in two. This was clearly meant to goad the reluctant Earwig into the commission of an act he would surely regret. He stared at Roger, still refusing to respond. 'Come on,' said Roger dancing wildly, ducking from left and right, 'see if you can hit me.'

'I don't want to,' said Earwig.

'Come on, come on! Or are you a coward like Ben?'

Something flashed in Earwig's countenance. He sprang forward, throwing a clumsy punch at a spot where Roger's head had been a second ago, but Roger had stepped aside so quickly it was like watching a magic trick. Earwig recovered his balance and turned with the stupidity of a bull being taunted by a matador, and swung once more, hitting the empty air to his left, but Roger had melted away like a will-o'-the-wisp and stood dancing to his right, urging him to punch him. Again Earwig took a swing, but this time Roger punched him back with a piledriver to the stomach that left him on all fours, fighting to suck in air. I stood up and walked briskly over.

'See here, chaps,' I said as I approached. 'I think this is going a bit too far.'

'It's only horseplay,' said Spaulding. 'Just a bit of fun.'

'Perhaps that's best left to horses.'

Roger turned towards me and looked me in the eye. He was smiling but there was something unnerving about his smile, as if it did not betoken the same warmth and geniality for him as it did for other people. The thought flashed across my mind that he might actually be insane.

'What's up with you?' he said.

'I dislike seeing a chap picked on like this.'

'We're not picking on him,' he said.

'It rather looks to me that way.'

'And what way is that?'

'You know jolly well what I'm talking about.'

'No I don't. Perhaps you should explain.'

'Very well then, bullying.'

'Bullying? We are playing.'

'It's clear you are quite a boxer, Roger. And very strongly built. Mr Earwig is no match for you and clearly does not *wish* to match you. It behoves you as a gentleman to respect his wishes.'

He paused, and swallowed. It was difficult to divine what was going on in his mind. 'What about you, then, Wenlock? Are you a boxer?'

'No, I am not, or at least not unless I have to be.'

'What if you have to now?'

'I would be severely disinclined to engage in such vulgar behaviour on an occasion such as this. We have ladies present and an invalid child.'

'That's convenient,' he said, trying to provoke me. 'I think you are just scared.'

'I'm happy for you to think whatever pleases you.' I gave him a long and unflinching look. He held my gaze and it was as if a thousand words passed along the line, as two men peered into each other's souls and sized each other up. Spaulding interrupted.

'It's all right, really. He enjoys it, the rough and tumble,' he said, and reached out his hand to Earwig. 'Don't you old sport? We're only playing, you know that.'

Earwig took the hand and dragged himself to his feet. 'It's OK, Wenlock, it's just … it's OK.'

'See?' said Roger, still holding my gaze. He walked closer to me and feinted a jab at my nose. Still, I held his gaze, unmoved. He laughed and turned away.

'I think I'll go for a dip,' said Earwig. Roger and Spaulding began to walk away, laughing. Roger half turned. 'One day, Wenlock, one day.'

I returned to the main party and sat with Mr Webster.

'Watching Hoshimi takes me back,' he said.

'Yes,' I said, 'I should imagine it does. Were you terribly fond of Japan?'

'I used to be the chaplain on Tinian Island.'

'Where's that?' said Jenny.

'It's a small island in the Marianas, south-west of Saipan. Interesting place. There used to be some people living there. Forty thousand or so I believe. Then they received a visit from a Spanish missionary by the name of Diego Luis de San Vitores. He gave them the surprising news that the islands on which they were living – the Marianas – had been named after the Queen of Spain.

'The Spanish had the islanders removed so they would have somewhere to graze their pigs in peace, and a few hundred years later the Germans had the Spanish removed. Then, round about the end of the First World War, the Japanese removed the Germans, and then the Americans removed the Japanese in 1944 and turned the island into one of the world's biggest air bases, with forty thousand people working there. They laid out the streets on a grid following the streets of Manhattan and even named them after the original. The base hospital was in Central Park. Obviously you need a good chaplain to minister to all those souls, and I got the job.' If there was more to the story, Mr Webster did not seem inclined to reveal it. A silence ensued.

I decided to take the opportunity to approach Sam Flamenco. He was standing with Miss Connemara on the veranda of the summer house where the treeline began. I trudged through the sand up to them.

'Mr Flamenco,' I said as I approached.

He was holding a cigar in one hand and looked displeased to see me. 'You again?' His eyes narrowed as if he were struggling to recall exactly where he knew me from. 'I thought I told you to go jump in the lake.'

'I don't remember you saying that.'

'I think I did.'

'I'm sorry, Mr Flamenco, I think you must be confusing me with someone else.'

'That's what you said the last time, in Chicago.'

'I've never been to Chicago.'

'Well you sure as hell look like someone who has. You'll get nothing from me.'

'I suspect you are confusing me with … you see, we did meet once, very briefly, but not in Chicago. It was on a ship, the SS *Pandora*.'

'Never heard of it.'

Solveig Connemara, who had been watching proceedings with a bemused smile, interjected. 'I think that was the boat we took to Port Said, honey.'

Mr Flamenco seemed reluctant to concede even such a small point. 'Anyone can find out the name of a boat. These people do it all the time: discover a few things about you any fool could find out, then turn up claiming to be your long-lost brother or something. It always comes down to money in the end, of course.'

'I don't want money, Mr Flamenco. I just want to ask about a mutual friend.'

His eyes flashed in anger, as if my denials were cast-iron proofs of his accusations. 'Oh so now we got a mutual friend. Who is he? Santa Claus?'

'Mr Curtis. From Singapore. I understand you and—'

'Curtis! That son-of-a-bitch! You a friend of his? Oh boy! I've heard it all now. If you knew the money I've lost because of that … that joker you would swear you didn't know him. I had to hire a screenwriter in L.A. Got tired of waiting. If it was down to Curtis, we wouldn't even have a script. Curtis Schmurtis. Pah!' He threw his cigar onto the floor in disgust and turned his back on me, to walk into the summer house. I was pretty sure he had no business in there but was simply making a suitably dramatic exit. 'Curtis!' he snorted again as he entered the building. It was clear if there had ever been a friendship between the two men, it had long since turned into the opposite.

There was an awkward pause. Then Miss Connemara held out her hand.

'Solveig Connemara.'

'Wenlock, Jack Wenlock.' We shook hands.

'Don't mind him, Jack. He's spent his whole life with his head up his ass, he ain't going to take it out now.'

'That's quite all right, Miss Connemara—'

'Solveig.'

'Solveig. I expect it must have appeared a trifle impertinent.'

She gave a laugh that was quite gay but contained a hint of bitterness. 'He wouldn't even know how to spell impertinent. He just likes to be rude. You really a friend of Curtis?'

'More an acquaintance, really,' I said, determining that honesty would work better. 'I know his mother, and she is … is worried about him.'

'Yeah, if I were his mother I would be too. Amazed he found his way out of the birth canal.'

'I expect he had help.' I had not intended to say something funny, but it seemed to come out that way.

Solveig laughed and asked, 'Shall we join the others?' It was less a question, more the act of someone informing you of a decision that has already been reached. We walked back down the beach. 'If it's any help,' she said, 'we heard he's in Bangkok. He owes Sam a lot of money, and Sam doesn't take people owing him money all that well.'

As we walked we watched Earwig emerge from behind a group of trees wearing a bathing costume. He put his clothes down in a pile on the sand and walked towards the sea. He was chubby and pink and there were four bruises on his back, like the spots on a die. He walked into the sea and carried on until it was up to his waist. He dived under the water, rose, flicked his head and swam in a languid crawl that bore witness to many hours in cold school swimming baths, and in a manner suggesting that he was more at home in this element. I had a sudden vision of him swimming endless lengths alone each morning before school started. Perhaps the water was less cruel than the world beyond it.

As he swam, the two chaps reappeared and picked up his clothes and walked over to a coconut tree. Roger took off his own linen jacket and removed his white cotton shirt. He had the well-muscled torso of a circus strongman. He drew himself up in the sort of act of preparation someone about to dive off a very high board does, then threw his arms around the bole of the tree, gripped it between his knees and began to shimmy up. Roger made it look impossibly easy, but I knew such a feat took great strength. Midway he stopped and, hold-ing on with one arm, reached down to Spaulding, who handed him Earwig's clothes. Roger carried on up the tree. In the sea, Earwig stopped swimming and watched. Roger reached the top and bedecked the leaves with Earwig's clothes and then slid slowly down to the ground.

Earwig traipsed back from the water, with the reluctance of one walking towards a problem he has no idea how to solve. It was quite certain that no one else in our party had even the slightest chance of being able to climb the tree and rescue the clothes, least of all Earwig, who was as likely to perform the Indian rope trick as climb that tree. And where in such a place would you find a ladder?

Then a curious thing happened. The air behind Earwig darkened, and turned a fuzzy sort of grey, and within a few more seconds the canvas of our tent began to flap angrily. A few raindrops fell, big fat globes of water that you could almost see your face in, one or two or three, each making a dark stain in the sand the size of a halfpenny piece. The sand became dappled, and within a few seconds a torrential downpour engulfed the beach, driven by a fierce wind that caused Kilmer and me to grab hold of our tent. Up in the treetops the wind tore Earwig's clothes, his trousers and shirt and underlinen, and swirled them all up into the darkening sky, spiralling madly like a newspaper caught on a bonfire. The party gathered under the canvas awning and watched transfixed as the effigy of Earwig flew up and out to sea, getting smaller and smaller, until the clothes were lost in the storm.

It was all over in a couple of minutes, like a squall at sea, the storm passing as fast as it came. The sun re-appeared, burning fiercely in the washed-out blue of the sky, and the beach steamed. Earwig had stood the whole time, rooted to a spot midway between the sea's edge and the tree from which his clothes had disappeared.

I stood up and walked past him, over to the tent where Hoshimi was sitting. On the table before her lay a pack of Benzedrine tablets. The intent was clear and exasperating: to make her fold faster. It was apparent that Earwig's life had been filled with suffering, and yet normally one finds those who suffer have great insight into the sorrows of others. Earwig however betrayed little understanding in that department. I smiled at Hoshimi and put the Benzedrine in my pocket, explaining that they would make her poorly.

'Oh it's quite all right, Mr Wenlock,' she said. 'I wouldn't dream of eating them. Mr Earwig and his friends, I feel, are not trustworthy. Do you know, I am not a great fan of Winnie the Pooh?'

I laughed at the simple innocence of the remark. 'No I didn't. I hope you won't be disappointed to learn I have never read it.'

'You have saved yourself a tedious experience. The story is very sentimental. I much prefer *Swallows and Amazons* by Mr Ransome.'

As we prepared to board the flying boat, Hoshimi's father drew me aside on the pretext of wishing to talk to me in confidence. 'Hoshimi has lost a milk tooth,' he began. 'An incisor. She has been reading about the custom of the tooth fairy in your country and is most keen to give it a try. We do not have this tradition in Japan. I wondered if you might be willing to sell me an English coin. I could put it under her pillow during her afternoon nap.' His face as he spoke was almost comically solemn, and reminded me a bit of the expression on the face of a bloodhound.

'Sir,' I said, 'nothing would give me more pleasure, but unfortunately I do not have any English coins.'

'Jack,' said Jenny, 'you do have a spare Gosling's Friend badge in your luggage.'

'By Jove,' I said. 'Indeed I do.'

Hoshimi's father had no idea what the badge was, but seemed very keen on the idea once it was explained. He agreed to accompany us back to our hotel room on our return and collect the badge.

During the short flight back to the hotel I brooded upon our situation. Curtis was certainly in Bangkok or had been, and my instinct told me he was still. But so elusive had he become, he might just as well have been in Australia. I was fairly sure the chaps did not know where he was but would greatly like to. I had no idea what their interest in him was.

It was plain, too, from Sam Flamenco's behaviour, that he and Curtis were no longer on good terms, and moreover he was not kindly disposed towards me on account of what appeared to be a misunderstanding. Solveig Connemara seemed more sympathetic.

And what of the man with the burned face? Had we succeeded in eluding him?

Chapter 16

THE ST GEORGE'S DAY party began at seven that evening. I watched events on the lawn below from our window. A string quartet played in the marquee as waiters carried trays of gin and tonic. A few balloons had been tied to the canvas. Guests in evening dress and ladies in gowns filtered out gradually from the main building, across the lawn. I had been given to understand there would be a performance of song and dance acts by some of the guests, with Kilmer acting as the compère. Due to our arriving only the day before we had been excused from performing.

Jenny returned from the bathroom wearing a lemon-tinted trouser suit. The last one left. 'Ta-da!' she said. 'What do you think? It's all right, I already know what you think.'

'It's ... it's ...'

'Swoony?'

'I was going to say "fetching" but that will do just as well. Swoony.'

'You don't approve, I know. But I like it.'

'I don't mind in the least, I'm sure there isn't anything you could wear that I would not like.'

Jenny joined me at the window and rested her head on my shoulder. 'Did you ever imagine you would visit a place like this?'

'It would never have occurred to me in my wildest dreams.'

'Me neither.'

'To tell the truth, I'm really not sure we should be here at all.'

'Why?'

'I feel I have led you into some terrible danger.'

'I'm not scared.'

'Well perhaps you should be. I jolly well am. This chap with the burned face will surely not take long to work out where we went. He may already have done so.'

'I'm sure Curtis can't be far away.'

'But we have no idea how to find him! I thought it would simply be a case of coming to The Garden of Perfect Brightness and there he would be. In truth, we find ourselves embroiled in an impenetrable mystery. A chap who never once said boo to a goose all his life goes off the rails in Singapore and sets off on a quest for fragments of a screenplay. He buys a ticket for Bangkok. Soon after he arrives he apparently commissions a photograph of a buffalo and inscribes on it the words *The horror! The horror!* He orders a circus ringmaster's outfit and omits to pay for it, then attends Spaulding's birthday party wearing a necklace of human ears. There he

258

does something so scandalous that no one will talk about it.

'Reportedly he falls in love with a blue-eyed girl and goes missing one night after a row with the same Mr Fink who took the photograph of the buffalo. That night there was a break-in at the hotel and a vase and a rug were taken.' I stopped, as Jenny nestled her head next to my left ear and stroked my right ear softly with her fingers. Was it really sensible to bring the girl who had brought me such joy into this perilous adventure? Was I being an utter fool?

'But we are so close.'

'How can you know we are?'

'I just sense it.'

'We really have no idea where to look. My understanding is that the plane will take off the day after tomorrow. All these people who you say know where he is will be on it. The three chaps will leave Bangkok. In the meantime, should the man with the burned face arrive, I don't think … I am pretty sure I could not kill him in cold blood. I could not kill anyone in cold blood. And I am not sorry.'

'We must hold our nerve, Jack.' She pulled herself away. 'Would you like me to change into something else?'

'Not at all, as long as you don't mind standing out.'

'We already do, Jack. Surely you must see that? Let's both get squiffy and then we won't mind.'

We descended the stairs and out on to the lawn. Earwig was standing alone, clutching a drink and looking deeply troubled by the events of the afternoon. Sam Flamenco and Solveig Connemara walked across the lawn. Mr Flamenco wore a cream suit with a pink cravat, and dark glasses. He walked stiffly with a cane and his face had that artificial tautness that they say comes from the surgeon's knife. Miss Connemara wore a sequinned evening gown and a white stole upon her shoulders. A microphone had been set up before the string quartet and Mr Flamenco stooped towards it and spoke.

'Folks, I'll keep this brief, parties are for drinking, not making speeches. But I have a short announcement. After fifty years of telling me to go and jump in the lake, Miss Connemara has agreed to be my wife. Anyone who has the slightest inkling of just how wonderful a person she is will understand that I am utterly consumed with happiness. My wedding present will be to make her once again the star she never stopped being in my eyes.' He then proposed a toast to his betrothed. A thin scattering of guests on the lawn raised glasses and said, 'Solveig!' There was polite but passionless applause.

A hand touched mine, so gently it could have been a passing butterfly. I looked down. It was Hoshimi, for once standing without the need of her chair. She was wearing the Gosling's Friend badge pinned to her frock. She grinned at me in delight, revealing unintentionally the gap where the incisor had been.

'Thank you so much, Mr Wenlock,' she said. And before I could say it was nothing she held her hand out, fist balled in a manner suggesting it contained a secret she wished to pass to me. I put my open palm under her fist and she released something into it. I looked down. It was a small brown shrivelled thing that instinct told me was a human ear. She indicated that I was to follow her, and led me out onto the terrace and down the lawn.

She walked to a pile of junk and bric-a-brac near the water towards the edge of the grounds where a crumbling wall marked the boundary with the neighbouring building. In England it might have passed for a compost heap. She pointed at something in the pile and I took a closer look. It was a piece of string. I tugged and drew out the necklace of human ears that Curtis had stolen from Kilmer. There was also a scrap of cloth.

I tugged at this experimentally at first, and then with greater confidence. The cloth took shape, appearing to be some sort of jacket. Finally it came free. I unfolded what indeed turned out to be a jacket and held it up. It was a scarlet circus ringmaster's coat and had five puncture holes on the front. The cloth around each hole was darkened with a stain that must have been blood. I divined in an instant the significance of the holes. At the same time I realised that I would indeed be able to take part in the guest performances tonight. I would be able to put on a little show that even Hercule Poirot would have been proud of.

I returned my gaze to Hoshimi. She stared at me without expression, her eyes glistening.

'Thank you,' I whispered and, raising my finger slowly to my mouth, said softly, 'Shhh!' A furtive smile stole across her face.

I rolled the necklace of ears and jacket up into a bundle and returned to the hotel, where I sought out the manager. I asked him to provide for my little routine a number of items: a boy from the kitchen, a white chef's tunic, and a pot of strawberry jam. I also asked that the spiked rattan ball be brought down but kept hidden from view under a cloth until a certain moment in my performance.

Satisfied with the arrangements, I wandered over to the party and caught the middle of Mr Spaulding's conversation. He was holding forth to a group of guests.

'You probably think he was an awful rotter, but the Mongols to this day revere him as their George Washington. Balkh in Afghanistan was even worse. A beautiful ancient city of temples, observatories, galleries, gardens, palaces, libraries. Birthplace of Zoroaster, admired by Marco Polo and Alexander the Great. There's nothing there now, just windswept ruins. They didn't even spare the dogs.'

'I do think it is terrible to destroy libraries,' said Jenny, interrupting him from behind.

'These are the realities of war,' Spaulding replied, turning round. 'If you spared libraries, the enemy would hide in them and shoot at you.' It was then that he noticed Jenny. His throat tightened. 'Have you not had the chance to change?'

'Change what?' said Jenny.

He swallowed hard, and said icily, 'Your outfit.'

'What's wrong with it?'

'This is St George's Day.'

'He won't mind, he was Turkish wasn't he?'

I forced a laugh. 'Ha ha! By Jove, I didn't know that. Was he really?'

Spaulding blanched.

Earwig joined us. 'So glad you could make it, Wenlock,' he said, as if the party was his. A thought troubled his countenance. 'She hasn't folded anything today, so I guess that's it.' He spoke in the manner of someone who had spent the time since our return from the beach in the bar.

'It still strikes me as wrong,' said Jenny, 'to blow up a whole city. I'm sure we would never do things like that.'

'Of course we would. In fact, this hotel is named after just such an occasion. Do you know where the name The Garden of Perfect Brightness comes from?'

Neither of us did.

'It was the old imperial summer palace in Peking. Fifty square miles of temples and pavilions, pleasure palaces and gardens. Museums filled with antiquities, art galleries filled with gorgeous paintings and tapestries and jade sculptures. More libraries than you could shake a stick at. Probably few places on earth to compare to it. Well, it's gone now, not a trace of it remains.'

'Why?' I asked. 'What happened to it? Was there a fire?'

'Yes, I suppose you could say·that, the fire in the loins of the doughty British infantryman. Stout men every one, sacked the whole place.'

'That sounds horrible,' said Jenny, shocked.

'I'm sure it does to you, because you don't under-stand these things. I suppose you would have preferred it if we had put the people to the sword instead.'

'Of course not!'

'We showed them clemency, that is more than most would do.'

'Why destroy such a beautiful thing in the first place?' I asked.

'It was a reprisal, you see. Some Chinese ruffians attacked a handful of British merchants. An example had to be made. The Earl of Elgin ordained that rather than shoot a load of worthless peasants he would be merciful and sack the Summer Palace. Remarkable man.'

'Why did they attack the British merchants?' asked Jenny.

'A dispute over opium. They stopped buying it.'

'Who did?' asked Jenny. 'The Chinese? I thought they liked opium.'

'Oh they did, too much. The whole country was greedily sucking on the pipe, no one went to work. They were in a pretty sorry state of affairs, so the authorities banned the import of it. We had large tracts of land in India under cultivation with the crop. Being a woman you are squeamish about the measures that it is sometimes necessary to take, you prefer not to know, or not to know about what might happen if they were not taken. When nations go to war they fight worse than dogs. We talk a lot about honour and fair play but it is the biggest beast who wins.'

'It used to be the case,' Jenny objected, 'that civilians were spared in times of war.'

'You have a very selective understanding of history if that is what you believe.'

'Even if the enemy you face is a brute,' I said, 'I don't see that it is much of a victory to become a brute yourself.'

As I spoke, Kilmer walked in, spotted us and strode over. Spaulding acknowledged him without warmth.

'That's because you were brought up in an orphanage,' said Spaulding. 'You can't expect to get a proper schooling there.'

'You know,' said Kilmer, 'when you tell a Siamese person how you abandon your children at the age of seven and send them away from their mothers for most of the year, they think you are joking.'

'Seven?' said Spaulding. 'Roger was sent away to school at four! It didn't do him any harm.' He continued: 'It's called sacrifice. A word, I suspect, that is unknown to Mr Wenlock. He lives in a civilised country with museums and libraries, law and order and a fine police force – perhaps one of the very few in this world that cannot be bribed – a blessed realm of hospitals and football matches where he enjoys many fine freedoms and countless other wonders that are the envy of the world … but who pays for it? Do you, Mr Wenlock? What have you ever done to merit your place in all this? The wealth that pays for it comes from peasants in other lands who break their backs in the noonday sun and live short lives on your behalf.'

'You should be more grateful, Jack,' said Kilmer.

Spaulding responded before I had a chance to. 'Tell me, Mr Kilmer, what is it you do for a living?'

'I work for the Military.'

'Yes, I know, but which branch?'

'Many branches.'

'In what capacity?'

'Lots of capacities.'

'All rather conveniently vague,' said Spaulding, draining his glass and standing to leave. 'If you ask me you are up to no good. What actually are you doing in Bangkok?'

Kilmer smiled. 'I'm here to keep an eye on you.'

We all laughed, but it was slightly forced because one strongly got the impression that he was telling the truth.

During the course of the conversation the waiters had been quietly wending their way among us bearing trays from which drinks were regularly lifted. Roger arrived, looking sweaty, with a slightly unhinged gleam in his eyes, and said, 'Rather!'

Kilmer turned to Jenny and said, 'I like your outfit.'

'Why thank you, sir!'

'Reminds me of Katherine Hepburn. Yes, I'd say it was pretty … lalapalooa!'

'Lalapaloosa!' said Jenny raising her glass. 'Spoony even!'

'Totally Fifth Avenue,' said Kilmer.

'Super-colossally fantabulous!'

'Snazzy!'

'Cheezle-goddam-peezle.'

I listened with a sense of growing despair. It was wrong to be discomfited by this, and yet I was.

'I say, Wenlock,' said Spaulding quietly. 'Have a care to your wife.'

'What do you mean?'

'She's making a bloody fool of herself. And of you too.'

It was odd. The exchange of American slang with Kilmer had disconcerted me, but the idea of Spaulding expressing disapproval of Jenny made my gorge rise. 'My wife,' I said in a steely tone that I hoped left no doubt that he had better watch his step, 'is behaving in a perfectly acceptable fashion, and I'll thank you to mark that.'

He was about to respond when he spotted Mr Fink approaching. 'Well, of all the cheek!'

'Happy St George's Day!' said Mr Fink.

'So now we have the deserter and a lady dressed in trousers,' said Spaulding. 'Some St George's Day this is turning out to be.' He gestured with his drink at Fink. 'What in blazes do you think you are doing here?'

'Come for the party.' He wore a supercilious smile that suggested he was already a bit tipsy.

'This is no place for a deserter, your presence dishonours our patron saint.' Spaulding's face was dark with repressed fury. He whispered as if it would be letting the side down if the natives heard them disputing.

'I have my own patron saint,' said Fink. 'Saint Martin of Tours. He refused to be conscripted into the Roman cavalry in AD 334, saying, "I am the soldier of Christ: it is not lawful for me to fight."'

'They have a patron saint for cowards?'

'Conscientious objectors.'

'What nonsense! Where would we be if everybody behaved like you?'

'In a world without war.'

'In chains you mean. Those chaps you abandoned fought on, risked their lives so you could take your silly photographs and mock the country that bore you.'

'Why should I go and fight chaps with whom I have no quarrel?'

'So they don't dishonour your sister, you bloody fool.'

During the heated exchange, Kilmer, perhaps with an eye to calming things down, had moved over to the microphone. He blew on it and then announced the

268

beginning of the performances. He called on Mr Fink to take the first turn. Fink walked over to the microphone and explained that he would make a recital about St George, with the theme: *How can we be sure he was English?*

Spaulding lost whatever was left of his patience. 'Of course he was bloody English!'

Mr Fink grinned provocatively. 'Are you sure, now? He was born in Cappadocia, to Greek parents, and never visited England.'

'Yes he did, he came to our school,' interjected Earwig. 'I mean, the place where it was later built.'

'The legend of the dragon was added a thousand years after his death and is believed to be a mistranslation of "crocodile".'

Again Spaulding objected, but some of the guests were rather enjoying the mild blasphemy and encouraged Mr Fink. Although he clearly did not need any. 'He is also the patron saint of syphilis sufferers.' The audience tittered and exchanged looks of mild shock.

'But there is one way we know he must have been English,' continued Mr Fink. 'Because in the third century AD the Emperor Diocletian threw George in the dungeon and tried to test his faith by sending him a beautiful damsel to spend the night in his cell. And it's what he did to her that tells us he was an Englishman.'

'Did he make her a cup of tea?' shouted one of the guests.

'Even worse,' cried Mr Fink. 'He converted her.'

There was more laughter. Spaulding looked on, unable to impose his will on events, aware that they were running out of control.

As the applause died down, Mr Kilmer called on Hoshimi, who had requested to be allowed to participate. The mood changed and softened as she walked up to the dais. One could sense everybody willing her to do well. The mike was lowered and she stood as straight as a sentry.

'Dear people, you know that my health is not good, so I will make this very short. I hope you like it.' She paused, her face betraying the effort of concentration. 'A small recitation,' she said. Took a breath, and then said:

'Hush hush, nobody cares!
Christopher Robin has fallen downstairs.'

She paused, then bowed to show her piece was ended. Enthusiastic applause broke out as soon as it was understood there was no more.

After this, the three chaps recited a verse.

'The sand of the desert is sodden red,—
Red with the wreck of a square that broke; —
The Gatling's jammed and the Colonel dead,
And the regiment blind with dust and smoke.
The river of death has brimmed his banks,
And England's far, and Honour a name,
But the voice of a schoolboy rallies the ranks:
"Play up! Play up! And play the game!"'

The next act was Mr Webster, who declared he wished to recite a short piece entitled 'Why I decided to stop shooting Jesus'. This was met with more polite expressions of feigned shock, and once more Spaulding objected that such a subject was unsuitable. But Mr Webster disagreed.

'On the contrary, this is the story of how I lost my faith and here today have rediscovered it. I'm sure St George would be delighted to hear it.' So it appeared was everyone else. Mr Webster began:

'My story begins in Japan in the years before the war. I was seconded to a mission in Japan attached to the Catholic cathedral. It was a very nice one with two towers and an Angelus bell, and lovely statues of Agnes holding a lamb. It was called Urakami Cathedral. Christianity had arrived in the sixteenth century with the Jesuits, who taught the locals about the Crucifixion only for the locals to promptly crucify twenty-six of them. I guess that's what you call irony.'

There was a smattering of laughter.

'The beautiful cathedral was built in a lovely city on a bay overlooking the sea whence those Jesuits had first arrived. And it was there in the apse that I met a Japanese girl called Izumi. It was the Feast of the Assumption of Mary and the girl, seventeen years old, was standing there in a modest navy-blue serge skirt and the blue and white sailor collar top that the girls wear to school over there, staring at an alabaster statue of the Virgin Mary and crying. What man could fail to be moved?'

271

The laughter died and was replaced by the concentrated gazes of the audience who, one sensed, had divined that this story came genuinely from the heart.

'For a while, I stood transfixed and simply stared. Eventually, I went over to ask what was the matter. Her English was poor and she was unable or unwilling to explain her tears. I took her for a cup of tea. By the end of that cup of tea my heart had been ravished. A genie had been released from the bottle of my heart. When she left, I knew she would never return, but I was wrong. The next day, she came back and looked for me and stammered a few words of broken English, no doubt having pored over the dictionary all night; she thanked me for my kindness. We both came to the conclusion that she needed some coaching with her English, and after wondering for a while who might be able to tutor her, we agreed that I would perform that office.'

The room was silent now. There was a sincerity to Mr Webster's words that I had never heard from him before. As he spoke, two members of the staff carried between them, behind our group, an object covered in a sheet. I knew it to be the rattan ball, but no one else at the party paid the slightest attention, so engrossed were they in the story. Mr Webster continued:

'After that, we met regularly under the pretence that our meetings were about English lessons and nothing more, but our hearts knew differently, as hearts always do. Then, in early December 1941 I travelled home to the States to speak to my parents and sound out their reactions should I decide to break with the Church and bring home a Japanese bride. When I arrived back on US soil, the papers were full of a place called Pearl Harbor. The Japanese were being rounded up and interned. It was not a pretty sight. I'm not sure exactly what happened after that. I got caught up in the tide that swept hundreds of thousands of young men into ships and boats across the sea.'

The people listening were gripped by his tale, no one stirred. The only movement came from the manager, who was quietly setting up a small table, much like a magician might use. He covered it with a silk cloth, and where there might usually be a top hat he placed a jar of strawberry jam.

'I assumed I would land in the European theatre of war,' said Webster, 'but I found myself instead on Tinian Island. There I was called upon to bless a special bombing mission, a B-29 Superfortress called Bockscar that took off on the morning of the ninth of August 1945 carrying a new type of bomb called Fat Man. It was my duty. I blessed the crew and their mission and thought no more about it. It wasn't until the next day that I saw the photographs and learned that the aiming point for the bombardier had been that prominent landmark in the centre of the city, Urakami Cathedral. It was full, too, because they had been holding a Mass to mark the Feast of the Assumption of Mary.' The audience responded with soft gasps of indrawn breath. 'That was the day I fell out with Jesus. And spent the next three years calling him all manner of names. But today, my friends, I have made my peace with Him. I realised it was not Jesus who designed that bomb, but we sinners. It was seeing the innocent beauty of Hoshimi's face that drove it home to me. I just want to thank her. She's an angel.'

He mimed a little applause to Hoshimi and this was enthusiastically taken up by the rest.

Kilmer proposed an interval and both he and Webster rejoined our group.

The night air became filled with the song of a man singing, coming from the river. A boat had moored containing a group of blind musicians, the same people I fancied had played outside the hotel the chaps had taken me to the night before. One of their number held out a tin cup and some guests walked over to donate. The words, 'You good heart,' drifted over.

'I have to say, Mr Webster,' I said, 'I found your story very affecting.'

'It was totally cheezle-peezle,' said Jenny.

Spaulding scoffed. 'Wearing trousers and talking like a GI. Would you believe it?'

'Something wrong with GIs?' said Kilmer.

'This is a dull party,' said Roger. 'Let's liven it up.' He sauntered off.

'Only with their morals,' Spaulding responded to Kilmer. 'It's a wonder they found time to clean their rifles, things they got up to. Personally I wouldn't have allowed it.'

'Yes,' said Kilmer, 'it's a wonder they found time to save your sorry Limey asses!'

'I'm not aware they did any such thing, too busy chewing gum, and making GI brides. That's on the rare occasions they thought to marry.'

'Why must you put such a sour complexion on something so … it's a beautiful thing, isn't?' said Jenny.

'What is?'

'Two people falling in love.'

'I hardly think love came into it,' said Spaulding, 'not if the bacchanals that I witnessed during the blackout were anything to go by.'

'I don't know what that word means,' said Jenny, her voice starting to crumble, 'but as far as I can see it is the most natural thing in the world for young men and women to fall in love. It's the oldest story in the world, and I wonder that your heart can be so cold as to disparage it in the way you do.'

Hearing the mounting anguish in Jenny's voice, I made a desperate attempt to divert the conversation. 'I say, I heard an interesting story the other day. Did you know on the main route of the trans-Siberian railway there is a spur line between Buyant-Uhaa and Borhoyn Tal leading to a small garrison of soldiers. It goes nowhere else. And the soldiers of the garrison have only one purpose. Their job is just to sweep the line clear of sand.' I laughed. 'Isn't that jolly?'

No one took any notice of me. Spaulding said to Jenny, 'For the arrangement you describe I prefer the word miscegenation. As for the sort of love that can be bought for nylon stockings, I prefer the word harlotry.'

The colour drained from Jenny's face. 'Please excuse me,' she said in a voice soft as a whisper. 'I'm going indoors for a while.' She walked off towards the main hotel building.

'Mr Spaulding,' I said, 'I must insist that you stop being so impertinent in front of my wife. I have already warned you once.'

'Impertinent in what way?'

'You know exactly what I mean. Your tone and manner is disagreeable to me and insulting to my wife. If you do not change your ways it will be the worse for you.'

'Really? And what will you do?'

'I have a mind to give you a bloody nose.'

'What about Roger? Think you could give him a bloody nose, do you?'

'If he makes himself disagreeable in the same fashion I shall extend the same courtesy to him. For all your talk about cowardice and desertion it seems you are a man who gets other chaps to fight his battles for him.' Our voices had risen considerably and I became aware that all eyes were on us.

I directed my attention to the people watching. 'So,' I said, 'since I have everybody's attention, this might be a good time to perform my little act. I have decided on the title "Whatever happened to Mr Curtis". I hope you like it.'

The rattan ball was hidden beneath a drape. I indicated to the kitchen boy that he should approach, and he did, having been rehearsed in his part by the manager.

'You may recall,' I began, 'there was a burglary at the hotel on the night of Mr Spaulding's birthday party. This was also the night that a certain Mr Curtis scandalised you all by turning up at the party wearing a necklace of human ears. Mr Curtis has not been seen since that night, and I propose to demonstrate to you what I think happened to him. You will observe my assistant is a boy from the kitchen. Note the shining white condition of his tunic, which has come straight from the hotel laundry. Now, see here!'

I whipped the sheet from the rattan ball with the drama of a stage magician. There was a slight gasp from the audience, even though there was nothing much to gasp about.

'Many of you will know this rattan ball is usually positioned on the first floor landing. Now watch carefully.' I began applying the strawberry jam using a spoon as my brush to the tips of the inward facing spikes.

'Bloody pointless theatre,' Earwig said, but seemed reluctant to take his eyes off it.

Flies began to buzz around the spikes.

At my request, the boy in the white tunic climbed carefully into the ball and crouched. He then got out and stood up. The jam had left its imprint on his tunic.

I held up the jacket that had been worn by Curtis. 'See the similarity of the pattern of holes?' I asked.

'Bravo!' said one of the guests.

'Completely different,' said Earwig.

'Do you really think so, Mr Earwig? It seems to me to be remarkably similar.' I returned my attention to the audience. 'In the burglary a vase and a rug were stolen. It is my surmise that there was no burglary. I believe instead this rattan ball tumbled down the stairs and knocked the vase over at the bottom. It is further my belief that the unfortunate Mr Curtis was inside the ball. The rug was used to wrap up his body and remove it from the building, perhaps in the back of a motor car.'

Earwig snorted and walked towards the main door, passing close to me and hissing in a voice of repressed anger, 'You'll get what for, Wenlock.'

'Perhaps so, but I suspect so will you. I have already this evening placed a call to the Chief of Police and explained the situation. You can be sure he is most interested.'

Spaulding was now some distance away, moving towards the main hotel. He scoffed in an exaggerated fashion. 'Mr Wenlock, if you telephoned the Chief of Police and found him at his desk at nine p.m. then you must have accidentally phoned a different country. In Siam you would need to phone his mistress!' The three chaps disappeared into the main building.

Webster approached me. 'That was smart thinking, Jack.'

Before I could answer our attention was diverted by a scream. It came from Hoshimi, uttering a cry that pierced the heart of all who heard it. It was followed by shouts from the hotel and we detected the smell of burning. We rushed across the lawn. Through the French windows of the reading room we could see the flare of a small fire. We arrived in time to find hotel staff dousing the conflagration with water from a saucepan. Someone had set fire to all of her cranes.

EXT. OCEAN, OPEN BOAT. NIGHT
The boat drifts through a gentle swell
beneath a night sky ablaze with stars.

SQUIDEYE

The natives call him Chomghuürgha,
the abominable yeti told of old.
Twelve foot high, fiercer than a pack
of hungry lions, he eats sheep whole
as if they were Turkish Delight.

But we will no longer go there, we
sail instead for Singapore.

MILLIE

After all the monsters of the deep
you have battled?

SQUIDEYE

The monsters of the deep are nothing to the monster deep within our hearts, which we must learn to overcome.

Since that brigand SCARFACE plucked out my eye, I see more clearly. All my life I have been blind, and yet now I see with that inner eye of the heart.

I have squandered all the Lord's precious gifts. He was right to take away my eyes because I misused them. I could see but was blind; now blind I finally see.

MILLIE

If you go to Singapore they will
hang you!

SQUIDEYE

And you will find passage home to the land you love and there perhaps find your son.

MILLIE

I fear they mean to hang me too!
They said I was a spy.

SQUIDEYE

Why would they think such a thing?

MILLIE

There were strange goings on at Wisskirriel Hall in the years before the
Great War. Secret meetings held at
night. The Graf von Scharnhorst came
often and was always very welcome even
when the papers were full of stories
of the coming war. When Archduke Fer-
dinand was shot the Master received a
telegram from the Graf saying the
single word, Rejoice! I delivered it
to the Master. He told me to forget I
had ever seen it, and never to breathe
a word about it to anyone.

SQUIDEYE

In that case we will sail to my home
on the island of Tepu Nui in Polynesia.

CHO LEE

            Captain Squideye, look!
POV CHO LEE: Ahead a thick impene-
trable bank of fog.
C/U: Compass needle spins wildly.

MILLIE

My God!

POV CHO LEE: Out of the fog shapes appear. Warriors armed with spears stand on the beach.

EXT. MOUNTAINTOP. DAY

MILLIE is alone on the plateau. She stares up in awe and terror at CHOM-GHUÜRGHA. He looks down at her, pounds his chest, and ROARS.

MILLIE SCREAMS.

CHOMGHUÜRGHA jumps down onto the plateau. MILLIE backs away in fear but finds herself standing on the cliff's edge, unable to back away any further.

In a flash CHOMGHUÜRGHA swipes and grabs her in his big paw.

MILLIE SCREAMS

CHOMGHUÜRGHA brings her up to his face, peers at her with a puzzled frown on his brow.

MILLIE SCREAMS. The SCREAMS peter out. CHOMGHUÜRGHA stares in deep fascination. MILLIE begins to calm down.

Her hands rest on the index finger that enfolds her. She looks down and notices a thorn embedded deep in CHOMGHUÜRGHA's flesh. It has clearly been there a while and become infected. MILLIE puts her hand round the thorn. CHOMGHUÜRGHA starts in pain.

MILLIE

There, there!

MILLIE slowly pulls the thorn out, and lets it drop. CHOMGHUÜRGHA is deeply moved. He emits a soft whine of contentment. He reaches up and places MILLIE gently on his shoulder, where she sits holding on to his fur. CHOMGHUÜRGHA moves carefully to the cliff's edge and looks out.

POV: the NATIVES down below. They watch in astonishment as CHOMGHUÜRGHA appears, with MILLIE sitting happily on his shoulder.

NATIVES

Chomghuürgha! Chomghuürgha!

NATIVES throw themselves to the ground in prostration.

EXT. THE COTTAGE OF SQUIDEYE AND MILLIE. DAY

TITLE: 13 YEARS LATER

SQUIDEYE lies in a hammock strung between two palm trees, smoking. In the distance we see a little cottage, and behind it a smoking volcano towers up above the trees. A little girl playing at the water's edge discovers some flotsam washed up. It is a sea chest. She opens it and finds inside a typewriter, a sheaf of paper and a manual on How to Write Motion Picture Screenplays.

INT. THE COTTAGE OF SQUIDEYE AND MILLIE. DAY

MILLIE, watched by the little girl, inserts a piece of paper into the platen and begins to type the words: 'FADE IN'

                    MILLIE
Well, little Jackie, it is time to write the story of your brother Jack.

Chapter 17

A N ACRID SMELL OF wet burned paper hung in the air. The fire had been small and easily extinguished. Word reached us that Hoshimi was sleeping. A box of matches found nearby, Bryant and May 'England's Glory', suggested very strongly that the fire had been deliberately set. I suspected Roger.

The party had resumed, but with noticeably less effervescence. It was getting on for ten and the combination of the heat, the alcohol and perhaps the obvious stupidity of the ritual had taken its toll on the spirits of the guests. I found Jenny sitting quietly in the hotel lobby and went to sit next to her.

'Jenny, you must not think I mind about your American chap, Cooper.'

'I know you try not to.'

'I try very hard.'

'Yes.'

'I do not blame you for walking away, Spaulding is a most—'

'I did not leave because of him. I don't care a damn for him. It's what he said, about GI brides. It … it reminded me … something I've wanted to tell you, for so long, but I was scared.'

'You must never be scared of me.'

She paused for a long while and then said, 'Do you remember me saying about your mother, I said I knew how she felt?'

'Yes. And I thought it was jolly big of you to take her side.'

'No, Jack, no—'

'Yes! A lot of people can be … quite snooty about such matters. '

'I don't mean like that, I mean, *I knew*.'

'Yes, you knew. You knew, of course. What do you mean?'

'I knew what she felt like because … once … a similar thing happened to me …'

'You?'

She said 'Yes' in a voice so soft it was almost inaudible.

'A similar thing?'

She whispered, 'Oh Jack, I knew how she felt, the poor thing, I knew what the world thought of her and how keenly she knew what they thought, how terrified she must have been, how she knew she had to tell Lady Seymour but knew there was no way in the world she could, I knew, Jack, how … how utterly alone in all the world she felt. With no one she could turn to, no one she could trust who could tell her, she who knew nothing of the world, knew only how completely she was doomed, and all for something so innocent, something that … strangely everybody else did but you

286

weren't allowed to, and those same people who did it would cast you out for doing it too … oh I knew, Jack! A girl so young … where could she go?' She stared at me, eyes filled with anguish. 'Who could she turn to?'

'But … Lady Seymour would have …'

'She would have cast her out. She would have been alone in the world, in winter, with child, can't you see? What terrible fears must have filled her young heart? You can't imagine it, you can't. But I can, I knew. What could she do? Perish? The only thing she could think of, even worse than dying, was to give you up. So you could have a life. She must have thought hers didn't matter any more, it was over. At sixteen. How it must have broken her heart to give you up, Jack!'

'Do … do you really think … it was like that?'

'Oh yes, yes, I do. I know. She did it because there was no other way. Pity her, Jack.'

'Oh I do, I do. Of course I do.'

'She must have loved you so much,' she said, her voice a whisper of such intensity it was barely audible.

'Yes, that is … is such a wonderful …'

'Pity her.'

'Yes.'

She placed her hand gently on my cheek and turned my head to face her. 'Pity me.'

There was a pause. From far off came the thin sound of the string instruments, the hubbub of drunken conversation. After an eternity, I spoke. 'Where is your child now?'

'I lost … it.'

'Lost it? Where?'

'Not like that. I miscarried.'

'Oh. I see. Yes, yes. I see.'

'It's quite common.'

'I'm so sorry …'

'I was scared of what you would say. And then when you bought the train set on the boat for … our son I—'

'Yes that was inexcusably clumsy, I—'

'No, Jack you must listen. There is more. Please listen. When you talked about … our son I … I …' Jenny's voice became constricted to a whisper of unbearable intensity. 'Oh Jack, I can't have one. At least, the doctor said it was … very unlikely.'

An unutterable silence followed. Even the distant background din of the Bangkok night subsided. I felt like the man in an electric chair who survives the first lightning bolt that flashed through him and so they press the lever again. Finally I spoke.

'You … you didn't tell me.'

'Jack, how could I have? When could I have? There was never a time when … Do you remember that New Year's Eve when you proposed? We sat in the train to Bristol … I think we might have been the only ones on the whole train, it certainly felt like it. I didn't want the train to stop, ever, I just wanted us to travel on and on through that lovely moonlit snow-filled night. And then you asked me to marry you in that terribly silly serious loveable way you have, asked if I would mind terribly if

288

we did it on the footplate of a Great Western engine, and you apologised for the unseemly haste but said we needed to perform the ceremony before midnight, when the Great Western Railway would pass out of existence. And I wanted to tell you, "Oh shut up you daft brush! I will marry you now this very minute if you can find a priest!" But we needed no priest, you had something better in mind. The driver of a train, with a book of common prayer in his pocket, one he had carried all his life in expectation of just such an emergency. I don't believe there was a happier girl alive that night. How? How could I possibly have told you?'

I stared into her eyes, but said nothing.

'Well,' she said. 'You must think about it. Decide what you think. And if … if you find it changes things, too much … well then it is up to you. But remember whatever it is you think of me,' her voice rose in pitch, 'I did nothing worse than your mother.'

She stood up and walked back towards the party. I made no attempt to stop her, but sat on the chair there for a while, my thoughts fizzing like bees in a hive that has been kicked over.

My attention was drawn to a couple of chaps walking across the lobby behaving strangely. It was Roger and Spaulding, visibly inebriated and giggling and shushing each other. Roger was carrying a catapult. They crept towards a small room that served as a library, but was seldom visited. I became aware of a gleam from the gloom within, like a storm lantern at night. I stood up and followed and saw a strange sight. Inside the darkened library there were some candles burning, and Webster, wearing a dog collar and black shirt beneath his jacket, was sitting in a chair, holding aloft a golden cross. Before him, kneeling in supplication with head bowed, was Earwig. It seemed Webster was blessing him, or taking his confession.

Just then an egg smashed into Earwig's ear, exploding in a slap of yolk on his cheek. Earwig cried out in shock. Roger and Spaulding collapsed with laughter. Webster spun round with a face livid with anger, jumped up and ran to the door. As he reached it, he delved into his jacket and drew out a semi-automatic pistol. Roger and Spaulding had been laughing too much to escape and already it was too late. Webster pushed the pistol into Roger's face and said, with cold fury in his voice, 'Get on your knees, you crazy fuck!' The laughter stopped instantly. And for the first time since arriving here, I saw Roger lose his expression of supercilious detachment and genuine fear filled his eyes.

'On your knees,' said the priest again, and Roger obliged, sinking to the ground.

'Steady on, old man,' said Spaulding, alarmed. 'It's just a bit of harmless fun.' It was plain that Spaulding had spent his life inflicting cruel jokes on people and then obliging them to regard it as harmless fun or risk being called a bad sport. But tonight he was out of his depth, for once unable to control events.

'Pray to the Lord,' said Webster, ignoring Spaulding, 'pray to be forgiven for your blasphemy or you will be meeting Him face to face with six bullets in your brain. Pray! I said.'

Roger began to mumble the Lord's Prayer.

'Lower your eyes,' said Webster. Roger did so, dropping his gaze to the floor. A second passed. Then Webster raised the pistol and cracked it down hard on Roger's head. Roger fell forward onto his face and groaned. 'If you disturb us again,' said Webster, 'I'll shoot you both.' He returned to the writing room to pick up, it seemed, where he'd left off. Roger began to revive and Spaulding helped him to his feet and they walked off to the main entrance.

I pretended not to have noticed the scene that had just unfolded, even though it was impossible that I could have missed it. In the lobby one of the hotel staff had erected an easel and was pinning to it photographs taken earlier of the party. I asked him if he had seen my wife and he directed me to the lounge. Then I noticed the photographs. One in particular stood out. It showed a guest who had newly arrived, leaning casually on the reception counter, a suitcase at his feet. It was a man with a burned face.

Chapter 18

I HEARD JENNY'S VOICE BEFORE I entered the room. She was standing before Earwig, with her back to me. He sat in an easy chair, clutching a tumbler of whisky so far from perpendicular it was on the verge of spilling its contents into his lap. He looked confused, with the air of a drunk who can no longer focus his gaze and lacks the energy to care. He did not notice me enter.

'You gave her the Benzedrine,' said Jenny. 'You could have killed her.' She sounded tired and exasperated, as if trying to explain something that should need no explaining: the obvious cruelty of Earwig's behaviour.

'Only Panzer-Schokolade,' he whined.

'What difference does it make what you call it?'

'I don't see what bloody business it is of yours or that sap of a husband of yours.'

'Don't you dare say that about him!' said Jenny. 'He's a good man.'

Earwig gave a sour laugh.

'He's worth ten of you.'

'So what? I'm not worth anything. Besides, if you like him so much you should tell him to mind his step, or he'll get what for.'

'Who from? You?'

'Roger.'

'He wouldn't stand a chance! Jack knows how to do Chinese Temple Boxing. They did it at school.'

Earwig's face creased up in confusion. 'What are you talking about?'

'At the orphanage, one of the masters had been a missionary. He knew Chinese Temple Boxing and taught it to the boys.'

He shook his head as if what he had just heard was irrelevant. 'He wouldn't last five minutes against Roger.'

'He'd knock Roger into Kingdom Come.'

For a moment I stood transfixed by the strange conversation. Jenny was clearly exhausted, yet finding the strength to speak of me with fierce pride.

'I doubt it,' said Earwig, with barely the energy left to speak. 'Roger once fought a boy to death at school.'

'I don't believe you,' said Jenny scornfully. 'Schoolboys don't fight to the death.'

'This one did. The other boys wouldn't let it stop, the fight went on for three hours. Then his heart gave out. It was his first day.'

'I … I don't believe you,' said Jenny in a voice that suggested she did. 'Boys don't do that in English schools. They would be arrested.'

'Who by?'

'The … the police!'

'Shows how much you know about English schools,' he sneered. 'I daresay they would in the sort of ghastly place you were dragged up in, but in a decent school

294

the police wouldn't even find out about it.' Earwig became animated, as if the memory of this horror from long ago gave him the strength to be bitter. 'Such things are hushed up of course, or parents would stop sending their little boys and the place would fold.'

'Someone must have informed the police, it's … it's the law,' Jenny persisted.

'The boy had a weak heart and simply collapsed on his first day. Why would you call the police?'

In the gloom I sensed rather than saw Jenny stare at Earwig in a sort of bewildered shock, a shock I shared. It was as if we knew the events Earwig described could not possibly have happened, and yet the manner in which he related them left one in no doubt he was telling the truth.

'Mr Earwig,' I said, keen to draw Jenny's attention to my presence. 'We are very sorry to hear about this.'

She turned and said in a whisper, 'Jack.'

'No you are not. How could you be? You couldn't even begin to imagine.' He stopped, drained his glass and went to place it on the floor next to his chair. As he reached down it slipped from his grasp, hit the floor and rolled away. 'Here!' He reached for his wallet and took out a photo. It was the photo of his nanny in China and two small boys. I remembered the play-acting on the beach when Roger had torn up an imaginary photo in front of Earwig, trying to goad him into violence. 'That's him, on the left.'

'Your … your brother?' said Jenny.

'Yes. Roger was the county junior boxing champion. He knocked Ben down two hundred and thirty-four times in a row.'

'That's just so horrible,' cried Jenny. 'But why?'

'Ben snitched on Roger's brother for starting a fire. He liked fire-setting. That's why be burned the cranes.'

'Mr Earwig,' I interrupted, 'Is Mr Curtis dead?'

'Not as far as I know.'

'Why did you put him in the rattan ball?'

'To shut him up, the bloody fool. It was just to shut him up. Just horseplay, really.' That word again made him peer once more at the photo. 'That's the thing about photographs, isn't it? We're better off without them. They don't let you forget anything. Whoever invented them should be shot. Here, see? Here's another one for you, for your scrapbook.' He slid out another of his nanny, and as he did, a photo lodged behind it slipped out onto the table. It showed a dingy room with a bed and a single ceiling fan. On the bed a naked girl lay draped across a man. The man was me.

There was a moment's silence. Jenny gasped. I said, in a stricken voice, 'Jenny!'

Her eyes flashed as if she had just spotted an oncoming car. She flinched, and turned and ran out. I rushed after her. She ran through the main door out into the night. I raced in pursuit but a line of drunken conga dancers came between us and refused to let me pass, insisting instead that I join their childish game. I struggled free of them and bolted into the night.

It was like running into an oven. The night was filled with the din of a thousand noises. Choirs of cicadas fried like bacon, car horns tooted, and music drifted in from all corners. I reached the lane and looked up and down, but the night was a carnival of people urgently going about whatever business it was they had.

They had slipped something in my drink at that nightclub we visited. Why did they do it? Did they fear me looking for Curtis? Feel a need to restrain me? Or was it just the sort of thing they did at a school where boys were boxed to death? Horseplay.

None of that mattered, the only thing that was important was the urgent need to find Jenny and tell her how I had been tricked like that. Surely she could not believe that I ... but then what did she know of me? It was only four months ago that we first went to the Lyon's Corner Shop for a boiled egg, and Jenny, showing off the slang she had learned from the GI, had asked for water by ordering dog soup. I think it was then that I realised that my life had changed utterly in a way that I couldn't imagine. Jenny was the only girl I had ever known, the only one I ever want to know, the only girl I have ever taken out and bought an egg for.

A lot of chaps, sporty types I suppose, have in the past found this disclosure to be somehow amusing, as if it revealed an inadequacy in my character, but I never greatly minded this. It is the action of a fool to resent what he has become when he had no choice in the matter. During my years as a detective on the railways I have encountered many chaps behaving disagreeably and showing great disrespect for their lady companions. I freely confess it gets my goat, and there have been times when I have deemed it necessary to box a chap's ears on account of this. Men like Spaulding and Roger and Earwig think being mean and spiteful is a sign of manliness, a form of strength, but I knew that it really shows weakness of character. It is designed to conceal the coward within.

A lot of people supposed that life in an orphanage must be hard and severe, like an institution from Charles Dickens, but this was not true. At the St Christopher's Railway Servants' Orphanage there were disagreeable masters and unpleasant incidents, but in the main I would describe the atmosphere we were brought up in as firm but kind. And I know why, too. In contrast to the parents who sent chaps like Spaulding to a school – people who arrived in their Rovers and shook hands with their little boys before abandoning them – in contrast to them, the men and women who paid for the keep of us orphans were poor. Mostly they were the hard-working men of the railway who donated a small fraction of the wage they toiled so hard for, a pittance they could barely afford, to bestow kindness upon children whose parents had worked on the railways and perished.

This kindness, I believed, communicated itself to the school in ways we cannot fathom. It was love, because only a man with love in his heart can so visualise the pain of an orphaned child, one whom he will never meet, and so pare from his meagre wages a few shillings. It was the same love that caused the men in the engineering works to make miniature, fully functioning steam engines and tracks to give to us at Christmas. They did it in their spare time, and if you had asked them why they would have had no answer.

I hailed a tricycle rickshaw. The driver looked about seventy but was probably only half that, his face set in the permanent rictus of a man straining under loads too heavy. He wore a vest that might once have been white, and canvas shorts. I indicated to him that he should cycle round the neighbourhood, as I was looking for my wife. I got in and, without a word, he stood up on the pedals and forced the contraption forward and out into the stream of people in the lane.

He did not ask for any further information but pedalled confidently against the main stream of the throng towards the river. The smell of incense in shadows sweetened the night as we passed the temple where dim figures could be discerned paying obeisance to a glinting shrine. The track became rougher, the suspension squeaked and the driver struggled to make headway. He turned right into a lane and then left and left again. We drifted away from the thoroughfare. There were no lights now, and no people, a road so dark it was a wonder the driver could see to cycle. Maybe he was so familiar with these streets from the daytime, or maybe he had cycled them for so many years that lights were hardly necessary.

It reminded me of driving a train at night. Few passengers had any idea of just how blind the driver and his fireman are at night. We hurtle along at 80 mph, hurled forward with the momentum of a train hauling many tons that would take a mile or so to bring to a halt. There is nothing to be seen ahead, and apart from the occasional cottage light glimmering like the lantern of a traveller lost on the heath, there is nothing to be seen to the left or right. If there is something in our way that should not be there, the only consolation is that we will not see it and, in contrast to the horror that such a sight unleashes during the day, will not have to endure the sickening minutes heavy with the knowledge that we are bound unavoidably for death, nor confront the decision that no man ever wants in his lifetime to face: to jump from the cab or not?

At night we are given a sort of grace, the same grace that a man who dies in his sleep is given. Surely this is the kindest way to die? Without pain in the body or in the heart. At night, one crashes on in a tiny world of lovely clanging din, and sees no more than does a man in a coal cellar. One doesn't even see the way the track is heading. At night there is no light at the end of the tunnel.

After ten minutes the driver returned me to the hotel. I realised after I had calmed down that he had not understood a word of my wild instructions. How could

300

he have? I got out and paid him. I knew it was a forlorn task. I wandered out onto the hotel lawn. The proximity to the river gave the air a slightly cooler quality, a gentler one. If this were England, one might expect dew to be forming on the grass, sparkling dimly at one's feet like beads of glass.

The tranquillity was starkly at odds with the storm in my breast. I could not ever remember a time when my soul had been exposed to such torment as this evening. I suddenly realised a simple truth. The quest for my mother was a fool's errand. I had never known her, but I did know Jenny. We were both alive and had each other and no one needs more than that. All we had to do was leave this city. But into what danger might she now have accidentally fallen? What if I were now to encounter the man with the burned face? I felt tonight, for the first time, that I could kill him. But I knew that would make the situation more desperate. They would catch me and I would spend years in a prison world where the smell was so strong it could knock a man unconscious.

I could hear the water lapping, and as my steps brought me closer to the water's edge I discerned the figure of a man sitting in a chair next to the tin of syrup. It was Roger.

He looked irritated, as if he were enjoying the late-night tranquillity and did not want to be disturbed. Or maybe he was just befuddled by drink. 'What do you want, Wenlock?' he snapped.

'I might ask you the same question. What are you doing at this late hour sitting in the garden?'

'What's it look like? I'm enjoying the sun.'

'I've always regarded sarcasm as a cheap form of humour.' My voice was absurdly calm.

'Have you indeed. Thanks for letting me know.'

'You look to me rather like a chap acting as a guard.' He picked up a revolver lying in his lap. 'I am.'

'Is that a Webley?'

'What does it matter?'

'I'm not sure. What's in the tin?'

'Syrup.'

'I see. Mind if I look?'

'It's sealed, I'm afraid, like your fate if you don't start minding your own business.'

I stepped closer to the tin, and peered at it. 'How exactly is it sealed? Can't we open it?'

Roger laid the gun down and stood, squaring up to me. 'It's completely sealed, there is no lid, the top is like the base of the tin. There's nothing in it, it's just a prop for the film. Empty.'

'Why guard it, then?'

He flinched, and I could see in the dim light the throbbing Adam's apple of a man swallowing anger. 'Because someone might steal it, of course. Props are expensive. Now clear off before you get what for.'

'What if I want what for?'

'The way you've been asking for it, you certainly seem to.' He stepped closer to me, until there was less than a foot between us. He smelled of cologne, with a hint of whisky. 'You'll do what I tell you,' he said.

I stared into his face. He placed his hand on my chest and shoved, and I stepped back with one foot to brace myself. He pushed harder and my supporting foot dug into the lawn. A member of the hotel staff, a waiter, came out on some errand and stopped a few yards from us, arrested by the sight.

'You're getting my goat, Wenlock,' he said, and grabbed the lapels of my jacket. 'It's time to teach you a lesson.'

The waiter cried out in alarm.

Roger, for all his power, was not a skilful fighter and signalled clearly his intention to smash his forehead into my nose. I swung my arm over his, as I had been taught at school, and broke the hold of his hand. We fell to the ground, and began trading blows in the most uncivilised fashion, most of them missing their mark in the confusion. The boy ran back to the hotel, and there we squirmed on the lawn, grappling and writhing until eventually the matter was settled when Roger grabbed his revolver and brought the butt crashing down onto my head.

Chapter 19

I OPENED MY EYES AND found myself in a bare stone room, lying on straw. Instinct told me the stone floor should have been cold, but it was blood-warm. The air was moist and hot, and it stank. Far away a man cried out in pain, a faint but harrowing sound that chilled the bowels, fading like the wail of a man thrown from a high tower. I could not discern whether it was the cry of a man being beaten or one simply fed up with the indignities of the world.

In the far corner of the room stood a boy. He was dressed like a Dickensian urchin with torn and ragged trousers that he had clearly outgrown. Though a child, he wore a waistcoat under a shabby bottle-green jacket. His face seemed a stranger to soap. It was Ben Hawkins, the boy who appears from time to time in the dreams of all railwaymen.

Once, long, long ago on a cold winter's night when all eleven-year-old boys should be warm and snug in bed, he was shivering in the engine shed, cleaning the locomotives, and finding one in which the firebox was still warm from the day's exertions, he climbed inside for a while then fell asleep. The next day they shovelled in the live coals and that was the end of him.

'You must not give up, Jack,' he said.

I closed my eyes and slept again. It was morning when I next opened my eyes. My body throbbed with pain. It felt as if I had been given a good kicking by Roger, or maybe he had used the revolver to deliver the blows. But I did not appear to have sustained serious damage. I passed out again.

When I woke again it was evening and I found myself sitting in a chair staring into the smiling face of Lieutenant Colonel Nopsansuwong.

'You, Mr Wenlock, are in what you call hot water.'

I struggled to gather my thoughts. I had been fighting with Roger, but before that Jenny had run away. Because of a photograph. I remembered her telling me about her miscarriage, and a bolt of pain shot through me as I recalled, in turn, the thoughtless gift I had given her on the boat. For our son.

'Very hot water.'

'I feel as if I have fallen from a tall building.'

'You are bruised, but it will heal. But what about your reputation? Two men, Europeans whom we are brought up to respect, fighting like labourers. You could go to prison for a very long time for this. Do you want to be the second-most lonely man in the world?'

My mind turned to our first visit when he had outlined the terrors of this fate. 'I was only defending myself against Roger.'

'He said he was defending himself against you.'

'He would do.'

306

'The hotel boy confirmed his story.'

The simple statement hit me like a punch. 'No!' I said in despair. 'It can't be true ... the boy must have been bribed.'

'Do you have any evidence for that allegation?'

'I can assure you, Lieutenant Colonel, I had more important things on my mind than starting fights. My wife ... after we had a disagreement she ran out of the hotel door into the night and ... and ...'

'What does that have to do with Mr Roger?'

'It's difficult to explain.'

'Tell me, why do you care about this man Curtis?'

'I have reason to believe he knows the whereabouts of my mother, who left my life the day I was born. Furthermore, I have reason to believe that Mr Spaulding and his friends may have killed Mr Curtis by putting him in that rattan ball that stands in the glass case at the hotel.'

'And what makes you think that?'

'The night he disappeared he had been wearing a circus ringmaster's jacket. I found it in the garden of the hotel. It had puncture holes in it.' I described the little demonstration I had performed with the kitchen boy and the pot of strawberry jam, aware as I did that he must surely have known all this.

The answer seemed to impress him. 'Mr Wenlock, would you describe yourself as an honest man?'

'Of course.'

He pulled a wan face. 'That saddens me, for as much as you are honest, so I am poor. We do things differently in this country. We prefer to help the poor rather than see them go hungry all in defence of a noble but empty principle. The police are poor.'

My stomach lurched as the implications of his speech became clear. 'Are you asking me for a bribe, Lieutenant Colonel?'

He feigned mild shock. 'Of course not! A consideration perhaps, some tea money … It pains me to be so blunt, but I know you do not understand our culture and must make allowances. It would be terrible if you were to end up spending the rest of your life in this most unpleasant place all because of a trivial misunderstanding.' He smiled, then stood up. 'I will be back in a short while. In the meantime I recommend you reflect on the decision that faces you.'

I sat for a while, aware only of the pounding of my heart. Again I heard the wail of the man being thrown from the tower. I thought of Curtis, and the chaps putting him in the rattan ball.

I did not need to buy an envelope from the post office to know that, in Mrs Carmichael's system of classification, Siam was a type-B country. A land where one could get into a lot of trouble if one failed to bribe the police. I remembered my indignation at catching Cheadle stealing coal. All my life I had felt that same sense of indignation, had chased chaps who stole coal, even though they must surely have done it for compelling reasons. Who but a desperate man steals coal? Was I wrong?

I took out the photo of my mother and examined it. I had still not got over the shock of seeing her; it was like a blind man who wakes up one day and can see. In the photo there was a sparkle in her young eyes, an impishness, the hint of a dimple in her chin. It was a picture of innocence and kindness. I recalled the pain in Jenny's voice as she related the bitter tale of the child she lost and saw clearly how I, though alive, was a child dead to Millie. It broke my heart to think of her suffering. What had they done to her? What had Curtis discovered here that made him inscribe the words 'The horror! The horror!' on his postcard? What could possibly be even more scandalous than turning up at a birthday party wearing a necklace of human ears?

Lieutenant Colonel Nopsansuwong returned and said, 'Well, Mr Wenlock, what is it going to be? A little tea money for a hard-working policeman?'

I raised my eyes to his. 'I have to tell you, sir, all of my life I have been utterly incapable of offering a bribe to a policeman. I condemned my friend for stealing coal in winter for his fire, for robbing the greater crooks who stole his life from him. That coal was more his than theirs. I disdain the attitude found among my fellow passengers on the boat to Singapore that foreigners are less honest than us, and that it is natural to bribe their policemen. It is born, I believe, of the misconceived notion that we alone are honest, when in truth very few people are and they do not all belong to one country. Hitherto it would have been impossible for me to contemplate such a course, but hitherto I passed my life in a stunted fashion, and that all changed when Jenny walked into my life. And though I find the prospect disagreeable, I am ready to offer you, sir, whatever you ask, within reason, although I must honestly tell you that I am disappointed – you have always struck me as an upstanding man.'

He stared at me long and hard and finally said, 'Are you sure?'

I assured him that I was, whereupon the policeman laughed. 'Your instincts were right, I have no intention of taking your money. I was just seeing how you would react. I have to say, I like your speech very much. I will have you driven back to your hotel.' He laughed at the look of puzzlement that stole across my face, saying, 'What else can I do? You are clearly an honest man, and therefore your account of your fight with Mr Roger must be true. In fact, I know it to be so because the hotel boy told me. Perhaps you think I would take your bribe because you have spent too long listening to Mr Spaulding, who has a very low opinion of me, and has indeed attempted to bribe me in the past. I'm going to drive you back to your hotel. And I will ask my men to search for your wife, they will be a lot better at it than you. Although I suspect it will be difficult for you, I suggest you simply wait at the hotel until you hear from us.'

I nodded.

'Might I also offer you a piece of advice? Take your beautiful wife away from here and forget about this man Curtis.'

I stared at him, looked into his eyes. He seemed to be genuine in offering his advice.

Nopsansuwong stood up. 'Let us return to your hotel.'

The policeman drove me back. I went to the lounge and ordered a Scotch. It was early evening.

Solveig Connemara walked in and joined me.

'You look how I feel,' she said. She pulled back a chair and sat down.

The waiter brought my drink and set it down on a side table next to the arm of my chair. There were five or six origami cranes on the table, and the waiter pushed them gently aside.

'I'm afraid I won't be much company for you,' I said.

'Buddy, when it comes to company my expectations are not very high. Besides, from the look on your face I'm not sure it would be safe to leave you alone.'

I forced a smile.

'You and your girl had a tiff?'

'Rather more than that, she … she ran away.'

'That's tough.'

'Yes.'

'It's none of my business, but don't let that stop you.'

'It's nothing really, it would probably bore you.'

'Until you've spent ten years in a funny farm, you don't know what boredom is.'

I explained to her the events of the previous evening. She evinced no great surprise, merely said, 'Well I'm sure the cops will soon find her and bring her back. Cops are good at that.'

'I don't imagine she'll ever forgive me.'

'For a lousy staged photograph? She'll forgive you in five seconds flat. Don't be an ass, Jack.'

I nodded. 'I would very much like not to be. You see, I can tell you frankly, I'm not a man of the world. I have lived a life that would be considered most unusual. I spent almost all of it never once imagining that I would meet a girl. I really have no experience.'

'Believe me it ain't that hard. All you have to do is love her, take care of her, hug her, buy her a dress once in a while, tell her she looks nice in it, trust her and forgive, especially for the mistake of being human.'

'She ... she had a child. Before she met me. With an American soldier. She got into trouble, if you see what I mean.'

'I hear it's quite popular, getting into trouble. Did you ever think about that word "trouble"? That's what you get when you do something wrong at school, or later you get it with the cops, especially if you are poor. At the same time it's the most natural act there is, without it none of us would be here. You had a mother, didn't you?'

'Yes, yes, I did, and rather a plucky one.'

312

'Everyone did. And all mothers did it. There wouldn't be anyone here otherwise. Calling it trouble marks your cards against you. It's like beating a dog for licking a bone. I've seen enough of this world to know it's not the people who get into trouble who cause all the pain, it's the ones who judge them.'

There was something deeply reassuring about Miss Connemara's words. We are so often taught that kindness is a form of weakness or self-indulgence, but these words coming from a film star in the twilight of her life, who had seen and suffered so much, carried a conviction that could not be doubted.

'Where's the guy now?'

'He fell in Normandy.'

'Oh. And the child?'

'She lost it.'

Solveig refilled our glasses with an unsteady hand. 'At least you still have her, and she has you. I had no one. Went to a fancy clinic to get rid of my child, even though it was all I ever wanted. Paid for by the studio. Doctors removed my heart by mistake. If I'd had a man to stand by me, who knows? Stepped out of that clinic and there was a bouquet of roses waiting for me. From Sam Flamenco. Can you believe that? What did he think I'd just been doing? Having a toenail removed? So I did what any decent girl in a situation like that would do, went to the liquor store.

'Still to this day I don't know what I did during that month. I was never sober. I was even drunk in my dreams. Spent some time in jail, no idea what for. After the third time, when they let me out, I had ten dollars left in all the world and a letter from the studio who'd cancelled the movie, saying they were suing me for breach of contract. So I jumped off Brooklyn Bridge. I don't recommend it, you just get wet and even more miserable than you were before you jumped. After that it was ten years in the funny farm, getting zapped with electric shocks every month. And one day they said I was cured and could leave. Where do you go after being in a place like that? The street. That's where I spent the next three years. Once a man approached me and told me they were shooting a movie about Solveig Connemara and I should audition because I looked just like her. I went but failed the audition, so I guess you could say it really was the story of my life.'

She stood up. 'Come with me, I want to show you something.'

I followed her. She walked out onto the lawn and down to the river. The night was hot and damp, and the black depths of the river gave off a palpable scent. Light glittered across the water, and ahead of us, too, in the darkness, the Empire Flying Boat glimmered like an animal glimpsed in the forest at night.

'You said, if you'd had a man to stand by you,' I said. 'Did the father of your child abandon you?'

'He never knew. I didn't tell him.'

'Pardon me, but I thought … I was told, the father was Johnny Sorrento.'

'Everybody thought so, including old Johnny, but it wasn't him. It was the boy from next door. He wasn't good enough for me, you see. Or so I thought. I was a star, what was he? Just a boy from the Bronx I'd grown up with. He wasn't ever going to be anybody, not like me. I was going places. I got that all wrong too, it was me who wasn't good enough for him.'

'Do you ever wonder what became of him?'

'Nope. It's too late, wherever he is now he will be as old and broken as me. I don't want ever to know.'

'The policeman said I should take Jenny away and forget all about Curtis.'

'Cops don't often offer good advice in my experience, but that sounds good. I wish you could see what I see. I wish you didn't have to grow old and broken in order to see so plainly. You and Jenny are the two luckiest people in this lousy hotel, do you know why? Because you don't need to take that goddam plane. Here we all are, one big dungheap of losers, flying off to find something you never find by searching somewhere else, you only ever find it in your back garden because you either carry it in your heart or nowhere.'

'If Sam Flamenco made you get rid of your child, why are you with him now?'

For a long time she did not answer and then said, simply: 'He's not the man he used to be.' She paused

315

and emptied her glass in one gulp, and then left. I watched her go and then let my gaze drop. My eyes came to rest on one of the cranes. It had a pattern of printed words. One word stood out. 'Fun'. I picked up the crane and looked more closely. 'Fune'. I unfolded the paper bird. 'Funeral'. It had been folded from a scrap of torn-up screenplay.

EXT. MILLIE TOOKEY'S FUNERAL. DAY

On the same promontory where MILLIE first drew the thorn from the mon- ster's paw, CAPTAIN SQUIDEYE stands in oilskins and sou'wester at the side of a grave. HE sings from a hymn book. Torrents of rain sweep in, and the drops trace the words, engraved on the headstone, MILLIE TOOKEY.

The monster CHOMGHUÜRGHA stands by, weeping.

SQUIDEYE

(Singing)

There is a place where hands which held ours tightly

Now are released beyond all hurt and
fear

Healed by that love which also feels
our sorrow

Tear after tear.

Chapter 20

I STOOD ON THE EDGE of a cliff so high there was nothing below except clouds. It overlooked the canyon of my own stupidity. What an imbecile I had been. How unutterably a clown. Like a fool I had allowed myself to be seduced into the preposterous belief that my mother was alive and that I should soon meet her. In allowing myself to be bought in this way I had been a dupe, exposing both myself and my dear wife to danger in pursuit of a chimera.

As I stood amid the rubble of my quest and began to comprehend the extent of my folly, I became aware of another feeling rising within me. A steely resolve began to form. There was still a prize I could salvage. Jenny. I must find her, and make myself worthy of her. I would implore her forgiveness, and with the money the Countess had given us we should go somewhere far away, a place where neither the Countess nor the man with the burned face should find us.

I walked back out into the lobby and into the path of Sugarpie, who seemed distraught. She took a look at my bruised face and said, 'Must go hospital.'

I assured her the bruises were superficial.

'No, must go. Madam have car accident.'

My stomach lurched. 'Do you mean Jenny?'

'Yes, but she OK, sir.'

We took the same rickshaw driver as I had taken the previous day. He cycled at a brisk pace through the darkness, down alleys in which the faint light of the sky glinted in the eyes of dogs watching us with suspicion. Other things scurried in the gloom and everywhere there was the smell of stagnant water, tar, rotting wood and charcoal smoke, jasmine, camphor and spices. The background hum of a Bangkok street – the tooting of horns, bark of dogs – became soothing. The choir of cicadas rose to a crescendo and then went silent as if answering the commands of an invisible orchestra conductor, before starting off again.

Before long we pulled up at a hospital. It seemed not greatly different to ones back in England: tiled floors scrupulously scrubbed; walls painted in beige and tan; swing doors opening onto long corridors, inadequately lit, and filled with the faint reek of disinfectant and lavatory smells. The nurses were smaller, but more numerous, and thronged the corridors in starched white tunics, skirts and aprons like flocks of snowbirds. Sugarpie spoke to a nurse behind a reception counter and after a phone call was made I learned that Jenny had been discharged in the company of a Mr Spaulding.

This revelation unleashed a paroxysm of fury within me. The blood rushed to my head so violently I had to reach out to a wall to avoid stumbling. When the turmoil passed it was replaced by a feeling I had never experienced before: the cold, calm certainty that I should soon kill a man.

When I returned to the hotel I was told that Roger and Spaulding were away, but Earwig was believed to be in his room. I was quite calm as I climbed the stairs. I knew with simple certainty that I should kill Earwig, but before he died he would tell me where they had taken Jenny. I had never possessed the intention to kill someone before and I was surprised at how normal it felt.

I imagined I could probably throttle him but thought maybe it would be better to go armed with something with which to club him, so I went first to my room to find a weapon. But there was nothing. Suitcases, a lamp, a chair, some shoes ... nothing that would be useful for the task I had in mind. The sight of Jenny's clothes draped over a chair filled me with a cold fury. I walked up the corridor to Webster's room and knocked. There was no response. I opened the door. There was no one in, but I could see his semi-automatic Colt 1911 glinting on the bedside table. I picked it up and pushed it inside the waistband of my trousers.

At Earwig's door I paused as if about to knock, but realised this was a foolish courtesy in view of the act I had in mind. I opened the door and walked in. Earwig was hanging by his neck from the ceiling. On the floor beside the bed was a knife he had used to cut up his bed sheets, and an upturned chair. I looked up at him and as he gently swivelled, our eyes met. His face was purple but the expression that entered his eyes upon seeing me showed that the pilot light inside him was still flickering.

'Mr Earwig!' I cried, 'You mustn't.'

I grabbed the knife, replaced the chair and climbed on it, embracing him with one arm and sawing at the bedsheet ligature with the knife. It tore easily and Earwig slumped into my arms and we overbalanced and toppled onto the bed. There we lay facing each other as close as a man and his wife.

'Mr Earwig,' I said, 'How could you do such a terrible thing?' I loosened the noose, my fingers pressing gently into his collar, into the soft and clammy flesh of his neck. 'Whatever possessed you?'

He stared at me, with wide wet eyes and the tears brimmed over and streaked down his cheeks, dropping onto the counterpane, beating out a tattoo like soldiers drumming in the street outside. He opened his mouth a fraction and a squeak came out, like a bed spring or a puppy that has lost its mother.

'I must ask you, sir, what have they done with my wife?'

He said nothing, his chest heaved with panting sobs.

'I regret the clumsiness of my manners in asking you at such a time, but you must understand, if you do not tell me where she is, I will kill you.'

He spoke in a whisper. 'But you just saved my life.'

I struggled to find a way to explain the paradox. 'But only so I could question you first. In truth I would kill you with as much thought as I would crush a beetle.'

He was silent, staring at me and blinking away the forming tears. He seemed unconvinced by my words.

'Jack, I didn't burn the cranes.'

'No,' I said gently, 'I didn't think you did.'

We lay there staring into each other's faces. I could feel his warm, damp breath on my face.

'Mr Earwig, when you went for your swim … on the beach, we saw … marks on you. Did they put you in the wicker ball too?'

'Yes, that was just larking about.'

'Horseplay?' I said bitterly.

'Yes. That's all.'

'Why do you stay with these men?'

'They are my friends.'

'Mr Earwig, I believe you know where Mr Spaulding and Roger have taken my wife. You must understand there is nothing I wouldn't do to protect Jenny.'

'Kill me?'

'I assure you I am serious.'

'I would be most grateful if you would carry out this threat. I think death must be rather fine, at least compared to the life I've had.'

'Mr Earwig, no! You must not say that! You must not give in to dark fears and imaginings, they work on your soul and make you see the world in a far gloomier light than the truth requires. I assure you from the bottom of my heart that things are never as bad as they seem, and one day—'

He groaned. 'I wish you would make up your mind.'

'If you sincerely wish to die, what reason can you have for withholding the information? Even Roger can't hurt you in the grave.'

'I know, but if you let me live, what then?'

He looked into my eyes and saw that I had no answer. If he were to die he could tell me, but if he were to live, he couldn't.

'It's probably best if you let me die,' he said.

'There is no reason for such a counsel of despair.'

'My whole life is composed of despair in one form or another.'

'It seems to me, that ... that is not necessary. I happen to believe you are a good man, Mr Earwig.'

'Do you? Do you really?'

'Yes, I do. A good man who has suffered terribly at the hands of two scoundrels.'

'Thank you. That means a lot to me. I ... I wish I was like you.'

'There is nothing special about me, in that at least we are not so very different.'

'But you have a wife ... I never get the girls, even Sugarpie threw my book away. Kilmer can have her any time he wants.'

'Are you not aware,' I said gently, 'that the book was probably not the most appropriate gift in the circumstances?'

'Wasn't it?'

'I'm not well up in the way things work out here, but I feel you would stand every chance of winning

Sugarpie's heart if … if … Tell me plainly, do you genuinely want to win her heart?'

'Oh yes!' A new light appeared in his eyes as he considered the prospect.

'As opposed to a quick, seedy conquest in which you enjoy her body for a night and no more?'

'Oh no, I would marry her at the drop of a hat!'

'In that case I would say to you the following: if you changed your approach, if you dropped this … this act of insouciant swagger with which the men out here, it seems to me, treat the girls as some sort of easy conquest, and showed to her that you cared for her and would take care of her, that you would be willing to insulate her from the terrible future of poverty … then I suspect she would marry you too at the drop of a hat.'

'Jack, are you serious?'

'Very much so.'

'But …'

'Mr Earwig, can't you see that a book about Winnie the Pooh is utterly meaningless to her, whereas if you had spent the same amount, or even a fraction of it, on gold … she would surely have loved you?'

'But isn't that terribly meretricious?' His face was creased with confusion but his voice became clearer. It was as if the vision I dangled before him – and assured him was attainable – had restored some of his vigour.

'Back home perhaps, but here it is otherwise. The interpretation. You would be signalling that you cared greatly for her welfare.'

325

'How can you know?'

'Mr Earwig, I know very little about affairs of the heart – I can diagnose a thousand different mechanical faults in a steam engine from the sound of the chuffs, but the workings of the human heart are largely a mystery to me. All the same, in this situation, it seems plain as a pikestaff to me.'

Earwig stared at me in wonder, the wonder that fills the heart of someone seeing something for the first time that was obvious to other people.

'It was my fault they put Curtis in the rattan ball,' he said. 'When he first arrived we became friends. We got drunk and I blabbed. I told him too much.'

'What did you tell him?'

'About the tin of syrup.'

'What about it? It's a movie prop, isn't it?'

He stared at me wild-eyed. 'Oh Jack,' he said in the sort of whisper one might use in a haunted house. 'Jack, it's … it's a bomb.' He squeezed his eyes tight and gulped, trying to suppress another wave of sobs.

I looked at him dazed with surprise. 'But what for?'

'They are going to blow up the flying boat.'

Astonished horror flashed within me. 'Are you serious, Mr Earwig?'

'I swear, Jack.'

'Who do you mean by "they"?'

'Room 42.'

'The chaps work for Room 42?'

'Yes.'

I struggled to assimilate this revelation. 'Why on earth? Why would they ... you mean with everybody aboard?'

'Yes. Because of the Scharnhorst Plan.'

'What's that?'

'I thought you knew.'

'I haven't the foggiest idea of it.'

Earwig stared at me. His eyes glistened like those of a scolded dog. 'I don't know much, Jack. The chaps don't trust me. It has to do with some very high-level, top-secret meetings that took place at Wisskirriel House when Curtis was a boy, in the years before the Great War. After the signing of the armistice they had to hush it all up. There was a boating accident in which all the staff who were there at the time died. The Scharnhorst Plan is mentioned in the screenplay, so anyone who has read it has to be bumped off.'

'Are you saying Room 42 deliberately killed all the domestic staff from Wisskirriel House?'

'Yes. That's what they said.'

'This is an extraordinary tale, Mr Earwig.'

'When I told him the truth about the bomb Curtis became really crazed. He had always suspected the boating trip was no accident. That's when he turned up wearing the necklace of human ears.' His voice rose slightly and he swallowed as if suppressing a sob. 'We didn't mean it, Jack. We put him in the wicker ball, to frighten him. To shut him up. He was making a scene. He wasn't supposed to tumble down the stairs like that.'

327

'Are you saying it was an accident?'

'We had the ball perched on the top of the stairs, with him in it. We were making it see-saw on the edge, saying, "Are you going to be a good boy now, Curtis?" We were all a bit drunk. Then we stopped with it resting on the edge. Suddenly Roger kicked it and shouted, "Goal!" Down it went. It crunched each time it hit a step, and seemed to get faster … It's a wonder Curtis didn't wake the hotel with his cries. We rushed down, he was in a bad way, but he wasn't dead. There was blood seeping onto the rug, and the vase was broken. We got him out and took his jacket off to examine his wounds. He was in a lot of pain, and no one knew what to do. So Spaulding and Roger rolled him up in the rug and put him in the boot of their car. They told me to bury the jacket and the shards of broken vase, which is what I did.'

I watched with strange fascination the track of a tear on his cheek. It formed on the lid of his eye, welling up slowly like a balloon being inflated. It clung heavily to a lash like snow overburdening a tree branch, and then it fell and slid slowly down the cheek to a point where it dropped onto the taut cotton of the pillow, making a sound like the 'tock' of a clock.

'Now they are really scared,' he continued, 'in case Curtis goes public with what he knows. That's why they are desperate to find him. That's why they're worried about you, Jack. They don't know who you are. Roger thinks you are a detective hired by somebody to find Curtis. Spaulding thinks you work for the Russians.'

I stared in disbelief at this man whose face lay inches from mine, resting on a pillow wet with his tears. He raised a hand to dab them from his cheeks, and I saw how small and pudgy his hand was, almost like the flipper of a sealion.

'Why on earth would he think that?'

'Lots of reasons. Do you remember telling him about that spur line on the trans-Siberian railway? He says only a Russian would know something like that.'

'That's preposterous, everybody in my school knew it.'

'Why do you care about Curtis, Jack?'

'Millie, the woman who wrote the screenplay, was my mother.'

Earwig's eyes widened in astonishment. 'Oh my word. Oh my word.' He paused and stared at my face as if seeing it for the first time.

'I have discovered that she is dead.'

'No, why do you think that?'

'I found a fragment of the screenplay that described her funeral.'

'No, Jack. That was a forgery. Curtis made it. I saw him do it. When he found out they were hunting for Millie he gave Spaulding the fragment describing her funeral. But Spaulding knew straight away it was fake, it was pretty poorly done. So he screwed it up and threw it away.' He paused and wiped away a tear. 'I honestly don't know where they are, but Roger said he was going to see Mr Fink tonight. He was going to make him talk.

He said, if Fink knew where Curtis was hiding, he would find out. And if he didn't, it would be all the worse for him.'

I looked into his face. The passion that caused him to make an attempt on his own life seemed to have passed. In its place was another persona, the boy with the puppyish desire to please. I knew he was telling the truth.

I sat up and indicated to him that he should do the same. 'Mr Earwig,' I said, 'I feel that tonight I have finally come to understand you. I would go so far as to say I regard you as a friend. If I leave you now, will you give me your word as a gentleman that you will not attempt another desperate deed like this?'

'I swear, Jack. I swear I won't.'

I thanked Mr Earwig and returned to the lobby, my thoughts chasing after each other like moths around a lamp. A few hours ago I had been grieved to come by news that my mother must be dead. Now it appeared she might still be alive. I strode through the lobby in such a passion that I nearly bumped into the blind musicians who had been playing earlier and were preparing to leave.

A girl, hearing me pass, held out her cup and raised her eyes. I looked into them and found my gaze transfixed. The affliction that had taken her sight had also erased the distinction between iris and pupil. In its place was a featureless faintly bluish translucence, the colour of milk into which the tiniest drop of blue ink had fallen.

Suddenly I understood the cause of the bad blood between Curtis and Mr Fink, the dispute over a girl with blue eyes.

'You good heart, sir.' she said.

'Yes,' I said. I dropped a coin into her cup and thought, *Roger will not think so when I have finished with him.*

Chapter 21

THE DESK CLERK HAILED a boat that was long and thin, like a pencil, and gave the boatman directions for Mr Fink's house. The boatman stood in the stern and rowed with a single oar, like a gondolier.

We crossed the river and entered the mouth of a broad shipping canal, before turning off and entering a channel scarcely wider than the boat. The stillness was broken only by the soft plash of the oar and the tinkling – like the highest notes at the far right of the piano keyboard – of water breaking against the side of the hull. On either side of us stood low wooden houses fronted with plants and statues of the Buddha and apricot-coloured earthenware tubs. Oil lamps shone softly from each dwelling. There was no sound. Now and then the sweet scent of incense pricked the nostrils.

Smoke always carries within it memories of other times. When you thunder across a landscape on a spring dawn, and all the world still sleeps – only the footplate team and rabbits in the fields are awake – you feel a joy in your heart that you see in young lambs when they frisk and run. Or in the depths of winter when snow lies thick upon the ground, all the fields are hidden beneath its blanket and the trees spread white. Nothing moves, all is bleak and frozen, still as stone. Or perhaps you pass a lane in which a lone man plods, and wonder keenly about him and the life he leads. At such time the chuffs seem deeper, more sombre, and the whistle more forlorn, but you shovel your coal, deeply contented by the knowledge that behind lies a string of warm compartments, cut off from the cold landscape, warmed by the steam from your boiler, illuminated with dim yellow light in which travellers head towards adventures as yet undisclosed. Few things have such power to move the heart as smoke.

Finally we stopped at a house made of teak, where a veranda overhung the water, and here sat Mr Fink next to a table with a lamp and mosquito coil lit. He was drinking whisky. I climbed out of the boat onto the veranda. The incense of the mosquito coil mixed with the stench of putrescence that pervaded the district even more powerfully than on the eastern side of the river.

The boatman departed to wait at some discreet distance and for a while there was utter silence. The sky was mauve, and everything beneath it was black. Just then out of the night came that dearest of sounds, the wail of a steam engine. It was clear Mr Fink lived close to the narrow-gauge railway line we had seen from the air during our flying boat trip.

'Mr Fink,' I said, 'I hope you will forgive this intrusion and the dramatic news I have to convey. I have information that Roger will come here tonight and use violence against you in an attempt to gain from you information about the whereabouts of Mr Curtis. If you would be kind enough to allow me, I propose to turn the tables on Roger and use violence against him in order to find out where he and Spaulding have taken my wife. I would need your cooperation for the plan to succeed.'

'Really, Jack? Roger used to be a boxer, you know.'

'I know, but I used to fire a King-class 4–6-0 from Paddington to Bristol Temple Meads. The movement of the right arm with the shovel is the same as the punch to the ribs that breaks the heart of the prizefighter and makes him kiss the canvas like a sweetheart.'

He made an expression that suggested he was impressed, but it was difficult to know whether it was genuine or mockery.

'Besides,' I added, 'I propose to shoot him, not box him. I think you are a good egg, Mr Fink—'

He laughed softly. 'I'm sorry to disappoint you, Jack, but I am not really a good egg.' His voice had a strangled quality that it did not normally possess. It was the voice of one in pain. 'In truth, I am a pretty poor sort of chap. In that matter, Spaulding was right.'

'If you are referring to your having deserted from the army on a matter of conscience, I have to tell you that this in no way lowers you in my esteem. I once knew a chap who refused to serve, and the ordeal he consequently suffered on account of his conscience left me in no doubt about his courage.'

He let out a sour laugh. My impression that he was in pain grew stronger. 'I agree. It is surprising how sympathetic folk are when you tell them, particularly the people you would least expect – such as soldiers who have been wounded in action. It's humbling. But, alas, I do not deserve to be held in such high regard. In truth, I did not desert His Majesty's Armed Forces but left Brighton under such a cloud of infamy that I dare never return. You see, old Finky used to steal purses. From pensioners.' He paused. 'Can you believe that?'

'I confess your revelation surprises me.'

'I targeted the public lavatories on the Promenade. The cubicle doors had handles, you see. The old dears would go to spend a penny and hang their handbag on the door handle. It was an easy trick to give the handle a sharp twist and make the bag fall; then pull it out through the gap under the door. I did all right for a while until one day I stole a bag belonging to the local bobby's mother. Next time I did it, he was waiting. I was given a good kicking in the cells and had my face featured on the front page of the *Argus*.'

He touched his broken nose. 'I was no boxer. It was the bobby who gave me this. The accompanying story in the newspaper hinted that the police suspected me of being responsible for a string of other crimes, extremely unsavoury ones about which feelings had been running high all summer. The lying swine. I spent six months in the Scrubs, and was warned in no uncertain terms never to show my face in Brighton again.' He stopped talking and reached for his whisky tumbler, but then halted and withdrew the hand.

'Mr Fink,' I said softly, 'I can assure you I do not judge you. But time presses, where would you suggest the best place for me to conceal myself …'

'I'm afraid, Jack, it is a little too late.' The last two words were gasped as if a jolt of pain had shot through him. Blood frothed at his mouth. 'Roger has already paid me a visit.' He looked down. My eyes followed his gaze and noticed for the first time the blood soaking the shirt covering his stomach.

I drew back, startled. 'Mr Fink!'

'He was looking for Curtis. I said I didn't know where he was. He didn't believe me. He shot me.'

'Mr Fink! You poor man. We must get you to hospital straight away. I have a boat.'

'No Jack, no. You need your boat. You must use it to find your wife. They will have taken her to the beach house, the one we visited in the flying boat. The boatman will take you to the night market and from there you will be able to find a taxi.'

'Mr Fink, I cannot allow you to die. We must take you to the hospital first.'

'I'm fine,' he croaked in a voice that abjectly contradicted what it said.

'Surely,' I said, 'you understand me well enough to know it would be unthinkable for me to walk away and leave a man bleeding to death here?'

He considered my words and eventually gave in, clearly without the energy left to fight, and said there was no reason we might not do both. We could visit the night market on the way to the hospital.

I helped Mr Fink into the boat and he gave instructions in Siamese to the boatman. The man showed no emotion on seeing a white man with a blood-soaked shirt climb into his boat.

We drifted gently downstream as Mr Fink slowly died in front of me. 'I have some money,' he said, 'a little. In my house. If I don't make it … would you be kind enough to give it to … Curtis's girl?'

'Am I right in understanding,' I said, 'that his girl, the one over whom you bickered, the girl with blue eyes, was not a European as Mr Spaulding told me, but a blind Siamese girl?'

'Yes,' he said, speaking more to the sky than to me. 'The first buffalo. I misled you when I said it was Curtis's first buffalo. In truth it was mine. That's why I was so disturbed when you brought the postcard to show me. Do you remember I told you about all her tricks and wiles, and I said I had come to accept them and knew they were the result of expectation laid upon her? But when she intimated that there might be something wrong with her eyes, such dishonesty struck me as too much, and so I cast her away. But then Curtis met her and fell in love. It wasn't a hard thing to do. After all, I had done the same thing. When he found out about my betrayal, how I had cast her away for feigning

338

blindness, he said it was caddish and we argued about it. This was when he first arrived in Bangkok.'

'And of course, she wasn't feigning, was she?'

'No. I found out a year later. I had reason to visit Mueang Samut. She heard about it and asked me to go and see her. I took the bus. I'll never forget the day. It was just the same as all the previous times, the bus made its way through a sea of people and bullock carts into a dusty main street on which a few concrete shacks stood, and a cheap hotel and a tree with a bench encircling it by the river and the customs house. I saw through the bus window an old lady sitting on the bench, and I thought that it must be her mother. This old woman sat like a statue, with a stillness that set her apart from all the other people bustling there on a busy market day. She seemed to be unaware of what was going on around her. But then at the sound of the bus she made a movement, her hand reached down to clutch her bag and it was noticeable she did this without looking down. I watched it all as if in slow motion, the way time slows down in a motor-car accident. Her hand missed the bag slightly, then she corrected her grasp, again without looking down. Then I knew she had been listening for the sound of the bus, a bus she would never see.

'The last time we'd met she had the most beautiful brown eyes, like the eyes of a horse, dark and conker-brown and sparkly, and this old woman who was no old woman turned at the sound of the bus and I saw her eyes – they were milky blue.'

We continued to drift along. If the boatman discerned any urgency to our errand he betrayed no evidence of it in the manner of his rowing. Chaps like Spaulding would have instantly mischaracterised this as laziness or a deliberate ploy to exasperate the foreigner. I did not think so. I sensed it was more the wisdom innate to residents of hot countries, where to rush is never advisable and seldom achieves more than the same purpose performed at a languid pace. I recalled a poem by Kipling we once studied at the orphanage that said as much:

A Fool lies here who tried to hustle the East.

'Is it very much farther to the hospital?' I asked Mr Fink.

He continued to stare at the sky and spoke in an exalted way, as if he were becoming feverish. 'Hospital? Yes, did you know, Jack, if you go to hospital here your girl will come and sleep on the floor at the foot of your bed because she can't bear the thought of your being lonely? Are these people not the most wonderful, warm, cruel, honest, dishonest, corrupt, pure-hearted things that ever lived? Nowhere on earth is there such a voluptuous concentration of vice and pleasure and hedonism and loveliness and rottenness and heat and stink all jasmine-scented, perfumed with incense and madness, and loud, louder and noisier even than the foundries of Gomorrah ...' From somewhere deep within Mr Fink had found a strength to utter the words with intensity, despite the pain, as if nothing was more urgent than this.

340

'Sometimes I feel like a fly who lands on the calyx of a flesh-eating plant and knows he cannot escape but realises to his surprise that he doesn't greatly care to, for he stands ankle-deep in a gorgeous sticky substance that tastes divine. He licks the nectar off his boots, unaware that it is actually an enzyme that is slowly dissolving him. What a grand consummation! In this beautifully stinking, utterly corrupt and toxically lovely city of glory and degradation.'

Despite his pain and fading strength his voice grew in intensity. He spoke as if he beheld a vision and was struggling to describe it to me, aware that I saw nothing but the water and the sky. I knew I should counsel him to be quiet, to conserve his strength, but some instinct told me there was no point, nothing mattered more to him now than delivering his final verdict on his life. That slow-motion fall from the cliffs of Beachy Head he had mentioned during our first meeting was drawing to its end.

A pain shot through him and made him gasp; his frame quivered, but he continued with greater urgency. 'They call it the Big Mango, you know, but really it is a poisonous and beautiful tropical flower, scented like the moon and coated in the sweet nectar that is the joy of life distilled, and we know in our hearts that it is destroying us, and love it all the more. This is the great secret of the Siamese: they have taken the instant death of the moth in the candle flame and made it last for years.' The intensity in his voice subsided, like an oil lamp being turned down. The last words were no more than a whisper. 'This … this is the unique, pure and un-destroyable bliss of Bangkok.'

Ahead of us, a glow resolved into a small night market next to the bank. The boatman pulled up and called out to the people there. In turn they shouted to people we could not see, and before long a car that would serve as my taxi appeared. It was a dusty Japanese sedan with a broken headlight. I shook Mr Fink by the hand and clambered ashore. I gave the ferryman a coin, a fee which it transpired would be well earned tonight, because at some point on their journey to the hospital the candle flame of Bangkok finally consumed the moth of Mr Fink.

Chapter 22

IT TOOK ABOUT TWENTY minutes to reach our destination. We pulled up alongside a teak house, with a banister and veranda that encircled the whole bungalow. The door was open, leading onto a hall. I heard voices coming from a room on my left. The Colt 1911 is said by many to be the finest pistol ever made. Simple, reliable, effective. It shoots where you point it and, unlike many similar pistols, always goes bang when you pull the trigger. I released the safety catch and stood to the side of the door, and from outside I formed the impression that there were only Jenny and Spaulding there. I pushed the door gently, it moved an inch. I waited and listened. Then I pushed it again until a two-inch gap permitted me to peep within. I had been right. I walked in.

There was a simple table, set with chairs. Jenny sat at the table, playing patience.

'Oh, it's Sir Galahad,' said Spaulding with laboured nonchalance.

'Jack!' Jenny leapt out of her chair and ran to me. I embraced her with one arm and swung her gently to my side in order to keep the gun trained on Spaulding. 'Are you badly hurt?' I asked, speaking to her but staring at Spaulding.

'Only a bit,' she said.

'Plucky girl,' said Spaulding, in a voice that suggested he had taken a few drinks this evening. 'She stuck to your cover story the whole time.'

'I told him the truth, Jack.'

'I rather think you have the wrong idea about us, Mr Spaulding. It is true I am or was a detective, but only on the railways. And it is equally true that I have been searching for Mr Curtis – I had reason to suppose he could help me find my mother. But I have now abandoned that quest.'

'Pah!' Spaulding expressed his contempt. 'You'll have to do better than that, comrade. You don't fool me for one minute. You are as Russian as they come. You know what gives you away? This phoney British gentlemen act. The "cheerios" and "By Joves", and "I say, old man". The imbecilic obsession with trains. I knew it the moment I first set eyes on you. There was something false about you, something shifty, I could tell from the way you avoided a chap's gaze. I'm never wrong about these things … I have to tell you, Wenlock, or whatever your real name is, your British accent stinks. And as for that damn fool Curtis …' He then put on the voice of a mimic. '*Turned out fine, again, what?* If I ever hear another man say that another time I will shoot either him or me.'

The phrase *turned out fine again* flashed inside me. I had heard another English chap say it just recently, in Hotel 90 on my night out with the chaps … Was that

Curtis? Some instinct told me it had to be. 'It really is rather comical how wrong you are,' I said.

'Is it? You find it comical do you, counterfeiting an Englishman in order to undermine the King's realm?' As he spoke his eyes darted to the right, for the tiniest fraction of a second, as if spotting something behind me. Then I felt the cold hardness of a gun barrel being pressed against the back of my head.

'Drop the gun, Jack.' It was Roger's voice. 'Or I shoot you and your wife.'

'If it makes it any easier,' said Spaulding, in the supercilious tone of one for whom the cup of life always tastes bitter, 'we are not going to shoot you. You are in luck, comrade. You're going to be spared. There's a very important man in town, a man with a burned face. He's arranged a spy exchange. You for one of ours. You're going back to Russia. So put the gun away, there's a good sport.'

'Three seconds,' said Roger. 'Three, two ...'

I put the gun down on the table and raised my hands. Spaulding picked up the gun.

'Of course, if it were down to me,' he said, 'I would shoot you with as much compunction as I would drown a rat. But apparently it's not good form to shoot your spies, because then your people shoot ours and very soon no one wants the job. It's a sort of gentleman's agreement, which is ironic when you consider how rotten your English gentleman act is.' He stood up to leave. 'We are going to leave you here. Someone will be

345

sent to collect you. If you want to see Mother Russia again, I'd stay put.'

He moved towards the door. Roger removed the gun barrel from the back of my head. I sensed it was done with reluctance. Spaulding stopped and gave me a final look, the sort one would give to an insect found in one's soup.

'You know,' he said, 'it beggars belief when you come to think about it – when you look at what a catastrophe your doctrine of Mr Marx has been for the poor bloody folk of Russia – that you want to help us achieve the same disaster in our own country. Did you never stop to think of that? Eh? What about those precious bloody railways you are always going on about? They are owned by the working man now. God knows what sort of hash they will make of the job.'

'I'm sure they will do a very good job,' I said.

'You think so? And what about the men who owned the railways and from whom they were stolen?'

'It wasn't theft, they were compensated.'

'Yes, with their own bloody money! The very money they paid in taxes was used to compensate them for the theft of their own property. Where did the working man get the money to buy a railway?'

I looked Mr Spaulding directly in the eye. 'The working men paid for the railways with the blood of their fallen comrades. The blood of the men who fell on the beaches of Normandy and all the fields between there and Berlin.'

346

He laughed bitterly. 'You seem to have forgotten the English gentleman act, what ho?'

They both left. A minute later we heard the sound of a car leaving.

I turned to Jenny and she collapsed in my arms. 'Oh Jack.' We remained there embracing for a while.

'Roger is going to kill Curtis tonight,' said Jenny into my chest.

'Yes,' I said. 'It appears he has already put a bullet in the belly of Mr Fink.'

We walked outside. Our taxi had gone. Somewhere in Bangkok tonight was a man who knew the whereabouts of my mother and a man called Roger intent on killing him.

'How will we get back?' said Jenny. 'There are no cars or buses.'

The whistle of a steam engine sounded from somewhere close.

I looked at Jenny and said, 'Are you ready?'

She made a mock salute and said, 'Yessir!'

Chapter 23

THE STATION WAS DESERTED. The only activity was the gentle steaming of a wood-burning German Krauss 2-4-0T, still warm from the day's work. With luck there was steam enough to carry us back to the city.

We climbed aboard. I opened the firebox door and placed in two shovelfuls. Jenny released the brake and grabbed the regulator lever, like the big hand of a clock, and pushed it sideways. We began to move. Hardly perceptible at first, but then quickly gathering pace, until the night outside was gliding by. Jenny eased back slightly on the regulator, I put in another shovelful. She ran well. All grew dark on the footplate, apart from the copper-red glow from the firebox at our feet. Every time I opened the firebox door to throw in more wood it was as if a giant had struck a match. Our speed built, we lurched gently from side to side and up and down, the metal creaked and groaned, soon we were drenched with sweat. The din was deafening and glorious, it filled our ears and pumped our stomachs with the deep rhythmic chuffa-chuffa-chuffa-chuffa. The rhythm built and built and our eyes gleamed, our nostrils pricked with delight at the sweet, sweet smoke, and we worked as a team without need for words. The obedient train roared and wailed as Jenny pulled the whistle cord, roared and wailed and roared. We felt it deep inside us.

'Oh Jack,' said Jenny, turning to me with eyes sparkling, 'it's ... it's ... oh my! Oh Jack! It's ...'

'Yes!' I shouted above the din, 'yes! Isn't it?'

'Oh yes, yes, yes, oh my, oh Jack, golly! Oh yes, it's ... it's ... oh Jack, it's so ... oh, oh, oh, oh, oh, oh, oh, oh, oh, oh, oh, oh, Jack ... yes, yes ... Oh!'

Chapter 24

WE EMERGED FROM THE railway station onto
the square. The same one Lieutenant Colonel Nopsansuwong of the Royal Siamese
Police, Foreigner Division, had brought me to on my
second morning in Bangkok. We had parked outside
three buildings, the railway station, the prison and
Hotel 90, and he had told me the loneliest man in all
the world was in there, and given me to understand he
meant the prison. Did he know the truth? I suspect he
did.

The blind girl stood by the entrance and turned
towards us, alerted by the sound.

She held out her tin. 'You good heart, sir.'

'Yes,' I said, putting a coin in. 'We are friends of Mr
Curtis. We have come to see him.'

'Curtis,' she said simply and turned to walk inside.
We followed her. We ascended the stairs in her wake
and walked along the landing to the room from which
the man with the chamber pot had emerged last time
and bidden me a cheery greeting: 'Turned out fine
again.'

Outside the door, we paused for an instant and then
went in. I did not know what to expect, perhaps a man

351

living in squalor and degradation of the worst sort. Instead I found neatness and cleanliness, but in the man residing there a different sort of degradation, that of the soul. The room was tidy and simply furnished, like a monk's cell. A bed, a bedside table, a window leading on to a balcony. A chamber pot. And a chair in the corner in which sat a man. Curtis. Bright yellow waistcoat, bright blue trousers, blue bow tie and hair in a permanent wave. Lips that were rouged. Only the red ringmaster's jacket was missing. And I saw what it was that had so scandalised the guests at Spaulding's party, even more than the necklace of human ears.

'You ... you have dressed yourself as a golliwog,' said Jenny.

It was true, although he had not applied boot blacking to his face as the seaside entertainers do.

He nodded, sadly. 'Are they not hateful things? I oversaw their making for five years and never realised. When I arrived at Spaulding's party, they were appalled, calling me all manner of things. And I said, "Why? What is it you dislike about them? You are happy to have them on the backs of your jam jars." They didn't understand, of course. They couldn't. Do you?'

'I'm not sure,' I said.

'I think I do,' said Jenny.

'For many years in Singapore, I worked in the Colonial Service. Then one day I discovered they were not what I thought they were. They were ... rotten. Can you imagine what that might be like?'

We both stared at him without answering his question.

'Empire is rotten. Or at least it is for those who break their backs in the noonday sun to pay for it.'

'I think we should leave here straight away, Mr Curtis,' I said. 'Roger is coming here. He intends to kill you.'

'Yes, they want to kill me. Mustn't let folk find out about the Scharnhorst Plan.'

'Am I right in believing, Mr Curtis, that these people – Room 42 – arranged the boating accident, and are planning a similar fate for the flying boat?'

'Oh yes,' he said simply, as if passing a remark about the weather. He took a longer look at me. 'So you are Jack. I doted on your mother, did you know that?'

'I thank you for those kind words. Might it not be a good idea if we removed ourselves somewhere safer to continue our discussion?'

'Really doted on her,' he said, ignoring my last remark. 'We all did. You know where she is now, don't you?'

'I confess I would be most—'

'Hello, Curtis.' We all turned to the door. It was Roger. 'Nice to see you again. And Jack, too! You sure get around.'

'No!' cried Mr Curtis, and jumped up and ran to the window.

Roger fired a shot that missed. Curtis ducked out of the window onto the balcony. There was a water tank adjacent and he clambered onto it. Seeing this, Roger ran back the way he had come, clearly aiming to take the stairs and catch Curtis at the bottom. I ran to the window in time to see Curtis scramble down onto the ground and get up.

'Stay here,' I said to Jenny and went out to the stairs on the landing. She ignored what I said and followed.

We heard a shot being fired and a man cry out. We saw Curtis limping into the railway station with Roger in pursuit. We ran after them. Roger stopped and turned, framed by the entrance door. He smiled and pointed the gun at me.

'Sorry, Jack,' he said. 'Spy swaps are not really my thing.' He took three steps towards us, so close that he couldn't miss. 'Time to say—'

A gunshot rang out. They say if you hear the report, it missed. Tonight I heard the report and it was Roger who didn't. The bullet struck him in the right eye. He turned to stone and stood there for a second before toppling forward like a felled tree crashing to earth.

Jenny and I both turned to see who had shot him. We found ourselves facing a man with a gun. A man with a burned face.

'Hello, Jack,' he said.

'If you are going to shoot me,' I said, 'would you be kind enough to let my wife leave first.'

'I'm not leaving,' said Jenny.

'I haven't the slightest intention of shooting you,' he said. 'It would be a rather pointless thing to do

354

considering the particular trouble I have taken to save your life, even making up a cock-and-bull story about a Russian spy swap. I am only pointing the gun at you in order to ensure you are not tempted to do some mischief before you have read what I wish you to read. After that you can shoot me if you like, and with my blessing.'

I looked at him, mystified. 'You killed my friend Ifan.'

'If you mean the Welsh miner who died at the engine sheds, I can assure you it wasn't me who pushed him into the path of the train.'

'You were there that day asking for me!'

'Yes, indeed I was. But I went there to warn you.'

'Is there any reason why I should believe that?'

'No, not yet. That's why I'm still training the gun on you.'

He drew a folded piece of paper out of his jacket pocket and threw it across.

'Mrs Wenlock, perhaps you will read it to us.'

Jenny took the paper and read.

EXT. THE MANOR HOUSE IN WISSKIRRIEL.
NIGHT

TITLE: APRIL 1913

A fire at night. Flames engulf the
west wing of the house. MILLIE, the
maid, stands on the balcony of her

room in terror. There is no way back
through the fire, and she dare not
leap.

MILLIE

(Screams)

CAPTAIN SEYMOUR appears on the balcony next to MILLIE'S. He leaps across
and takes her in his arms. He begins
to climb down the ivy, while holding
on to her. A crowd has gathered below,
they gasp. As the climbers reach the
first floor a gust of wind blows a burning curtain and wraps it around
CAPTAIN SEYMOUR. He drops MILLIE, who
falls safely into the raised arms of
the people below. CAPTAIN SEYMOUR
falls heavily to the ground, engulfed
by flames. Onlookers race to fetch
water to douse the fire.

TITLE: MAY 1913

EXT. THE LAWN. DAY

MILLIE pushes a bath chair across the
lawn. CAPTAIN SEYMOUR, wearing pyjamas and dressing gown, is seated in

356

it. One half of his face is badly
burned. They reach the summer house,
the main house no longer visible. She
wheels him in and positions the chair
so that the CAPTAIN is afforded a view
of the Downs and towards the sea. It
appears that this is an established
ritual. MILLIE slips her arms around
his neck, and presses her head to
his, again in a manner that suggests
this too is an established ritual.

                    MILLIE
        Alone at last, my darling!

'I don't imagine this will be very welcome news to you,
Jack, but I'm your father.'

I stood rooted to the spot, with no idea what to say.
What was I to make of all this? Eventually, I said rather
stupidly, 'I thought my father was the stable boy.'

'That's the story I circulated. It's one of the many
reasons Curtis hates me. He's got a long list of reasons.
I spoke to him earlier, but I'm afraid he has disowned
his father.'

'Is there any reason why I should not do likewise?'
I said.

'That's for you to decide, Jack, but this really isn't the
place. I can tell you about your mother, and indeed

where to find her, but we need to do something about this corpse here before we are discovered. Would you be kind enough to help me drag him to the car over there?'

I looked at him dubiously.

'Jack,' he said, 'surely you can see we need to get away from here?'

He put the gun into his pocket, and I realised there was little point holding a discussion here. We dragged Roger over to his car. There was another man lying across the back seat. It was Spaulding, and he had a bullet wound in his temple.

'It's been a busy night,' said the man with the burned face.

We put Roger in the boot and propped Spaulding upright in the back seat, leaving room for me to sit next to him. Jenny sat in the passenger seat and the man with the burned face drove us to a destination he had clearly worked out in advance. It was a deserted warehouse next to the river's edge, with a jetty that ran out into the river. We drove the car onto the edge of the jetty, left the brake off, and pushed it into the river. It slowly disappeared under the water.

———

Once back at the hotel, we sat in the bar while my father ordered three whiskies and explained about the Scharnhorst Plan.

'You see,' he said, 'the common man thinks that the ruling families care about him. But the truth is that the ruling families of Europe are loyal to each other, not to the peoples of the countries they happen to live in. For a start, they are all related to each other. So they watch each other's backs. They understand only too well how easy it would be for the masses to turf them out of their palaces. What baffles them is why the masses don't see it.

'Marxist socialism had raged like wildfire through Europe, and the ruling classes realised they needed to do something about it, put down something of a fire-break. And so the plan was envisaged, to have a sort of bloodletting of the proletariat, winnow them out a bit. Take the wind out of their sails. This was one of the hidden aims of the Great War. But of course, no one had any idea about trench warfare at the time. They assumed it would be over in three months. No one imagined it would go on for four years, and that twenty million men and women would die fighting for the pos-session of a piece of land not much bigger than a football field.'

He paused and observed my reaction. I looked at him. If I assumed him to have been in his twenties when he sired me, it would make him now around sixty or so. But he looked older, as if the weight of the secrets he was now disclosing had been hard to carry across the years.

He made a gesture with spread hands, to signal the scale of the calamity that might ensue if word of this wicked plan became public knowledge. 'Just imagine it! What people would say if they knew it had all been engineered! It was imperative that when hostilities ended all evidence of this plan was destroyed. It was my father who arranged the boating accident.'

'Was he in Room 42?'

'Yes. I didn't know about any of this at the time. I found out later. That appeared to be the end of the matter: your mother was understood to have perished when her ship to Australia foundered.

'But when it appeared more recently that she might perhaps be alive, Room 42 reopened the case. I think I have succeeded in closing it again. I have furnished them with proofs that Millie died on the island and that the Scharnhorst Plan is not mentioned in the screenplay. I've also sent them a picture of her gravestone, which I had faked. As long as she stays hidden and quiet she should be fine. Well, I will leave that to you to arrange.

'I am also going to give you a dossier containing everything I know about the Scharnhorst Plan. Names, dates, minutes of meetings … You can use it to bargain for your freedom, if the need ever arises.'

'What about Curtis?' I said.

'Curtis hates me. He hates me for what I did to Millie, and the stable lad. Because I was the one who urged him to sign up. And to be honest, I don't greatly mind

360

about Curtis. You only have to look at him to see that he is not my son. The Countess had a passionate side to her in those days. And I think she suspected that I was the father of Millie's child – this may be the reason she persecuted her. But she could not be open about it because she knew that she had committed a similar indiscretion in bearing Curtis.

'I think that's all I have to tell you, Jack. As I said, I do not expect you to admire me. I was a cad. I abandoned your mother. The paradox is that had I been willing to do the right thing by her, if I had given everything up in order to be with her, I would have had a far happier life than the one I have had. I don't deserve to have led a happy life. I shall end it by my own hand tonight.'

'No!' I said feebly, more from convention than conviction.

'You need not concern yourself. My life has reached its final act anyway. I have a condition you see, a degenerative condition of the brain. The doctor has given me six months. I could hang on longer, but eventually one loses the ability to care for oneself. I would rather get out before I reach that stage. Trouble is, you cannot know with any certainty when, so it is better to get out sooner rather than later. You know the custom. When the time comes, retire to Room 42 with a bottle of whisky and a revolver. I have booked Room 42 and the time has come. If you should meet your mother, could you tell her I am sorry? Nothing more.'

'How shall we find her?' asked Jenny

'I have posted to your room the final page of the screenplay, which contains some clues for you to follow. And now I will take my leave. Would it be asking too much to shake you by the hand, Jack?'

And so I shook the hand of my father.

That night a thunderstorm raged over Bangkok. The storm crashed and banged for hours. One of those bangs was accompanied by a muzzle flash from Room 42.

Chapter 25

'I NOW PRONOUNCE YOU MAN and wife,' said Webster. The marriage was between Mr Earwig and Miss Sugarpie.

'Sell book buy lady gold,' she had said to me earlier, demonstrating an arm jangling with gold. She looked incandescent in a white wedding dress. Earwig wore an expression of beatific pride. He was a man transformed utterly, whose fortunes had taken a turn for the better in a manner he had never in his life dared hope. I was best man. This was an office I had never occupied before.

It was a beautiful morning. The sky was pink and duck-egg blue. The sun had not yet fully risen, but already there was enough light to fill the world. The Empire Flying Boat shimmered, the river water lapping softly against her hull.

A week had passed. Spaulding and Roger's deaths had not been discovered. It turned out that Mr Kilmer had known all along about the bomb. He told me he had been informed about it by old friends working in a newly formed wing of military intelligence called the Office of Strategic Services. I asked him how they knew, and he replied that they knew everything. The bomb now lay safely in pieces at the bottom of the Chaopraya River.

After the wedding ceremony was complete, guests began to board the flying boat. Kilmer sat at the controls. Next to him on the bridge, Webster took his position as co-pilot. Solveig Connemara and Sam Flamenco were on the jetty, walking to the hatch. Mr Flamenco leaned on the arm of his wife, his unsteady gait exacerbated by the gentle sway of the jetty. Solveig had been right that night in the garden about the photo. Jenny needed no convincing that it had been staged by the chaps. She said there was nothing to forgive, although that did not stop her from teasing me about it.

Mr Kuribayashi wheeled Hoshimi out and past. She was still wearing the Gosling's Friend badge.

'Mr and Mrs Wenlock, might I just say what a pleasure it has been to meet you both, albeit so briefly?' said Hoshimi.

'We have so enjoyed meeting you, too,' said Jenny.

'It's such a shame we cannot persuade you to join us.'

'We will be thinking of you,' I said.

'And I of you! Parting is such sweet sorrow, is it not?'

'It certainly is,' I said.

She looked over towards the plane. 'I do hope Mr Earwig will not hold it against me – for what I said about Christopher Robin.'

'I'm sure he won't,' I said. 'My feeling is, he is far too chuffed with life to worry about a thing like that.'

'Yes,' said Hoshimi. 'He is as pleased as Punch.' She reached out and shook my hand solemnly. 'Adieu!' she said.

'*Sayonara!*' answered Jenny.

On board there was an urn containing the ashes of Mr Curtis. We had spent many hours searching for him later that night, but found no trace. It was the following day when the buzzing of flies – in a manner reminiscent of the story in Lieutenant Colonel Nopsansuwong's book *Washing Away of Wrongs* – indicated the trail of blood that led to the spot where he must have hidden. His remains were discovered in the firebox of one of the engines in the station. No doubt seeking to escape his murderous pursuer, he had chosen it as a hiding place, and fallen asleep, or fainted through loss of blood. So it seems he suffered the same fate as the engine-cleaning boy, Ben Hawkins, and next morning had been chuffed to death. I fancy there are worse ways to go.

His ashes were removed and placed in an urn. I sent a telegram to Lady Seymour telling her what we had discovered, and received a reply from Mr Bates to say that Her Ladyship had died in the night four days ago. He sought to reassure me that she had made the necessary approach to Princess Elizabeth. All that was needed was to stay out of the clutches of Room 42 until she became Queen and I could apply for a pardon.

Mr Earwig walked up to me and spoke, raising his voice above the noise from the plane's engines.

'Jack, Jenny, I have enjoyed meeting you so much.'

'We have enjoyed meeting you, too,' said Jenny.

'Are you not tempted to join us?' asked Earwig.

'Tempted, yes, and we are very jealous of you all,' she answered. 'But we have a pressing engagement.'

His expression grew serious, as if to say he understood. Then he said, '*My pen ry.*'

We both gave him looks that encouraged him to expand.

'It means never mind.' He seemed proud to display his knowledge, even though one sensed it had been newly acquired. 'Finky used to say it a lot.'

'Yes,' said Jenny. 'He said it the day we met. To me it sounds like a ... a counsel of despair. Isn't it good to mind things?'

'I don't think so,' he said. 'It's a counsel of acceptance. It's a Buddhist thing. Instead of demanding that the world changes to suit you, it is better to adapt to how the world is.'

'I'm not sure I understand,' said Jenny.

'Think of an old lion who has been cast out by the other lions. He has a wounded paw so he can't hunt. He slowly starves and dies. He mutely accepts it. A man in that situation would rail against his fate. "Why me? This isn't fair! This shouldn't be happening! Something should be done! What have I done to deserve this!" All of which makes no difference to his fate. But it does increase his suffering.'

'You don't have a wounded paw,' said Jenny.

'I said that to Finky and he said we all have wounded paws of one sort or another.'

I recalled the words of Mr Simkins in Singapore, about the awareness that afflicts you in the middle of the night when you rise to answer the call of nature.

That's when it strikes you: you only have one life to live and you've thrown it away.

Curtis must have felt this keenly. I wondered if this story of him falling apart, of being an unwitting victim on the path to his own destruction, was perhaps not entirely accurate. Perhaps he willingly undertook it and decided to go out in a blaze of glory. For the first time in his life he did something truly adventurous. I suspected he knew perfectly well how mad his quest was, but he didn't give a fig.

It was no doubt true that the fate of my mother had haunted him all his life and would account for the prompting of his heart to find her. But there must have been more. For the first time in his life he was enjoying himself and was well aware that the road led to his ruination. And he didn't care. Was his quest not a version of that slow motion drop from Beachy Head that Mr Fink had described with such relish? Late-flowering Bohemianism, yes, and so what if it were? Better late than never at all.

This had also been the message of Cheadle's life, he who so joyously blotted his copybook in Ilfracombe. I had been a stuffed shirt most of my life, I knew, but it is never too late … In my pocket the final page of the screenplay grew hot and moist under my fingers. I turned and looked at Jenny and became giddy with love for her, and my only regret was that we were already married and could not do so again. She saw me looking and with her eyes sparkling, pushed herself under my arm and threw her arms around me, signalling that she had no intention of ever letting me go.

'I have something to tell you,' she said. 'I'm late.'

I laughed. 'Hardly. You are never late.'

'That's the point. But I am. Late … late.'

'I'm not sure I understand.'

'Lady late. Oh Jack! I think we may soon be hearing the patter of an atomic train driver's feet.'

My heart leapt within me as I understood her meaning. 'But … you can't!'

'Why can't I? I can if I want.'

'No, I mean, you … you said …'

'It looks like the doctor was wrong.' She opened her handbag and showed me nestling inside the atom-powered toy train that she must have rescued from the bin and kept.

'By Jove!' I said. 'You kept it. By Jove … a son … We could call him Flash Gordon.'

'I don't think *she* would thank you for that!'

I laughed again. 'Ha ha, yes of course! Trust in God; She will drive the train.'

Jenny kissed me and held me tight, whispering into my ear, 'We will trust in God and let Her decide whether we have a boy or a girl.'

'Either will make me the happiest man alive,' I answered.

'I thought you already were,' she said with a grin.

'Then I will be doubly so.'

Shouts from the jetty drew our attention and we turned to watch as they prepared to cast off.

Kilmer revved up each engine, one by one, until he had all four throbbing and roaring. There were shouts, and the boys on the jetty released the ropes holding the white bird. She moved slowly out into the stream, eased round to face the south. Kilmer pushed the throttle and the plane began to cruise, sending a bow wave back towards the hotel. She picked up speed, faster and faster. She lifted from the water, fell back and then lifted fully, like a bird released from a cage. Stuttering and jumpy at first, but then she found an airstream and hit her stride. She banked and turned to the south-east, towards the sea, rising and climbing and getting ever smaller until soon she was just a speck in the serene, all-forgiving sky.

SAILING TO SHIMUSHIR

An original screenplay

by Millie Tookey

Dear Finder

The volcano beneath which we have passed so many happy years has forced us finally to leave. I put these precious pages in as many bottles as it takes and consign them to the sea. We will hand ourselves now to God's mercy and hope He will smile upon our quest to reach the island of Tepu Nui.

Millie Tookey

April 3, 1939

FADE IN:

INT. WEEPING CROSS ENGINE SHEDS. NIGHT

MILLIE ~~lies~~ in a bed set amid rows of engines gleaming in the gloom. NURSES wearing starched uniforms attend her.

They chafe her hands and dab the moisture from her brow. A whistle wails and out of the midnight gloom a steam engine rolls forward. The whistle shrieks; MILLIE lets forth a strangled gasp; a second later a baby cries.

A NURSE places the baby in the mother's outstretched hands.

MILLIE

You will be called Jack Wenlock. My darling boy!

Acknowledgements

I would like to thank my agent Rachel for all her help and support. Thanks also to fellow authors Tim Pears and John Williams for their help and advice. Thanks as well to my test pilots Lesli, Gwen, Lisa, Rachie & Squeaky.

Note on the Author

Malcolm Pryce was born in the UK and has spent much of his life working and travelling abroad. He has been a BMW assembly-line worker, a hotel washer-up, a desk hand on a yacht sailing the South Seas, an advertising copywriter and the world's worst aluminium salesman. He is the author of the bestselling *Aberystwyth* novels. He lives in Oxford.

@exogamist
www.malcolmpryce.com

Note on the Type

The text of this book is set in Baskerville, a typeface named after John Baskerville of Birmingham (1706–1775). The original punches cut by him still survive. His widow sold them to Beaumarchais, from where they passed through several French foundries to Deberney & Peignot in Paris, before finding their way to Cambridge University Press.

Baskerville was the first of the 'transitional romans' between the softer and rounder calligraphic Old Face and the 'Modern' sharp-tooled Bodoni. It does not look very different to the Old Faces, but the thick and thin strokes are more crisply defined and the serifs on lower-case letters are closer to the horizontal with the stress nearer the vertical. The R in some sizes has the eighteenth-century curled tail, the lower case w has no middle serif and the lower case g has an open tail and a curled ear.

The Aberystwyth Mysteries

The Aberystwyth Mysteries follow Louie Knight, Aberystwyth's best –
and only – private detective, as he takes on cases that throw him head-first
into the town's seedy underbelly, where encounters with mad nuns and axe-
wielding rabbit-hunters are as commonplace as a man, long presumed dead,
being spotted boarding a bus to Aberaeron.

Comedy and Noir collide on the rainswept streets of this sleepy seaside town.

BOOKS IN THE SERIES: